ELLEN ELIZABETH HUNTER

Ellen Eliz Hunter

MURDER ON THE CANDLELIGHT TOUR

D0064040

Magnolia Mysteries

Greensboro, North Carolina

This is a work of fiction.

Murder on the Candlelight Tour © Copyright 2004 by Ellen Elizabeth Hunter. All rights reserved, including the right of reproduction in whole or in part in any form.

Published by Magnolia Mysteries
P.O. Box 38041
Greensboro, North Carolina 27438

ISBN: 978-0-9755404-0-4

Cover design by Tim Doby

Also by Ellen Elizabeth Hunter

Murder on the Ghost Walk

Murder on the Candlelight Tour

Murder at the Azalea Festival

Murder at Wrightsville Beach

Murder on the ICW

Murder on the Cape Fear

Christmas Wedding

Murder at the Bellamy Mansion

Visit Ellen's website,
www.ellenhunter.com
Or contact her at:
ellenelizhunter@att.net

1

"He was murdered upstairs, in that front bedroom where you sleep, Ashley dear," Binkie said. "Stabbed in the back with a dagger as he frolicked with one of the 'girls.'"

Binkie struck a match to his pipe. He is history professor Benjamin Higgins, a septuagenarian, and one of the sweetest men I know. There are times when I wish I were an elegant matron—wavy white hair and ropes of pearls—so we could fall in love. But I'm twenty-four, and since Daddy passed, Binkie's been like a father to me.

"What are you talking about? Murder? In my house?" I wheeled about, unsteady in a pair of high heels. During the week, I wear sturdy construction boots for work. But this was Saturday, the first Saturday in December, and as tradition decreed, the weekend of the *Olde Wilmington by Candlelight* tour. My house was featured on the tour and in honor of the festivities I had put on a long narrow black velvet skirt with a red silk blouse. And dangerously high heels that tipped me off balance.

I flicked my lighter at the wick of a fat red candle. There were dozens of red and cream candles placed about the library, their wicks aglow. I have a master's degree in historic preservation. In the spring, I'd bought my first home, a charming Victorian dwelling in the heart of the historic district.

Binkie leaned against the cherrywood mantelpiece, a suede-patched elbow propped among fresh magnolia leaves, one Hush Puppy shod foot crossed jauntily over the other. He was a veritable centerfold for "GQ Seniors." His dark green herringbone tweed jacket and red silk cravat and pocket handkerchief spoke of Christmases past and present.

Lively blue eyes twinkling, he said, "Bet you didn't know your lovely home was once a bordello, an establishment for 'ladies of the evening' as they were called in those days."

"A bordello? In a minister's home!" I clapped my fingertips to my forehead. "So that's what Mama was talking about. She kept saying I had bought Belle Watling's house. Belle Watling. You know. The madam in *Gone With the Wind.*"

Mama has always been besotted with GWTW. I've often wondered if his name was what initially attracted her to Daddy, the late Judge Peter Wilkes. But then she'd fallen madly in love with him, for what woman could resist my darling father with his courtly, Old South manners. Mama had named me Ashley and my older sister Melanie. We've often laughed that it was a good thing we didn't have a brother, for surely Mama would have named him Rhett Butler Wilkes!

"Belle Watling! That's a good one. This lady's name was Suzanna O'Day."

"There *was* an S. O'Day listed in the archives as a former owner when I researched this house, although her profession wasn't listed."

"Nor would it be. Yet she is as a legend of this town as any founding father. Many a Wilmington gentleman left Miss O'Day's establishment early Sunday morning in time for church or mass. The good ladies of Wilmington rebelled, and rightly so. The Women's Temperance League organized to drive her and her harlots out of town. You see, that was the spring President Woodrow Wilson was expected to visit the manse at the First Presbyterian Church—his father had been the pastor there, you know, when young 'Tommy' was at Davidson—so the ladies were determined to restore the community to respectability. Those Temperance League ladies could be quite formidable when they chose." Binkie nodded his admiration, a snow white lock of hair falling over his high, intelligent forehead.

"And there was a murder here, you say? Why didn't you tell me this before I bought the house?"

"Why, I thought you knew. Believe me, Ashley dear, I'd have warned you otherwise."

"Well, I didn't know and no one told me. Oh, wait a minute, Melanie did mention something, but I wasn't paying attention. I was too caught up in the prospect of owning an authentic Victorian. Besides, people are always claiming that someone was shot or bludgeoned or poisoned or whatever within many old homes in the District. Makes for a good sales pitch."

"This is no sales pitch. With the Women's Temperance League hounding her, the story goes that a desperate Miss O'Day stole up behind a wealthy patron while his guard, as well as his ... ahem ... trousers, were down. She stabbed him in the back with a dagger, then snatched the pouch of gold coins from his pocket. Under cover of darkness, she rolled his body into the Cape Fear River."

"Oooh!" I exclaimed, wondering how I'd ever sleep in that room again.

Binkie went on, "Knowing that those paragons of virtue were determined to reduce her to penury, Miss O'Day secreted the gold coins somewhere in this house, intending to return for them. Then those Temperance League ladies escorted her to the depot, put her on a train, and warned her never to set foot in Wilmington again."

"And did she? Did she sneak back to get the gold?" I asked.

"I'm sure she intended to, but alas for Ms. O'Day, she was felled by the great influenza pandemic of 1918." Binkie paused, grinning mischievously. "So, if the tale is true, Ashley dear, and I vow I believe it is, for where there's smoke there's fire, somewhere in this ancient labyrinth, you've got yourself a fortune."

"Binkie, you amaze me!"

He removed his elbow from the mantelpiece carefully, so as not to disturb the garland there. Moving like a dancer—the result of a lifetime of amateur boxing—he settled on the leather sofa that faces my fireplace. To the left of the hearth, a ten-foot Fraser fir glittered with a collection of antique ornaments, furled gold lame ribbons, and sparkling fairy lights.

"Let's talk about this later. I want to hear more. But it's almost four and I've got to go to my post at the front door." I dropped the lighter into a drawer and swiped at the curls on my forehead. "Wish me luck."

Docents from the Historical Society were stationed throughout the house, prepared to recite the facts about its architecture and history. I wondered if the docent in my bedroom knew about the murder, and if she knew, would she tell?

"I do. Your house is the prettiest in the District. It glows, just like you, Ashley dear." He blew me a kiss. I blew one back and hurried from the library.

Dashing past the stairs, I entered the reception hall to greet my friend, artist Rachel Jacobs. We had worked on the decorations for two weeks, festooning five live Christmas trees, suspending mistletoe and boxwood kissing balls in doorways, draping mantels, banisters, and mirrors with swags of fresh green garlands. Red roses were tucked in among the greenery, and the air was scented with their sweetness, the freshness of pine, and the spice of bayberry and cloves.

"That's a pretty skirt," I told Rachel, admiring her plaid taffeta. Nervously, I checked the grandfather clock. "Ten minutes till four. We're not supposed to open the door until four on the dot."

Rachel moved to the window and drew back a lace curtain. "There's quite a line out there. Oh, and look, it's snowing!"

I peeked over her shoulder at the long line of people and large, soft snowflakes falling in the street. "Well, that's a first. Snow in Wilmington this early! And it's not even that cold."

"But it's so pretty, Ashley."

"Yes," I murmured absently. "Oh, I'm so excited, Rachel, I've got butterflies in . . ."

Binkie's loud, angry voice rang out from the library. "You murdered her as sure as if you'd put a gun to her head and pulled the trigger!"

Sheldon Mackie retorted with a roar, "That's not true and you know it! It was an accident and I've apologized a hundred times."

Had Sheldon, the docent assigned to the dining room, gone into the library to torment Binkie? I had to separate them. How had I been so naive to think that those two sworn enemies could co-exist under the same roof for even a few hours? I'd mistakenly assumed that out of regard for me, for they were both my good and loyal friends, they might suspend hostilities for several hours.

I hurried toward the library calling over my shoulder, "Be right back. I've got to do something about this. Don't open the doors till I return." Storming into the room, I saw Binkie with his fists up. It was almost comical. Dear, gentle Binkie is kindly to a fault to everyone but Sheldon.

In their youth, they'd been the best of friends, brothers-in-law, in fact. Sheldon Mackie, now the grand old man on Wilmington's interior decorating scene, had been married to Binkie's adored younger sister, Beverly. Early one New Year's morning, after a party where the revelry and libations had flowed freely, Sheldon, too drunk to drive but insisting he was able, crashed their car into the back of a parked delivery truck on Market Street. Poor Beverly had not survived the accident. Ironically, Sheldon walked away without a scratch. Binkie had never forgiven him. And in all fairness would I be able to forgive someone who took Melanie from me? From that day, Binkie harbored a hatred for Sheldon that bordered on psychotic.

Sheldon snapped, his face red with fury, "Put down your fists, you old fool!"

"Old fool? Who're you calling an 'old fool.' You're the one who's the fool. Destroyed every good and decent thing that came your way! Never were any good!"

Binkie feinted and sparred, egging Sheldon on. "'Born bad,' Mama used to say about you. She warned me. She warned Beverly too. Beverly was far too good for you. We did everything short of locking that girl up to prevent her from marrying a wastrel like you."

Working himself into a frenzy, Binkie swung a fist at Sheldon. But Sheldon was the larger man of the two, and at sixty, a dozen years younger. Nimble on his feet, he managed to sidestep Binkie's jabs.

"Stop it! Stop it, both of you," I cried, grabbing a fistful of Binkie's jacket and pulling hard. "I've got a throng of tourists at my door. Why do you two have to choose this moment to come to blows? I've dreamed about this day for years and I won't let you spoil it for me."

Binkie seemed to come to his senses and backed off. "Another day," he hissed at Sheldon.

"Any time and place, old man," Sheldon challenged, his chin jutting forward, his jaw clenched.

I caught my breath. "Sheldon, you're supposed to be in the dining room. What're you doing in here anyway?"

Sheldon looked mortified to be getting a dressing down from a person young enough to be his granddaughter, but he was smart enough to know he had it coming. Embarrassed, he said as he left, "I apologize, Ashley. The last thing I want to do is spoil this day for you."

"And you," I cried, staring down a shame-faced Binkie, "I expected better from you. Now I've got guests to greet, so see that you behave."

Binkie looked ashamed. "I'm sorry."

"Pull yourself together," I said gently and gave him a hug. "How about if we catch some dinner after the tour and you can tell me what's bothering you?"

He hugged me back, eager to make amends. "You're the daughter I never had."

2

When The Verandas B&B, just a few doors down Nun Street, was on the tour several Christmases ago, thousands of tourists had gone through the elegantly restored Italianate mansion. The three-story structure is listed on the National Register of Historic Places as the "Benjamin W. Beery House." During the Civil War, Captain Beery constructed a monitor on top of the roof where, with the aid of a telescope, he spied the Cape Fear River for Yankee ironclads.

The good folks at the Lower Cape Fear Historical Society didn't seem to mind that restorations on my historic home—its plaque identified it as the "Reverend Israel Barton House"—were not quite complete. So eager were they to include my Victorian dwelling on the tour, they happily accepted its not-quite-finished state. The colorful house, with its equally colorful history, has presided over Nun Street since 1860. The Society never could get the last owner, reclusive Dorothy Penry, to put it on the tour, but I'd jumped at the chance.

Opening my front door, I greeted the tourists with an enthusiastic, "Welcome to The Reverend Israel Barton House." A tall, distinguished, silver-haired man, carrying a silver-handled ebony walking stick, was the first to enter. He said hello to me and handed his ticket to Rachel. She appeared to recognize the second man to enter, for she greeted him with a breathy "hey" and beamed at him.

Two women came next: a solid, middle-aged type, followed by a sleek blonde wearing pink-tinted lenses. The stream of tourists who'd been waiting on the front steps surged into my reception hall.

"This is perfectly lovely, Ashley," Betty Matthews gushed as she brushed snowflakes out of her hair. "Don't tell anyone I said so because I'm supposed to be impartial, but I think yours is the prettiest house on the tour."

I'm very fond of Betty Matthews, the president of the Historic Preservation Society. Betty's banker husband Wayne kissed my cheek. "Congratulations, Ashley."

"Where's Sheldon?" the next woman in line asked irritably. I turned from Wayne to see MaeMae Mackie, Sheldon's wife, accompanied by her best friend Lucy Lou Upchurch. MaeMae and Lucy Lou appeared to be caught in a Sixties time-warp, when they were debutantes and the toast of Wilmington. Because the world had changed but they had not, they escaped into their little "drinkies." Judging by their style of dress, you'd think Jackie Kennedy was still the First Lady.

I checked the line for Melanie and wondered what was keeping her. She'd called earlier to wish me luck, but my moment of fame wouldn't seem real without her beside me to share my triumph. And where was Jon? I wanted him here with me too.

"Ashley?" MaeMae called sharply.

"Oh, sorry, MaeMae. Sheldon's stationed in the dining room. You can go straight back if you need to speak to him."

After that I lost track of MaeMae, not noticing if she'd followed the designated tour route, or cut through to the dining room. From four until eight, a steady stream of tourists and local residents came through my front door, including Jon Campbell, who kissed me on the cheek and told me that I and the house looked sensational.

Finally, day one of the tour was over and I sank gratefully onto the lower step of the front staircase. "Oh, my poor tootsies," I said, looking down at my swollen feet. I slipped off my shoes and rubbed my toes.

Rachel was in the kitchen, getting a Coke and taking a well-deserved break. I heard footsteps on the backstairs and thought that the last of the tourists must be leaving. We'd worked non-stop for four hours, and had just locked the front door.

But it was worth it, I thought, as I experienced the satisfaction of a job well done. People had ooohed and aaahed over the decorations. Tiny white lights twinkled on the small evergreen tree in its Chinese jardiniere that I'd bought just for the refectory table. The red and cream candles guttered and flickered. I sighed, deeply contented.

Then I heard it, a scuffling and thumping that came from the library.

I jumped up. "Oh, no. not again!" I dashed out of the reception hall and raced to the library in my stocking feet. The heavy mahogany paneled door stood ajar. I gave it a push and looked around it.

Binkie stood in front of the fireplace, looking every minute of his seventy-two years. His face was stark white like his hair. He was bent over, staring at something on the floor. The sofa blocked my view of the object. I scurried around the massive piece of furniture and came upon a grotesque sight.

Sheldon Mackie lay sprawled on the floor in front of the hearth. The pool of blood under his head had seeped into the oriental rug, vivid red blood mingling with vivid red wool.

Binkie stood over him, a brass-handled poker clutched in his hand. His eyes met mine across Sheldon's body. "I didn't do it. I swear on my mother's grave, I didn't do it." The poker slid from his grasp, striking the rug with a bounce. "I found him like that."

3

"Poor Professor Higgins," I moaned. "And poor Sheldon." It was after two A.M. and I was too wired to sleep. I sat propped up in bed on vintage linen pillows that cushioned my great-grandparents' ornate rose-wood headboard, while across the room Melanie studied herself in my cheval looking glass.

Dressed in nothing but a peach silk teddy, Melanie was critically appraising her center-fold figure. "Poor Professor Higgins, indeed! If you break out in a song over that daft man, I'll scream."

I jerked upright. "He is not daft! He has devoted his life to the University and to this town. No one knows more about the history and folklore of the Lower Cape Fear than Binkie."

Melanie scrutinized her left profile, then her right, then flung a haughty glance over her shoulder at the perfect bubble butt reflected in the mirror. She seemed pleased with what she saw, for she got a smug, self-satisfied smirk on her face. Patting her buttocks fondly, she said, "Not bad for a woman of twenty-nine."

"Thirty-two," I corrected absently.

She dropped her hands to her sides and cast me a defiant glare. "Don't you think I know how old I am?"

"All I know is I'm twenty-four, and you're eight years older than I am. That makes you thirty-two."

For sisters we're as different as night and day, with no familial resemblance between us. Melanie favors our mother, Claire Chastain Wilkes, with her creamy complexion and spun copper hair, eyes that are intensely green and gold. I take after Daddy, Peter Wilkes, having inherited his delicate heart-shaped face and eyes that are so deeply blue-gray they sometimes appear lavender. I've also got his abundant dark hair that curls tenaciously in Wilmington's humid climate.

"Mel, I've got more worrisome things on my mind right now than calculating your age. You can pretend to be nineteen for all I care. Poor Binkie. If it weren't for . . ."

She whirled around, hands on hips. "I hope you were about to say if it weren't for me calling Walt Brice, the best defense attorney in New Hanover County, your 'poor Binkie' would be rotting in jail right now."

"Yes, that *was* quick thinking, Mel. I'm sorry I'm in such a snit. It's just that I'm worried about Binkie. Everything looks so bad for him. I think Nick believes he's guilty."

For the past year, I'd been dating homicide detective Nick Yost. Our relationship was rife with conflict, but there was deep affection too, and a strong magnetic pull. The conflict arose when I got anywhere near Nick's cases because he worried I'd get hurt. Yet, there was no denying the charged chemistry between us, although we'd been dancing around it, neither of us ready to commit to a deeper relationship. Of course, that chemistry had exploded like lethal gas when Nick and a team of homicide detectives from Wilmington P.D. stormed into my house shortly after eight o'clock to find me sitting on the blood-stained rug, sobbing that I'd lost my dear friend Sheldon.

Nick, the senior detective and the first one in the library, had pulled me to my feet and wrapped his arms around me. But only for a moment. When the others reached the doorway, he'd let go of me. We went into the kitchen and he asked me to tell him what I'd seen. Had I witnessed the murder, he wanted to know. No, I'd told him. Then he'd hustled me upstairs and out of the way. Melanie arrived shortly after the police; she'd been sent upstairs too.

Now, she flounced across the room to the bed, pulled back the covers and slipped inside. "Thank God those police are gone. Now maybe we can get some sleep. Isn't this cozy? Just like when we were kids."

"I'm so glad you agreed to spend the night, Mel. Although I won't be able to sleep a wink, even with you beside me. I keep seeing Sheldon's face. His wide open eyes staring up at me. And poor Binkie. I thought he was going to have a coronary." I plumped up my pillows and slumped back onto them.

I'd called Melanie right after I'd called 911. She and Joel had been in his car, on their way to her house, having recently left mine. They'd been among the last guests on the tour. Melanie, in turn, phoned Attorney Walter Brice from her cell phone.

It had been the smart thing to do because Nick had taken Binkie to headquarters for questioning. Walt arrived in time to prevent Binkie from saying anything incriminating. Binkie had repeated his assertion that he was innocent, that he'd found Sheldon dead when he returned to the library. Walt agreed to represent Binkie and to defend him in court if that became necessary. Binkie is, after all, an admired and respected member of the community.

Melanie curled up on her side, one arm under her cheek, eyes fixed softly on my face. "You did a nice job restoring this house, baby sister. You've turned it into something really lovely. But you know its value just plummeted by half because of Sheldon's murder. Buyers are attracted to old houses with histories of long-ago murders, but not recent homicides."

Unexpectedly, she sat up and lobbed a pillow at me. "Even so, I'll never forgive you for cheating me out of a commission when you bought directly from the owner."

I'd bought my house directly from Mrs. Penry whom I'd met at Magnolia Manor nursing home where our mama was a patient. After we'd been forced to institutionalize Mama because of her dementia, we sold her house, in accordance with the documents Daddy had drawn up before his untimely accident. With his many years of seeing others make messes of their legal affairs, Daddy had had the foresight to prepare us for any eventuality. Mama's coastal property had sold for nearly three million dollars. The property consisted of our family home—a three story house with a two-tiered piazza and a widow's walk—the cute bungalow where I'd lived for a while after college, and a private boat dock and boat house located on the desirable Intracoastal Waterway.

Most of the money went into a trust to meet Mama's expenses at Magnolia Manor and future medical bills, but there was also enough to give us an advance on our inheritance. I'd used my share to buy this house.

"Melanie, I've explained a hundred times why I bought directly from Mrs. Penry." I felt guilty about excluding Melanie from the transaction and that made me defensive. "She insisted that the sale be handled privately. I met her when I was visiting Mama and we got to be friends."

Melanie flopped on her back.

"Mrs. Penry's in bad shape, by the way," I continued. "She might die. I didn't know people could die from asthma. Anyway, when I told her I restored old houses and that I was looking for one for myself, she wanted me to have her home. I've always admired it."

"Nothing you've just said would have prevented you from hiring me to represent you," Melanie protested.

"Mrs. Penry had her heart set on a quick, easy sale. No real estate brokers. No complications. You have to admit, Melanie, you realtors do have a way of taking a buyer who's eager to buy, and a seller who's thrilled with the offer, and turning them into mortal enemies. It's true. Admit it."

Melanie sniffed. "Well, it's true of some brokers. But not of me. I'd never have become a billion dollar producer if I didn't know how to close."

I sat forward suddenly. "Dear lord, in all the excitement, I nearly forgot."

Melanie was smoothing the coverlet over her legs. "What?" she asked incuriously. Melanie rarely reacts to my enthusiasm; what excites me rarely excites her.

"Binkie told me a man was murdered right here in this room by a madam who ran a brothel here in about 1918."

"Well, I tried to tell you about that but you wouldn't listen. Remember the first time you showed me this house? I told you then, but you were so gaga over it, carrying on about turrets and gingerbread and how the staircase split on the landing into front and back stairs."

I ignored her outburst. "Binkie says this madam hid gold somewhere and that it's still here."

"Pish-posh! I don't know why you listen to that old codger."

My heart was racing. I'd never be able to sleep. "Don't talk about Binkie that way."

She gave me a scornful look. "If there really was gold hidden here, don't you think you would have found it during the restorations? Why, you tore nearly everything apart, didn't you?"

My shoulders slumped. "Yes. That did occur to me."

Melanie snuggled under the comforter. "Turn off the light, will you, shug. And open a window. It's stuffy in here."

"But you can't go to sleep. I'm wide awake."

"Just watch me."

"Mel?"

"Hmmm."

"Why were you and Joel late tonight? I wanted you to be here with me."

Her eyelashes fluttered on her cheeks. "We had a business meeting that ran late. Besides, I had confidence in you. I knew the tour would go just fine."

"Business? Are you involved in Joel's business?" Joel is a real estate developer. When he lived in Los Angeles, he'd been a movie producer. I suspected that he missed the excitement of show business. After Los Angeles and New York, Wilmington ranks third in the production of major motion pictures, and I've always wondered why he'd switched careers. Must be more money in real estate. Melanie made tons.

Her eyes blinked open, then drooped shut again, as she murmured her answer, "I'm investing in his new project."

"What's that?"

"Joel wants to build a resort hotel. I'm looking for the right parcel of land for him." She yawned. "Now, goodnight. And turn off the light."

I tossed and turned, my brain reeling with images of Sheldon while Melanie slept peacefully. Finally, at about dawn, I succumbed to a dark and troubling dreamworld where dancing Christmas trees collided with faceless men brandishing pokers and canes.

4

I awoke with a start. Canes! The dream rushed up to the surface of my consciousness. One of the faceless dancing men had been cavorting with a cane, *a la* Fred Astaire. Then I remembered the first tourist yesterday, a distinguished older man who'd been carrying a silver-handled ebony walking stick.

Was there some test the police could do to determine positively that the murder weapon was the poker Binkie had been caught with so red-handedly? Or might they be able to identify another murder weapon, a walking stick, for example? I'd have to ask Nick.

As I considered the silver-haired man as a possible suspect, I had to admit the timing was off. Sheldon had been killed at eight P.M. The man with the walking stick had entered my house at precisely four and by eight would have been blocks away at the other end of the tour. Unless he'd doubled back.

Melanie was already up, looking refreshed and beautiful. She shook out her tumble of red curls and slipped into a fitted ginger-colored suit with a thigh-high skirt and high heels. Just as she was waving goodbye and about to dash out the door, the phone rang.

"Put my girl on," a man's voice said in my ear.

Girl? "What? Who is this?"

Sensing that the call was for her, she stopped in the doorway.

"Lemme speak to Melanie," he said. Not, "Good morning, Ashley, how are you?" Just, "Put my girl on."

I handed the phone to Melanie. "Charming Joel," I said, loud enough for him to hear.

But Melanie wasn't paying attention to me. She grabbed the phone out of my hand and breathed into it, "Sugah?"

Joel Fox was bad news. Melanie, always the one in control in her lust-laced relationships, had clearly met her match.

She giggled into the phone, murmured several "uh huhs," followed by more "sugahs," then, "I missed you too, sweetcakes, but I'll be back home tonight."

A few more giggles that included some strange body language, kind of a writhing and wiggling, and the twirling of curls around her finger.

She hung up, wiped a sex-suffused grin off her face, and was instantly restored to her business self. "I'm off to meet an important client," she called over her shoulder.

Each year when visitors come to Wilmington for the candlelight tour, a few always fall in love with our quaint city, buy houses and stay. Melanie is always hot on the trail of a hot prospect. Right now, she had an extravagantly priced listing at Landfall, the very posh, very upscale, gated community on the Intracoastal Waterway. Landfall had been developed on the former estate of the wealthy Pembroke Joneses who'd once hosted lavish parties there and at their Newport estate. They'd been two of Mrs. Astor's four hundred. When people talk about "keeping up with the Joneses," it's Pembroke and Sarah they're referring to.

Binkie had told me stories about the Joneses. Kindly and generous to a fault, Binkie had given so much to the community and had so much more to give. I refused to allow this miscarriage of justice to occur; I had too much of Daddy in me. I simply had to find a way to clear him. And that meant finding clues. And finding clues meant meddling in Nick's murder case. I hated to think of how that would set him off. I got up and went to Great-Grandma's rosewood dresser, picked up a hair brush, and started to brush my hair. Staring at my sleepy reflection in the mirror over the dresser, I whispered to myself, "Nick's right. Murderers are dangerous."

Inspired by Melanie's glamorous turn out, I took pains with my own outfit. Ordinarily, I'm dressed in what Melanie sarcastically refers to as my "construction-wear chic" — khaki pants, denim jackets, workshirts, thick socks, construction boots. Maybe I'd bump into her today and she'd see that I wear skirts too and I look good in them.

I buy my clothes at the Forum and Lumina Station boutiques — Oliver's and Jennifer's — and luck out at Marshall's and T.J.'s. I slipped into a black knit tube skirt by Donna Karan and low-heeled black leather boots, a magenta blouse from August Silks, and a cashmere cardigan. I gave myself a once over in the mirror and thought I should be in *Vogue*. I was meeting my friend and business associate Jon Campbell for brunch at Elijah's after church.

Before I left the house, I called Binkie to check on him and to invite him to join us. He confessed he couldn't bear to be alone but also felt he couldn't face a crowd. The memory of Sheldon's sightless stare was haunting him just as it had haunted me throughout the night.

"I think the police have me under surveillance, Ashley," Binkie said worriedly. "There's a car parked outside my house with two men in it, and it has been there all morning."

"Are you sure?" I asked.

"Well, no, I'm not sure. But they look like police to me."

And maybe they are, I thought. So Nick was treating him like a suspect, just as I'd feared. "Well, we'll just have to give them the slip."

He brightened immediately. "Sounds like a plan. Any ideas?"

"Only the most brilliant," I said with a cheerfulness I didn't feel. "How about this? I'm on my way to St. James. Meet me there. Let them see you entering through the front door. Then after services, we'll slip out the side door and leave through St. Francis's garden." I referred to the small garden behind the church where a statue of St. Francis, the patron saint of animals, stood guard over an earthly host of chipmunks, squirrels, and a variety of birds.

Shortly after twelve, Binkie and I left church by way of St. Francis's garden, as planned. Yesterday's surprise snowfall had vanished without a trace, and the noonday sun had warmed things up. I slipped my arm through his and we strolled cautiously around the block. When Binkie didn't see the car or the men he thought had been watching him, we crossed Third Street to the Burgwin-Wright House.

"A fine example of Georgian architecture," Binkie declared, "but just think of what's under it!"

"The old town jail, you mean?" I asked.

"More than a jail, Ashley dear, a dungeon. I've been in it." He gave a shudder. "It was inhumane of Lord Cornwallis to lock the patriots down there. You do know that he'd set up headquarters here during the War for Independence, don't you? He seized the house for himself, declaring it to be 'the most considerable house in town.' Then after the Battle of Guilford Court House, he retreated back here to Wilmington. Eighteen days later, he marched to Yorktown where, as you know, he was defeated and thus the war ended with his surrender. But he left some of our brave soldiers down there in that dungeon. Some were able to escape by means of the tunnel that leads to the river."

"I've heard rumors about a tunnel. So it does exist?"

"Oh, it exists all right. I've been in it. A truly gruesome place. Not for the faint of heart, nor anyone with claustrophobia. I can't imagine what it would be like to be locked up there. Or in prison."

His chin trembled. Overnight he seemed to have aged a decade. "You do believe I didn't kill Sheldon, don't you?"

I reached out a hand and patted the rough texture of his jacket. "Of course, I believe you, Binkie. You couldn't harm a fly. And the police will believe you, too. We have to find a way to make them see the truth. At heart, Nick is a fair man. It's just that he becomes overzealous when performing his duties."

"I hope you're right, Ashley, but it all looks bad for me. And I've only my ill temper to blame. I hated Sheldon, and everyone knew it. I attacked him earlier in the evening. You were a witness to that, and I will not permit you to lie on my behalf. Scores of people have heard me swear I'd like to see him dead." His chin dropped. "But saying you'd like to see someone dead and killing that person are worlds apart."

"I know, Binkie. Tell me exactly what happened. You didn't get a chance to last night."

He cleared his throat. "Well, the tour seemed to be over. Rachel came through on her way to the kitchen and said you'd locked the front door. I hastened upstairs to use the bathroom. That's the trouble with these old houses, only one bathroom to a house and it's always on the second floor. And the trouble with us old men is we have to use it too often."

He raised a palm in answer to my unspoken question. "No. No one saw me. The last of the stragglers was in one of the bedrooms. I heard someone moving about. When I returned to the library, the door was closed. I pushed it open and stepped inside, and immediately tripped over the poker. I didn't see it laying there on the floor."

"Did you fall?"

"Yes, down on my knees."

So that was the thump I'd heard. "Go on," I prompted.

"Well, I picked up the poker and carried it around the sofa to return it to the hearth. And then . . . then I saw Sheldon. He was lying so still, and there was so much blood. I think I froze."

"That's when I came in."

"Yes."

"Oh, I wish you hadn't picked up that poker. It is the most damning evidence of all."

"My wish, precisely."

"We're going to work this out. We'll make Nick see it couldn't have been you."

He looked encouraged. "I couldn't kill anyone, you know that."

I nodded and brushed his arm.

"As far as I'm concerned, Sheldon killed my baby sister, but I could never kill him over it. Yet, I couldn't forgive him either. He was no good, Ashley."

"He was always kind to me," I said thoughtfully, recalling how Sheldon had been instrumental in getting me the commission from the Historic Preservation Society that had launched my career. I still couldn't believe the illustrious Sheldon Mackie, Wilmington's legendary decorator, was dead.

The first stage of the grieving process, I recalled from when Daddy died, was disbelief and denial. Later, the tears would come. I knew that one day the flood gates would open and I would grieve freely for Sheldon.

But right now my major concern was for the living, for preventing Binkie from being prosecuted for a crime he didn't commit.

"Come, sit down," I said. We climbed the stone steps to the Burgwin-Wright House's front porch. No one was around. We sat on a bench.

Binkie, so distinguished with his thick white hair, his handsome herringbone jacket and knit tie, reached out to take my hand in his. "Yes, I know that Sheldon recommended you to the society. So did I. I'm a charter member, if you recall. You deserved the nomination. You're talented and dedicated, Ashley. It may have seemed like a magnanimous gesture on his part, but I can assure you he must have had an ulterior motive. Sheldon Mackie has never committed an unselfish act in his life."

"Binkie, don't you think you're being . . . well, unfair?"

"Not at all. Sheldon Mackie was a thief."

My surprise at this accusation must have shown on my face for Binkie exclaimed, "Aha! You didn't know that, did you? Sheldon Mackie robbed the Atlantic Coast Line payroll office back in 1960."

I blinked and shook my head. This was getting way out of hand. Sheldon's death had affected him more than I suspected. Binkie was off his head.

He continued, "Sheldon used his share of the money to set himself up in the interior decorating business. Fancied himself another Billy Baldwin. Hah! What a phony!"

An involuntary shudder flowed through me. Suddenly, I was very afraid for Binkie. What else might he tell the police? And would they use these flights of fancy against him? I had to alert Attorney Walter Brice. "If this is true, why wasn't he charged with a crime?"

"Because there's no proof. I can't prove it. But I know. And other people know too."

"Who knows?"

"His accomplices," he declared triumphantly.

Gently, I asked, "And who are his accomplices?"

He stared up at the porch ceiling. "I wish I knew."

5

Well-to-do tourists milled about the cobblestone street at Chandler's Wharf, peering into gift shop windows. Sunday brunch at Elijah's is a Wilmington tradition. With the town full of tourists, a line of ravenous people had queued-up on the boardwalk outside the riverfront restaurant. Folks wore sweaters and jackets.

Wilmington's climate is semi-tropical. We seldom experience truly cold weather, unlike the blustery winter days I had experienced as a student at Parsons School of Design in New York.

I'd had a wonderful roommate in New York, Delores "Kiki" Piccolomini, a fellow design student at Parsons. Without wanting to or even realizing it was happening, I'd lost touch with her. Where are you now, Kiki, I wondered. She'd been my best friend.

Now Jon Campbell is my best friend. I swept past the line and entered the restaurant. He was waiting for me at a window table overlooking the river. The sight of him—his golden hair, his ruddy complexion, his earnest face—was such a comfort after the horror of last night. We've been working together on restoration projects for over a year, and during that time have established a warm, trusting friendship.

He waved a navy clad arm at me. His golden blonde hair was brushed neatly to the side, but I knew that shortly it would flop onto his forehead. His face lit up when he saw me.

He jumped up and pulled out my chair. When I reached the table, he kissed my cheek. Over his shoulder I spotted Betty and Wayne Matthews, brunching at a corner table. We exchanged waves.

"How are you holding up, gorgeous?" he asked when we were seated. "Your cheeks are as rosy as poinsettias."

I felt my cheeks with my hands. They were warm. "Binkie and I were out walking. I guess I'm all right. I've got so much to talk to you about." I eyed his drink. "Is that a Mimosa?"

"Yes. How is Binkie holding up? He's such a nice old guy, one of my favorite people. And Ashley, I keep kicking myself. If I'd stayed with you through the evening instead of leaving to see those other houses I'd have been there when you needed me."

"I'll have a Mimosa," I told the waiter. "And decaf." I opened the menu. "Don't blame yourself. You couldn't have known. And Binkie's like you'd expect him to be. Nervous. Scared. I tried to get him to join us for brunch but he said everyone would stare at him. We were stared at in church. I'm worried, Jon. He doesn't look good. And he thinks the police are watching him."

Jon scanned his menu. "Eggs Benedict," he told the waiter who had returned with my champagne-and-orange-juice cocktail and filled my coffee cup.

"It looks bad for him. He's never made a secret about how he hated Sheldon and wished him dead."

I sensed the waiter's hesitation, could feel his ears perk up. Sheldon's murder and Binkie's involvement had made headlines in this morning's *Sunday Star-News*. I frowned at Jon and made a slight, negative motion with my head. "I'll have French toast with blackberries," I told the waiter.

After he left, I leaned across the table to confide, "Binkie told me about a murder that took place in my house when it was a brothel. About a madam who killed one of her gentleman patrons for his gold, then hid the gold in my house."

Jon's eyebrows arched. "Gold in your house? Well, where could it be? When we were making the restorations, we were all over the place. The walls, the attic, the basement, everywhere."

"Binkie said something else that's really got me worried. He told me Sheldon robbed the Atlantic Coast Line payroll office in 1960." I studied Jon's face. "Why would he say a thing like that? You know, I remember Daddy talking about the railroad and an old robbery."

Jon leaned forward, his palms braced on the table top. "That was before we were born, but it was such a big event, the town buzzed about it for decades. I remember my dad speculating with his friends. The oldtimers still talk about the glory days of the railroad. At one time, the Atlantic Coast Line was the largest employer in Wilmington. The day they announced they were moving to Jacksonville, Florida, is still known as 'Black Thursday' around here. Ashley, Binkie's your best source. He's the history expert."

"I know, but I'd rather not get him started on that subject again. Still, I'd like to know why he thinks Sheldon was involved."

Jon glanced across the room to the Matthews' table. "Well, what about Wayne? With his banking background, he'd have all the facts about the railroad and the payroll robbery."

I gazed across the room at the couple. Wayne Matthews was a good guy, a bit dour for my tastes, but solid and trustworthy. Betty was the outgoing one in that marriage, the high-flier. Wayne was the wind beneath her wings. "Sure, I'll give him a try."

Jon drained the last of his mimosa. "I remember overhearing my dad and his friend discussing the robbery. They said that afterward, everyone was watching everyone else to see who was spending big bucks. You know, some guy who never had two nickels to rub together suddenly parks a Jaguar in his driveway."

"And? Did anyone start spending large sums of cash?"

"No. No one. So the robbers must have stashed it somewhere to be spent later."

"Or, left town with it."

"That's a possibility."

"Well," I continued, "Binkie says Sheldon and his accomplices were the robbers. And that Sheldon used his share to set himself . . ."

Our food arrived, fragrant and hot. The waiter returned with a red-handled carafe and refilled my coffee cup.

After he left, I continued, "Set himself up in the decorating business." I lifted a forkful of sweet berries to my mouth. "This is divine."

Jon's usually cheerful brown eyes grew worried. "I see what you mean. I think I'd better have a talk with our Binkie."

"Oh, would you? He sure could use a friend. But, please, be discreet. He's so vulnerable right now. And you know how proud he is."

Jon cut into the Eggs Benedict and said, "Discretion is my middle name."

I dropped my fork. "Good lord, I don't believe it. There's Melanie."

Jon turned in his chair to look where I was staring. "So? What's with you? You look like you're seeing a ghost."

I grabbed his arm across the table and shook it. "Look who she's with, Jon. That man was the first person in my house yesterday. He carried a silver-handled cane. I have to find out who he is. That cane would make a pretty hefty murder weapon. Wonder if the police have talked to him?"

I fumbled in my shoulder bag for my cell phone. "I've got to call Nick."

"Don't bother."

"What? Of course, I've got to. Binkie didn't kill Sheldon. Someone else did. Maybe that man with his cane."

"Take it easy," Jon said. "Nick is here." He nodded toward the entrance.

I scanned the entrance area. Nick *was* there. I started to wave, then lowered my hand. The host was leading Nick to a table. My heart did flip flops at the sight of those broad shoulders. He was wearing a tweed sport jacket. Nick always dresses nicely. And he's handsome, with light ash brown hair, penetrating hazel eyes, and two dimples that are only visible when he smiles, which is rarely.

We don't have an exclusive relationship. I am free to date anyone I please. So is he. Why then did the sight of him steering a very pretty, tall, platinum blonde—his hand on the small of her back—make me feel ill? And, why did my heart ache when I saw how he looked at her—a look I thought he reserved for me alone?

Jealousy is a painful emotion. It makes you feel all tingly and itchy and sick. In that moment I forgot all about Melanie and the man with the cane. I wanted to swoop down on Nick and his little friend and do them bodily harm.

Outwardly, I remained cool, stayed firmly planted in my chair and did not reveal the fury and confusion that was overwhelming my senses. I patted my mouth with a napkin, withdrew my mirror and lipstick from my purse, and glossed my lips. As far as love relationships go, nothing much changes after high school. No matter how old we get, we react just as we did when we were teenagers. Angling the mirror just so, I spied on Nick and Blondie. The woman wasn't bad, not bad at all. In fact, she was hot.

I closed the lipstick tube with a pop. Now. Armed to do battle. I said innocently, "Since Nick isn't alone, I think we ought to talk to him over here at our table."

Jon gave me a blank look. Even the sharpest of men can be obtuse. "What do you mean?"

"Just go over there and ask him to join us for a minute. Tell him it's about his case. He won't turn you down."

With the aid of the mirror, I spied as Jon approached Nick's table. They exchanged greetings and shook hands. Nick turned in my direction. Blondie stared. In a minute, Nick was excusing himself to Blondie and following Jon. I dropped the mirror in my purse and pretended to be absorbed with activities on the river. The harbor master had elevated the center span of Memorial Bridge to let an enormous barge pass through.

I looked up when I saw Jon and Nick reflected in the plate glass window. "Hi, Nick," I said.

Nick grabbed an available chair and dragged it to our table. "Ashley, what's up?"

So that's how he's going to play it, I thought. Brusque and business-like. I was hurt. Not even a handshake, not even a light touch on my arm. I cleared my throat. "I'm surprised to see you here. I thought you'd be working the case."

He sighed. "I'm here on business, Ashley."

Uh huh, I thought, and my hobby is wrestling alligators.

"So?" he said. "You wanted to see me."

"I do, Nick." I pointed to Melanie's table. "See that man over there, the one with Melanie?"

Nick turned where I pointed. "Yes?"

"He was the first tourist in my house last night. He had a cane with a silver handle. That cane might be the real murder weapon. Do you know who he is and have you questioned him?"

Nick regarded the silver-haired man with interest. "No, but I will now. We're trying to locate as many of the people who were at your house yesterday as we can. If that man was there, I want to talk to him."

"Oh, he was there, all right."

"He may have seen something," Nick continued. "We don't have a witness to the murder yet. I'll see what he has to say."

Nick started to move away. I scrambled out of my chair to follow. Now I had a new worry: had my ploy just backfired? Was I making things worse for Binkie?

Jon grabbed the check from the table. "Hey, wait up, Nick. Ashley and I'll stop at their table and say 'hey' to Melanie. That way, your interview won't look too obvious."

I gave Jon a dirty look. He shrugged his shoulders like, Who, me? "Men," I muttered under my breath. I thought they were supposed to be the risk takers. While he and Nick were deciding who should go first, I stepped in front of them and led the way.

Melanie looked up as we approached her table, irritation plain on her pretty face. Now what's she in a snit about, I asked myself. I listened intently as she made the introductions, catching the new man's name.

"This is Earl Flynn," she said brightly. "Earl's an associate of Joel's. We've been out looking at houses." She patted Flynn's forearm and batted her eyelashes at him. "Something suitable for a man of his stature." She flicked her gaze at me, icicles glinting there.

Aha! So that's who he is, I thought. Melanie's hot prospect. And Joel's associate?

Flynn appeared to be in his fifties and had that fit, outdoorsy California glow. A full head of silvery hair framed prominent, handsome features. I wondered if he'd been in show business too.

Nick took charge. "Mind if I sit down for a moment?"

Melanie and Flynn exchanged looks. "Why, ah, not at all," Flynn said.

Nick snagged a vacant chair. "Ashley and Jon were just leaving." He cast a meaningful glance our way.

"Yes, we're leaving, aren't we, Ashley?" Jon gave me a nudge. "Nice to meet you, Flynn."

I lingered at Melanie's side long enough to hear Nick say, "I'm a homicide detective, Mr. Flynn, working the Sheldon Mackie murder case. I'm talking to people who were at Ms. Wilkes' house yesterday."

6

"I've never been so humiliated in my life!" Melanie hissed in my ear.

We were standing on the boardwalk outside Elijah's, Melanie teetering in high heels. Jon stood off to the side, arms crossed, studying contrails in the sky.

I scarcely listened. Melanie was not the focus of my attention right then. A short distance away, on Elijah's front porch, Nick and Earl Flynn were shaking hands. I took the opportunity to check out "blondie." Her makeup was flawless. She was well dressed—calculatingly so. I guessed she'd had her colors done, and she wasn't deviating from the formula by one scintilla of a hue. With her light skin and platinum hair, it would be easy for her to fade into the landscape. How I wished she would. But the right colors brought her out, enhanced her paleness.

Her hair was cut in one of those straight, forward swinging bobs, a style I wish I could wear. But forget it. My hair would just spring into unruly curls. She wore an expensive—I shop the designer boutiques enough to know expensive when I see it—raspberry jacket, superbly cut, over a matching silk blouse and gray silky pleated trousers. She was covetously thin so that the pleats fell in deep folds just as the designer had intended. I glanced down at my own poochie tummy bulge. I had to stop eating so much.

I couldn't take my eyes off her. She slipped her hand into her shoulder bag—soft, squishy, gray suede—and retrieved a pair of glasses with silver frames and pink-tinted lenses. She slipped them on, glanced my way, and caught me in the act of gawking.

I looked quickly away, but not before I recognized her. She was the fourth person to enter my house yesterday afternoon. When I looked back, Blondie was smiling my way, trying to catch my eye. I pretended not to notice. I wasn't feeling friendly and I knew exactly why.

Instead, I turned to Melanie, whom I'd been tuning out, and who was lecturing me. "You were behind that little charade. I just know you were. I was so embarrassed. Here I am trying to make a sale, not to mention trying to make a good impression on Joel's California associate, and you get that detective of yours to hound him down like a criminal!"

Hound? "Aren't we being a tad melodramatic?"

But Melanie is nothing if not mercurial. Nick, Earl Flynn, and Blondie joined us. In an instant, Melanie was all smiles and Southern charm. Jon murmured something innocuous about the weather to Flynn, but I wasn't listening to him either. Instead, I was registering the way Nick was presenting his new friend to us, like she was someone very special.

"I'd like you to meet Lisa Hamilton. Lisa is the police department's new public information officer. She just moved here from Georgia. And this is..."

He was about to say my name but Melanie stepped between us, hand outstretched. I thought she was going to shake hands with Lisa, but instead she offered the startled Lisa a business card. "I'm Melanie Wilkes, and I'm delighted to welcome you to our little community, Lisa." She linked arms with Blondie and drew her to one side. "Now, we'll just have to find the perfect house to suit a young executive on her way up like yourself. Naturally, you'll be doing a lot of entertaining." Inspiration seemed to strike. "Oh, I know. I've got just the house—in mint condition too so you can move right in."

"Why, why, thank you, Miss . . ." Lisa glanced at the card in her hand. "Miss Wilkes."

Jon took my elbow and tried to pull me away. I wasn't budging. I wouldn't miss this little bit of live theatre for anything.

"I'm Melanie," she said with saccharin sweetness. "Melanie Wilkes. Just like in *Gone With the Wind*." She laughed lightly. "Now you phone me, Lisa, and we'll do lunch, and then I'll take you on a tour of our best boutiques."

The group was breaking up, moving toward cars, Blondie with Nick. He never did complete the introduction.

Melanie grasped Flynn's arm possessively. "Come, Earl, let's take another look at that magnificent house in Landfall."

"Ashley, I'm so glad I caught up with you," Betty Matthews called. I turned back toward the restaurant to see the Matthewses hurrying my way.

"Hi, Betty, Wayne," I said. Jon greeted them too.

"Ashley, I just got a call from the Historical Society. I expected they'd close down your house today after what happened. Isn't it just awful? Poor Sheldon."

"Yes," I sighed, remembering. "Poor Sheldon."

"Well, imagine my surprise when I was asked to fill in for Sheldon and Binkie at your house. They made it clear they don't want Binkie there. He's going to be shunned until this is all cleared up."

"You mean my house is still on the tour?" I asked.

"Sure 'nuff. Can you believe it?"

"No, I can't. The police are agreeing to this?"

"They must be, Ashley, because you're supposed to open at four as usual," Betty replied.

"The candlelight tour is very important to our community," Wayne said.

"Let's take a walk," I suggested to Jon after Wayne and Betty left. "I need to clear my head."

He tucked my hand into his. "Where do you want to walk? Along the riverfront? At dusk the trees will be illuminated but it's too early now."

"Let's just stroll around town, look at the Christmas decorations."

"The town looks beautiful. I think you're worried about Binkie. I am too. But let's take some time out for ourselves."

We exited Chandler's Wharf into Nun Street. High atop a ballast wall, on property known as "Brow of the Hill," the handsome Federal-style Governor Dudley house, circa 1825, was decorated with fresh green wreaths in every window. The historic district, all two hundred blocks of it, had gone all out for Christmas — tiny white lights in trees and shrubs, candles in windows, wreaths with bright red bows.

On Front Street, volunteers were setting out fresh luminaries. They stopped to stare. I called hello. "As soon as we're out of ear shot, they'll be gossiping about us, Jon, and about the murder in my house."

He glanced back over his shoulder. "Don't let it bother you."

I shrugged. "I'll just have to get used to it. Everyone's talking about Sheldon's murder. And why not? Everyone knew him. He was popular." Everyone liked him. Except Binkie.

We walked aimlessly for a while, meandering up and down residential streets, and cutting through alleys. We ventured outside the historic district, into Palace Street. Here too the homes reflected the spirit of the Candlelight Tour, wreaths with berries and colorful bows on front doors, candles in windows, glimpses of Christmas trees inside.

Near the corner, four derelict houses seemed to lean into each other, a blight on the cityscape. "FOR SALE" signs dotted the tiny front yards. "Those houses have been for sale for almost a year," I said.

"They're not old enough to have any historic value, and it would cost too much to fix them up. They were rentals until the landlord started losing money."

"I suppose someone will buy them for the lots."

"I think you're right."

We followed the luminaries to Orange Street and the city's oldest house, the Mitchell-Smith-Anderson House, circa 1740. It was one of the few eighteenth-century homes to survive Wilmington's many fires. The rhythmic clip-clopping of a steady horse sounded in the street, and I turned to see the Springbrook Farms carriage, filled to capacity with tourists. The white horse had sprouted fanciful reindeer antlers.

Passing familiar landmarks, like the handsome Italianate Zebulon Latimer House, home of the Lower Cape Fear Historical Society, I felt my pulse slow and my breath come evenly. These old buildings are the touchstones of my daily life. I'm one of the lucky ones: I was born with a passion for history, with a desire to preserve the sound and the true, to restore dilapidated structures to wholesomeness. Now I'm doing just that. And managing to earn a degree of success I only dreamt about. Despite Sheldon's murder, despite Nick's perfidy, I felt my spirits soar.

"Look at that tree!" I exclaimed, pointing to the giant hemlock across Third Street at the First Presbyterian Church. The enormous evergreen glittered with thousands of tiny white lights.

"Stringing those lights wasn't easy," Jon commented. "They must have used a cherry-picker to get to the top of that tree."

Further along Third Street, we came upon the rear of the Burgwin-Wright House, the parterre gardens with their centuries old formal boxwoods, and the kitchen building.

"Binkie and I were here earlier. He told me he'd toured the dungeon and tunnel and that they were inhumane and gruesome."

"Every time they start a new construction project down by the river, they find another tunnel," Jon said. "There's a network of them under the historic district. During the Civil War, the blockade runners used them to smuggle munitions from the port to the railroad, then on to General Lee in Virginia."

"We're lucky some dedicated citizens got together to save the old sections," I commented. "Most other cities can't wait to tear down their old houses. I'm proud of Daddy for helping with the legal aspects."

Jon gave me a quick squeeze. "I love this place as much as you do, Ashley. The best part is that we're well paid for doing what we love. How many people can say that?"

We stopped, our eyes locking. "Yes," I said softly. "This is just what I needed. But, Jon, I'm so worried about Binkie. Do you think they'll really charge him with Sheldon's murder?"

He took my hand and we crossed Third to stroll alongside St. James Church. "Unless the police can find other leads, I have to admit it looks bad for him. I wish I could be more encouraging, Ashley. I know he didn't do it."

"But someone did, Jon. And he's getting away with it. Binkie told me he heard someone in one of the upstairs bedrooms after the tour. He thought it was a straggler. And I remember hearing footsteps on the backstairs. It must have been the killer, just waiting his chance."

So much for feeling good. "Nick thinks Binkie did it. Honestly, Jon, he's not much of a detective."

"Maybe you're being too hard on him. We don't know what he's doing behind the scenes. He's got to be investigating suspects we don't know about."

I removed my hand from his and, turning the corner onto Fourth Street, walked rapidly.

"Hey, slow down. Take it easy, Ashley. Okay, I take back everything I said about Nick. He's a lousy detective, and he's railroading Binkie. Feel better?"

I slowed to a stroll and couldn't help grinning up at him. "Do me a favor, will you?"

His arms spread expansively. "Anything. Just name it."

"Go talk to Binkie right now. Get him to run through the events of last evening. See if there's something he left out that we can use in his defense."

"Sure. I'll go see him as soon as I walk you home."

Swiftly now, shadows in the streets lengthened as the sun dropped behind Eagle Island. With the winter solstice almost upon us, nightfall was arriving earlier and earlier these days.

We reached my house where already a line had formed. "That was nice, Jon." I stretched to kiss him on the cheek. "You're a dear. I've got to get inside."

"I'll check on Binkie and see what I can learn."

I started up the walk, waving. "Tell him I'll pick him up at eight. We're going to see *The Nutcracker* tonight."

7

Candlelight behind lace curtains beckoned me to my own front door. Rachel was here and the docents too. Rachel had a key so she could let herself and them inside.

I turned my key in the front door just as she pulled it open for me. Over her shoulder I saw Nick standing in the reception hall. I dropped my sweater on a bench. "What are you doing here? And where's your little friend?"

"Friend? Oh, you mean Lisa. She's back at headquarters, managing the news releases. With this murder, we're all pulling double shifts."

"Then why are you here?" I challenged him, assuming he'd rather be at headquarters with Lisa.

"I thought I'd stay with you through the tour, watch the crowd for you."

My heart leapt with joy. "You haven't given up. You're watching for the killer. You think he'll return to the scene of the crime. On television, they always do."

"This isn't television! And we've got men watching Professor Higgins," Nick said.

So Binkie hadn't been imagining things. He was being watched by the police. He was still the prime suspect.

"I'm surprised we were allowed to open, Nick. Did the police go along with that decision?"

"The chief didn't object. There was no reason to close you down.

No safety issue."

"What about out of respect for Sheldon Mackie?" I asked.

"I don't know about that. That's not my area. Someone was quoted as saying he'd have wanted it this way."

"Someone was rationalizing a guilty conscience," I declared.

"Look, Ashley, isn't it enough that I want to be with you? I know this has all been upsetting for you, and I was hoping we could talk."

I sighed deeply. "Yes, it's been very upsetting. I've lost one good friend to a murderer, and the other to the police. What do you want to talk about?"

"Later. We'll talk later. There isn't time now."

Nick was an enigma, I knew that. I pretended not to care. But I did care. "Whatever," I murmured. "Your guys took the rug from the library. Hopefully, the real killer left evidence on it that will clear Binkie."

The doorbell chimed and I opened it to see Betty Matthews urging a crowd to stand back. "Let me pass!" she commanded in an authoritative drawl.

Once inside, she exclaimed, "Ah declare, Ashley, you will never believe what's going on out there. The entire tour is lined up at your house. The line stretches around the block."

"Oh, no! You mean there's no one at the other houses? Everyone's here?"

Betty was rearranging her mussed hair with her fingertips. "'Fraid so. Okay, just point me toward the rooms you want me to cover."

"I'll show you," Rachel said, guiding Betty toward the rear of the house.

The grandfather clock on the landing chimed four. "Well, this is it." I peered out the window at the crowd, and said to Nick, "Maybe it's a good thing you are here. There's a real crowd out there. And they look mighty impatient. Maybe this *is* a safety issue."

A chunky, pugnacious woman pushed her way in aggressively, her eyes darting first to the parlor, then beyond the stairs to the rear hall. Shoving her ticket in my face, she demanded, "Just show me where it happened."

"The tour starts in the parlor, ma'am. This way," I said firmly, my arm indicating the large, formal room where the docent waited.

"Skip it," the woman growled. "Just show me the library. I want to see where that decorator got snuffed!"

Eventually, Nick had to radio for a crowd-control team, complete with horses, to disperse the crowd, and we locked the front door and closed early.

"What a disaster," I cried, sinking down onto the bench. "I've waited my whole life to have a house on the candlelight tour, and now this has to happen. Poor Sheldon. Poor Binkie. And poor me."

"I'll make you a cup of tea," Rachel said, and went to the kitchen. The docents had left by the back door and Betty Matthews had called Wayne to pick her up on Third Street.

Nick sat down beside me and eased my head onto his shoulder. "I'm sorry, Ashley. I don't know what else to say."

I straightened up. "Well, Binkie and I are going to see *The Nutcracker* so I'd better go change and pick him up early."

"No, Ashley, you can't do that," Nick said.

A warning note in his voice made me ask, "Why not? Why can't I?"

"Ashley, I have bad news. That's the real reason I'm here."

"Tell me. Get it over with."

"Promise me you won't be upset."

"Nick, I'm already upset. I've been upset for the past twenty-four hours. Now, spit it out."

His hazel eyes narrowed. "Okay. Here's the thing. We did take a look at Flynn's cane like you suggested. I personally took it to the lab this afternoon. We rushed the lab results on the cane and on the poker. That poker is definitely the murder weapon. Mackie's hair and blood are on it. So are the professor's fingerprints. And no one else's."

I met his gaze. "I can't go to the ballet with him because you're going to arrest him. Right?"

"I'm sorry, Ashley," he said again.

I brushed away hot tears and dashed to the telephone. I reached Walt Brice at home—he'd never refuse a call from one of Judge Wilkes's daughters, even on a Sunday—and told him about Binkie's imminent arrest. I warned him that Binkie was making some pretty outlandish claims about Sheldon and that he had to get over to the jail right away.

36

8

The next morning sunlight streamed through the stained glass window in my bathroom, flashing a rainbow of colors on the white tile. I turned off the shower and reached for a towel. I may have only one bathroom but it is large and roomy, with a huge cast iron tub that sits up off the floor on wonderfully old-fashioned claw feet.

Again, I'd slept miserably, tossing and turning while plotting ways to spare Binkie a murder trial. In the clear light of dawn, all my ideas seemed farfetched.

As I reached for my terrycloth robe, I became aware of a scrabbling noise coming from somewhere below. At times noises on the street sound like they're inside the house. I tried to see down into the street but the stained glass made everything blurry and the wrong color.

Then the sound came again, a distant scratching. Mice? Or was someone in the library? Could the police be back? But no one could get inside, all the doors were bolted.

Good lord, it's the murderer, I thought. The blood in my veins turned to ice. I pulled the robe tighter around me, and dashed across the hall and into my bedroom where I grabbed the weapon of choice, a poker from the hearth. Creeping on bare feet across the upstairs landing, I peered down over the banister.

"Is someone down there? If there is, I'm armed!"

The scrabbling noise stopped, followed by a brief silence until I heard the dull thud of a car door slamming in front of my house. The doorbell rang shrilly and I jumped. Heart thumping, I raced down the front staircase to pad cautiously across the reception hall. Pulling back a lace panel from the sidelight, I peeked out on the veranda. Rachel.

"I'm so glad it's you," I said, pulling the door open.

"Who were ... ? What are you doing with that poker, Ashley?"

"Sorry." I lowered the weapon to my side. "I heard something, someone. I came down to investigate."

She dumped her paint supplies on the floor. "You should have called the police."

"And have Nick and his storm troopers stampeding through here again? No, thank you. I'll take care of this myself." I started for the back hall, brandishing the poker like a sword.

She scurried to catch up. "I'm coming with you."

We searched the first floor rooms, opened pantry and cupboard doors, checked closets, flung back the tapestry panels that curtain off a divan in my parlor, my interpretation of a Victorian Turkish Corner.

Rachel looked thoughtful. "Well, there's no one here, and nothing looks out of place."

"It sounded like scratching. Like a very large mouse."

"And you're sure you locked all the doors last night?"

"Absolutely. After what's been going on, I check the locks twice." I led the way through the kitchen and rattled the doorknob. Secure.

Filing through the back hall again, we reached the outside door that led onto the porte cochere. This was the door the tour group had exited through on Saturday and Sunday. It too was securely bolted.

"Okay, three down, one to go," I said.

"You've got too many doors. That'd make me nervous."

We checked the French doors that led from the dining room to the side veranda—all tightly locked with heavy bolts, no broken panes.

"Well, no one got in here. Must have been street noises. You know how sounds carry."

"Did you see anyone lurking around when you drove up?"

Rachel shook her head and her shiny black hair caught the sunlight. "No one. It's still early and fairly quiet for a Monday morning."

"What are you doing here so early? I'm not even dressed."

"I couldn't sleep so I thought I'd get an early start."

"I had a restless night too. I might as well tell you, it'll be all over the news. Nick arrested Binkie last night."

"No!"

I told her about Sheldon's hair and blood being on the poker, and Binkie's fingerprints on the handle.

"Oh, Ashley, this is all wrong. We've got to do something."

"I know. After the arrest, I called Walt Brice. He said he'd go right over to the station. Then I stayed awake for most of the night, trying to think of how to help Binkie."

She followed me up the stairs, saying, "I thought I'd catch up on the painting I'm doing in your guest room."

She went to work on hand-painting magnolias on the walls while I dried my hair, dressed, and made coffee. Carrying a large mug upstairs to her, I described how Nick had thought he was doing me a kindness by warning me of Binkie's impending arrest. "Honestly, Rachel, what did I ever see in him?"

WHQR was playing Handel's "Messiah" on the portable radio she brings with her when she's working. Hopping down off the stepladder, her long straight hair swung as she landed lightly on moccasined feet. The exquisite white magnolias on the mauve walls complemented the comforter on the antique rice bed that had been in my mother's family.

"What did you see in Nick?" she repeated. "Well, he's one sexy guy, for starters. There's a special kind of energy between you two. And he's nice, decent. But anyone who knows Professor Higgins knows he's no killer. I had him for history at the University and lord knows I'm brain dead when it comes to academics. Give me a paint brush and I'm a whiz . . ."

"You're a genius with a paint brush," I interrupted, standing back to admire the white blossoms.

"But the Battle of Waterloo or the Lewis and Clark expedition, forget it. Anyway, Professor Higgins was so nice to me. He's not a stuffed shirt like some of them. He gave me tutoring sessions in his office, made history fun. Thanks to him I passed a required course I would have failed."

"Binkie's a dedicated teacher."

Rachel appraised her handiwork for a moment, climbed back up on the stepladder, and dipped her brush into the paint. "Now he's in trouble and if there's any way I can help, just let me know."

"I wish I knew what to do," I said.

"Well, you know what they always say in the detective novels: follow the money."

"Yes, but what does that mean?" I asked.

"It means that murders are usually about money. So follow the money trail."

"Okay, but what money trail?" I asked.

"Find out who benefits from Sheldon's death?"

"That's probably MaeMae, but you've given me something to think about. Listen, I'd better go water all those thirsty Christmas trees."

We were startled to hear a man shouting from downstairs. "Rachel!"

Our eyes locked. "Who's that? Someone's in my house." I grabbed another poker from the guest room hearth, grateful for my many fireplaces. "The doors were all locked. You saw for yourself."

Rachel scrambled down the ladder. She put out a hand to restrain me. "I think it's Eddie."

"Eddie? Who's Eddie? And how did he get in my house?"

"I don't know but I'm going to find out," she declared.

"Rachel! Where the hell are you?"

"Eddie! I'm up here." We moved out into the hall, I clutching the poker.

There was loud stomping on the stairs, followed by frequent exclamations of the "F" word. I darted to the top of the stairs.

A head appeared, then a torso, then a man reached the top of the stairs.

I opened my mouth to ask how he got in, but his yelling drowned me out. He didn't even see me.

"Rachel, why the hell d'ya take the car when I told you I needed it? I had to walk all the way over here to find you."

Rachel exhibited a side of her personality I'd never seen before. She yelled, "*The* car? Don't you mean *my* car, Eddie? I had to get to work. *I* needed it. Besides, I wouldn't mind if you borrowed it if you'd put gas in it once in a while."

Despite his threatening demeanor, Eddie was a remarkably handsome man. Almost pretty, except for the sneer. He reminded me of an actor I'd seen on the late show, Tyrone Power, with curly black hair, arched eyebrows, long luxurious lashes. But the resemblance ended there. Eddie had a weak, mean mouth.

Suddenly I placed him. The second person to arrive on the tour on Saturday. Eddie had come in right after Melanie's client Earl Flynn, and before the solid, mature woman. I remember having the impression that he and Flynn were together.

"The keys, Rachel! Hand over the keys. Now! If you know what's good for you."

He raised a hand threateningly. He's going to hit her, I thought, and waved the poker at him. "Stop! Get out of my house now or I'll call the cops."

Eddie took a step back and for the first time saw me. "Who the hell are you?"

"I own this house you just broke into!"

"This is Eddie Parker," Rachel said, her tone surprisingly mild.

Eddie gave me a leer. "Well, hello there."

What did he take me for? A gullible female like Rachel?

"Your front door was standing open," he said in a wheedling tone. "I knocked but no one answered. Guess y'all couldn't hear me up here with your female yammering."

"You're a liar! The door was locked!"

Eddie didn't take offense. Guess he'd been called worse names. "Your house, huh?" He gave me another leer, like he thought no woman could resist him when he turned on the charm. "Some fancy crib. Come on, Rach, honey, get me the keys. I've got something big coming down. You don't want to blow it for me."

Rachel slumped, defeated. She picked her purse up off the floor, withdrew a key ring, slapped it into his open palm. "Don't bring it back with an empty tank."

Eddie went ballistic. He grabbed her by the arm and jerked her forward. "Get off my back, will you, bitch! You'll get your lousy gas. There's gonna be plenty of money for gas, and other stuff too, so watch your step."

Rachel pulled away and rubbed the red finger marks on her arm. "Leave, Eddie. You got what you came for. Just leave!"

"Get out of my house," I yelled.

In the background, the Vienna Chorus sang angelically as if to cajole evil Eddie into better behavior.

He sneered, gave us both the finger, then clumped down the stairs. When I heard the front door slam, I ran down to secure the lock. I went around the first floor again, checking every door.

Rachel was coming down the stairs. "How'd he get in here, Rachel? Did you give him keys to my house?"

She mumbled something and grabbed the handrail for support as tears streamed down her cheeks and her shoulders shook.

"Who is that mad man?" I asked and held out my arms.

She collapsed against me. Tears wet my shirt. "I'm so sorry, Ashley."

I took her gently by the shoulders and looked her full in the face. "What have you got to be sorry about, Rachel? You didn't give him a key to my house, did you?"

"No, no," she sobbed. "I'd never do that. I'm just sorry you had to see him like that. He's not usually that way. He can be so sweet. But, lately, well, Eddie's got a lot of pressure on him."

"Does he live with you?"

"Yes. I love him, Ashley."

I rubbed her back. And I thought I had problems with Nick!

9

"He looks so peaceful."

"Doesn't he though. They did a good job on him. You can't even see the head wounds."

The two women ahead of me took turns leaning into Sheldon Mackie's casket.

"How can they be so disrespectful?" I complained to Melanie who was standing behind me in line.

"What?"

Her gaze flitted around the viewing room and I knew I'd lost her. She was checking out the crowd that had lined up for Sheldon's "visitation." After assuring herself there was no one worthy of her consideration, she resumed her chat with me.

"What are you going to wear to the New Year's Eve gala? I hope you're not going to drag out that sorry black gown you wear to every formal occasion."

"There's nothing wrong with my black gown. It's a designer original I found on sale at Saks when I lived in New York."

Melanie arched her eyebrows. "Sure 'nuff, 'found' is the correct word. That old thing looks like the sort of dress anyone with a modicum of fashion sense would lose."

"Well, at least I have taste when it comes to choosing friends!"

She narrowed her eyes. "And what, pray tell, do you mean by that?"

"We'll discuss it later. And if you don't stop squinting like that, you're going to get wrinkles."

She gave me a startled look, then, instantly, composed her face into smooth planes.

The queue moved forward and I was next, and suddenly I was looking down at Sheldon's body. I glanced at him quickly, almost fearfully, then shut my eyes. It was true, his wounds were no longer visible. I remembered all the blood on his temple. I whispered the Twenty-third Psalm, then meditated on his good qualities. How kind he'd been to me when I was starting my career.

I opened my eyes and faced MaeMae Mackie who waited for me to offer condolences. She was dressed in black with pearls. Next to the casket, a larger-than-life portrait of Sheldon in his prime stood on an easel. I'd heard through the grapevine that an artist had worked on the painting for two days straight, going without sleep, and that the paint had not yet dried. MaeMae commissioned the portrait only hours after Sheldon's murder.

"I'm sorry for your loss, MaeMae. I'll miss him."

She clung to my hand, her frosted pink lips parted in a forced smile. "Thank you, Ashley. Sheldon lived a full life. I like to think he did it 'his way.' That thought gives me comfort."

"Well, if there's anything I can do for you, you have only to ask. I know everyone says that, but I mean it."

"I know you do, Ashley. You date that homicide detective. Tell him to lock Binkie Higgins up and throw away the key!"

Melanie and I moved into the lobby where a coffee urn was set up and helped ourselves to styrofoam cups. "Okay, what did you mean by that crack about my friends?" she asked.

"Just how well do you know this Flynn character?" I didn't bother to conceal my hostility.

"Shhh. Keep your voice down. He worked for Joel back in Hollywood, so Joel knows him well. And if Joel vouches for him, that's good enough for me."

She smoothed an arched eyebrow with one fingertip. "The truth is, Earl is one of us, a Wilmingtonian. He grew up here. Why, he even knew Daddy. He moved to California right after high school and with his good looks broke into the movie business."

"Well, I'd sure like to get my hands on that ebony cane of his," I said, still unconvinced that it wasn't the murder weapon.

Melanie choked on her coffee. "His cane! Have you gone mad? You really are getting bad." Despite my earlier warning, she narrowed her eyes, causing wrinkles in the outer corners.

"Why does he use a cane, anyway? He can walk perfectly well. I've seen him. What is it, a Hollywood prop?" Or a murder weapon? He could have washed it off, I reasoned.

"At least he's not a murderer!"

"How do you know that? Anyway, Binkie didn't kill anybody. Even you don't believe that!"

She had the decency to look contrite. "No, I never thought he did. But I'd stay away from him, if I were you. You don't want any part of this scandal sticking to you and ruining your reputation."

"I can't desert him, Mel. I'm going to prove he's innocent."

She screwed up her face again. She just couldn't help it. Wrinkles in the making. "How? By accusing Earl of killing Sheldon?"

She glanced around, then seeing no one of interest, turned back to me. "By the way," she asked with saccharin sweetness, "who put up Binkie's bail? As if I didn't know?"

I averted my face but she could always see through me.

When I didn't respond, she went on, "Oh, don't look so innocent. Walt Brice told me all about it. It was a staggering sum, and we both know college professors are as poor as sharecroppers. His little house on Front Street isn't worth a hundred thou. So where did the money come from, Ashley Wilkes?"

I heaved a sigh. "Oh, all right, I put up the bail money. But it was only ten percent and I'll get it back. Binkie'd never skip. Where would he go? And he'd never do that to me."

Then I realized I'd lost Melanie again. Lisa Hamilton was passing by and Melanie, flashing a megawatt smile, made a lunge for her. "Lisa, sugah, what a joy to see you again. And wasn't lunch today divine? You are such good company. We must do it again soon." She looped her arm through Lisa's and strolled with her toward the exit. "Now have you had time to consider the houses we looked at this afternoon? That darling ranch on Bradley Creek is perfect for you."

Soon they were out of earshot. I surveyed the lobby. The crowd was breaking up, heading out for the parking lot. In the viewing room, MaeMae was shaking hands with the final guest. I hurried to the Ladies Room.

Nicely appointed, the decorator in me noted, taking in the pristine marble vanity and the fresh floral arrangement. I stepped into the roomy handicapped stall.

Just then the outer door bumped open and I heard the clatter of high heels tapping on the marble floor.

"These shoes are killing me!"

That was MaeMae Mackie's voice.

"How much longer do I have to keep up this charade?"

"Just until the estate is settled," replied Lucy Lou Upchurch, "then you can do anything you please."

"Well, how long does probate take?" MaeMae asked over the gush of running water.

"Depends, but you should have it settled in about ninety days."

"Three months! You mean to say I've got to put on this grieving widow act for the next three months?"

I heard paper towels being yanked out of a wall dispenser. I held my breath and stood very, very still.

"It'll go fast, hon," Lucy Lou said. "You can do it."

There was the clitter-clatter of high heels as they moved to the door. Just before it swung shut, I heard Lucy Lou say in a stern voice, "You have to."

I waited a few minutes, then stepped out of the stall. I was shaken. MaeMae was glad that Sheldon was dead.

10

"Rhett proposed and I accepted," Mama announced on Wednesday morning. My mind had been wandering but that brought me back with a jolt.

I finished watering the Christmas cactus that bloomed on her window sill. The residents of Magnolia Manor weren't allowed to have poinsettias because poinsettia sap is as toxic as any of Blanche Moore's concoctions. I've often wondered why the North Carolina murderess fed her husbands arsenic, which could be traced, when all she had to do was chop up some poinsettia or oleander leaves and add them to the poor gents' salads. She'd never have been caught.

"That's nice, Mama," I said. "I'm glad you have a friend." The man she referred to as Rhett was in reality Maurice Dorfsman, a retired furrier from New Jersey and a fellow patient.

"I want you and Melanie to be my bridesmaids," Mama went on. "And Rhett's grandson is going to be the best man. He's a wizard."

I arched my eyebrows, but didn't say anything. I don't like to encourage her when she gets this way. "Do you need anything before I go, Mama?"

"A wedding dress, dear. The ceremony will be held on the Sunday before Christmas, in the social hall."

"Yes, Mama," I agreed sadly. I kissed her cheeks and promised to return soon.

I stopped at the manager's office and asked if she could spare me a minute. "Why, of course, Ms. Wilkes," Ms. Miller said, turning away from her computer screen. "What can I do for you? Your mother has really settled in nicely, don't you think?"

"Yes, Mama seems happy, and I can see she's well cared for. But," and I paused, choosing my words with care, "she's talking about marrying Mr. Dorfsman. I know she imagines a lot, but have you heard them talking about marriage?"

Ms. Miller slipped off her glasses and beamed at me happily. "Your mother and Mr. Dorfsman are so cute together. Holding hands like teenagers. It does the other residents a world of good to see them so much in love. Makes them all remember when they were young and in love and they lived in happier times."

"So that's all there is to it?" I asked.

"Well, we are planning a little ceremony for them right before Christmas. We'll have a party, but it'll be a mock wedding ceremony, of course. Our Chaplain, Reverend Goode, will preside. Naturally, under the circumstances, it won't be a real wedding, but he'll write a nice little ceremony where your mother and Mr. Dorfsman promise to love one another. That's all they want, really. The other residents are looking forward to it. I hope you don't disapprove. It's not like they're going to share a room or anything. It's all perfectly innocent. And your sister gave us permission."

"Melanie? Melanie gave you permission to hold a mock wedding with my mother as the bride?" I couldn't believe my ears.

Ms. Miller seemed a bit flustered. "Why, naturally, I telephoned Ms. Wilkes and got her permission before we proceeded with the plans."

Melanie approved this plan? Were we talking about the same woman? I dropped into a chair. "Tell me, Ms. Miller, exactly what did my sister say?"

Ms. Miller cleared her throat. "Well, actually, your sister made a kind of hooting sound. Then she told me that so long as it wasn't charged to your mother's bill, we could give her a coronation ceremony and crown her Queen of England if we liked." Ms. Miller looked nonplussed. "Those were her exact words. And, Ms. Wilkes, I assure you, the expense will not be added to your mother's bill."

I stood up to shake hands with Ms. Miller, who was obviously a good person with her patients' welfare at heart. "I like the idea. Mama's happy here. And of course, it's not legal. Mama's been declared incompetent by the court. She can't sign legal papers."

"No, no, of course not," Ms. Miller hastily agreed. "There will be nothing to sign."

"Well, I'll be here for the nuptials then. Thank you, Ms. Miller. I thought I'd stop in and say hello to Mrs. Penry. You know, I bought her house and I'm living in it now. Is she feeling well enough to receive visitors?"

Ms. Miller seemed glad that the subject of the wedding had been resolved. "Mrs. Penry is about the same. She'll be glad to have a visitor. No one ever comes to see her, poor dear. Just don't stay too long. She tires easily. You know the way. She's in the other wing."

I found Mrs. Penry resting in a chair. Her bed was made up and I was glad to see that she was not bed-ridden. The room was spartan: no draperies or rugs, just window shades and a clean tile floor. Those items that harbored dust mites had been banished.

She was hooked to an oxygen tank, tubes attached to her nostrils. But all in all, she looked better than the last time I saw her.

"Aren't you a dear to visit me," she said in a whistley undertone. "You must be here to see Claire."

I touched her arm in a gentle greeting. "Yes, I've been to see Mama. I guess you've heard about the wedding."

"Your mother and Mr. Dorfsman are an inspiration to us all. If they can find love this late in life, there's hope for the rest of us."

"Yes, ma'am," I said, beginning to see that Ms. Miller was right. "I can understand how you'd feel that way. Well, I'll be here with bells on."

Mrs. Penry coughed into her hand, and I reminded myself not to stay long. "I came by to tell you how much I love living in your house. My decorating is almost finished. You may have heard that it was on the candlelight tour." I wondered if she'd heard about the murder in the library. The patients here were insulated from the outside world.

"Yes, dear, someone did mention that to me. The historical society was always begging me to put it on the tour, but my health just wouldn't permit the stress." She grabbed my wrist. "And they told me that some-one was killed in the library. Is that so?"

Skipping over the gory details, I confirmed Sheldon's death. I didn't want to say too much. Talk of murder was much too distressing for some-one in her poor health. I tried to think of something to distract her. "You know, it's funny, Mrs. Penry, but Professor Higgins told me there's an old rumor about gold being hidden in your house. Have you ever heard anything so ridiculous?"

Mrs. Penry laughed, the laugh turning into a wheeze. The seizure passed and she breathed deeply.

"Maybe I should come back another time," I suggested.

"Oh, no, please don't go. I haven't had a good laugh in a long time. Gold, indeed. When he was in high school, my son Russell heard that story too, and I can tell you he turned our house inside out and never found a thing. Even ripped up some of the floor boards. Made the big-gest mess you ever saw. Then I had to have everything repaired."

"But he didn't find anything?"

"The only coins he found were some old pennies." Mrs. Penry laughed harshly. "Served him right." Her eyes widened and she started to cough. "He, he," she choked. Was she laughing?

A nurse came running. She bent over Mrs. Penry, adjusting the dial on the oxygen tank. "You'll have to leave now, Miss."

I walked slowly down the long corridor to the lobby. Was the asthma attack inevitable, or had our discussion about her son brought it on?

As I strolled out the front door and passed through the white columns, I replayed the conversation with Ms. Miller. Melanie never failed to sur-prise me. I reminded myself to call her later. Sheldon's funeral was taking place right about now, a private graveside service with only MaeMae and Lucy Lou. If I was going to find out who killed him, I needed to learn more about his private life, like who benefited most from his death. I had a plan. And I needed Melanie's help to carry it out.

11

On Thursday afternoon, I wandered up and down the aisles of the Harris Teeter supermarket. Panic was setting in. Displays featured Christmas toys and ornaments, paper towels and plates with holiday motifs. But where was the food? Grocery stores are foreign places to me. I dash into them only when I'm running low on toilet paper. The way I look at it, the same god who invented homecooking, cookstoves, pots and pans, also invented restaurants and professional chefs. I'll take the latter, thank you very much.

I wasn't sure what I was looking for but when I spotted the prepared entrees in the frozen food case, I knew I'd found it. Tossing two boxes labeled Chicken Divan into my shopping basket, I headed for the express checkout line.

At home, in my old-fashioned kitchen, I stretched on tiptoe to pull down my one and only casserole dish from a high cabinet. My gas stove is green and camel and sits nine inches off the floor on tapered feet. I've only used one burner and that was to heat water. I don't own a microwave. This is not a place where casseroles get assembled for grieving widows.

To my chagrin, the plastic containers inside the boxes were oval shaped, not rectangular. The Chicken Divan was frozen solid. I looked from them to my rectangular Corning casserole. Two oval blobs of frozen food set side by side in a rectangular baking dish would tip off anyone that I was offering tacky, commercial, frozen food to the bereaved.

A topping, that's what I needed. Something to conceal the oval outlines. When baked, they'd merge. Unfortunately, even if I could figure out how to turn on the oven, I didn't have time to bake them now. Jon and I had spent the morning reviewing blueprints and preparing an estimate for the owners of an antebellum mansion. Melanie was meeting me at the Mackie residence in thirty minutes.

I shoved the frozen Chicken Divan into my freezer, and zipped back to Harris Teeter where I purchased a shaker of seasoned bread crumbs and a packet of shredded cheddar cheese. Then I flew back home.

Running the frozen containers upsidedown under hot tap water just long enough to dislodge the blobs from the containers but not long enough to defrost the food, I then deposited the ovals in my rectangular casserole, side by side.

Tearing open the bag of shredded cheese, I sprinkled the frozen ovals generously with cheddar. Liberally, I shook bread crumbs on top of the cheese. Or should it have been the other way around? Bread crumbs first, then cheese? I didn't know which, so I combed my fingers through the topping, mixing it up and spreading it around. Maybe I should be dating a chef instead of a not-very-shrewd detective. The people in my life are as helpless in the kitchen as I am.

But the casserole, doctored up, didn't look half bad. I put the glass lid on it, slid it into a plastic bag, carried the offering out to my Aurora and placed it gently on the front passenger seat. For good measure I strapped the seat belt around it. Oh, why was I bothering? MaeMae Mackie would just shove it into her already burgeoning freezer and forget about it. Probably I'd never see my pretty casserole dish again. Well, no great loss.

I drove out Oleander Drive to the Bradley Creek community, then nosed down a narrow, very private road. The Mackie's one-level white French Provincial house sat high up on a bluff overlooking Greenville Sound. The garage door was closed but Melanie's Lexus RX-300 was parked in the semi-circular driveway. She jumped out when I pulled in behind her.

I opened my car door to say "hey."

"Where have you been?" she snapped. "I've been sitting here for hours."

"Hours? I think you exaggerate a tad, sister-mine."

Hands on hips, Melanie glared at me. "Ashley, what are you up to? This is positively idiotic. I don't care a whit about MaeMae Mackie and she knows it."

"Lower your voice," I warned as I stepped out. "She might hear you."

I gave Melanie a head to toe. As usual, she looked stunning. How was it she had inherited all of our family's fashion genes? She was wearing an olive green knit suit that showed off every nip and curve. Her jewelry was brushed copper and matched her hair. Her hose matched her suit. Her high heels, a mossy green suede, went with everything.

Carefully, I lifted the casserole in its plastic bag from the seat. "What's that?" she asked suspiciously.

"Oh, just something I whipped up. We can't pay a condolence call without a homemade food offering. Not in Wilmington."

"What are we doing here anyway? You said this was urgent." Melanie was already sashaying toward the front door, at the same time glancing at her watch. "I'm staying five minutes and not a second longer."

"Five minutes is all I need," I said, catching up.

Her perfectly manicured fingertip pressed the doorbell.

"Just keep MaeMae occupied while I take a look around."

"Keep MaeMae . . . have you gone ma . . . good afternoon, we're here to see Mrs. Mackie." She smiled sweetly at the housekeeper who stood holding the door open.

The haughty woman was primly dressed in a black uniform with a starched white collar. Tall and gaunt, she literally looked down her beaky nose at us, disapproval written all over her stern face. Good lord, I thought, MaeMae's housekeeper is Mrs. Danvers.

"Come this way," she said, taking the casserole I offered. She carried it with arms extended—and her arms were long—holding the plastic bag and its contents at a distance, as if it was nasty and smelled bad. As if she intuited that I was passing off store-bought as my own.

Behind her back, Melanie rolled her eyes toward the beamed ceiling. That look said: You're a fool for being nice. No good deed goes unpunished.

I looked around, taking in the decor. This was my first visit to Sheldon's home. Our meetings had taken place at the historical society or in public places.

A long, narrow hallway ran from the front of the house to the back. The oak floorboards were stained a deep chocolate brown. Walls were painted bright white. A glass and brass table under a Moorish mirror occupied one wall. The decor decidedly reflected the Seventies era.

Mrs. Danvers, for this was what I called her in my mind, led us through an open archway into the living room. Here again, the Seventies style prevailed and I saw Billy Baldwin's signature everywhere, except in this case, the signature was a forgery. Sheldon had copied Baldwin's classic rooms. I was disappointed. I had expected something original.

Long, floor-to-ceiling French doors looked out at an expanse of blue water and sky. Inside, the walls were upholstered in chocolate brown silk moire, the floor stained the same chocolate brown. Everything else was white, including the tuxedo sofa on which MaeMae and Lucy Lou sat sipping martinis with green olives. They looked up, startled.

"I'll just take this," Mrs. Danvers sniffed, "to the kitchen." She departed silently on little cat's paws.

MaeMae and Lucy Lou did not seem happy to see us. Neither said hello nor welcomed us in any way. They sat stony-faced, cocktails in hand, seemingly at a loss as to why we were there. Melanie cast me a cold, hard glint. I'd hear about this later. But I'll say one thing for my sister, she can handle any social situation with aplomb—even rebuff.

Her expression changed mercurially. Face wreathed in smiles, arms extended lovingly, she marched over to the sofa. "Now don't get up, you poor dears, and don't say a word. I know you're speechless. What you two have been through, why it breaks my heart." At this point, her right arm crossed her chest as her hand pressed over her heart. Then she reached down to MaeMae, hugged her neck, and kissed the air near her cheek.

"So good of you to come," MaeMae murmured, setting her martini glass on a tray.

Lucy Lou made a face. "Yes, aren't you thoughtful to remember MaeMae in her hour of need."

Hour of need? I was going to be sick. With my very own eavesdropping ears, I had heard MaeMae rejoicing because Sheldon was dead. But, coward that I am, I uttered appropriate banalities.

Mrs. Danvers appeared in the doorway conveying a pitcher of martinis and more glasses. "You'll join us in a little drinkie, won't you?" MaeMae inquired.

Melanie had settled in a French bergére that was covered in a zebra pattern, on the opposite side of the coffee table, another brass and glass item. She crossed her right leg over her left and murmured, "None for me, thank you." She patted her flat tummy. "I have to watch my figure and my skin."

"Excuse me," I broke in, reminding myself why I was here, "may I use your powder room?"

MaeMae looked like she'd swallowed a green olive. "Direct her to the powder room, will you, Velma."

Velma, alias Mrs. Danvers, escorted me out of the room. "Go down the hall and turn to your right. You'll find the powder room behind the second door on the right." She returned to the living room to oversee the dispensing of martinis, or so I imagined. I wondered if MaeMae was as intimidated by Danvers as I was. Or did she call her Danny in private? I suppressed a giggle.

At the end of the main hall, a side hall turned sharply to the right and I followed it into the back wing. Opening the second door on the right, I glanced in at a pink and brown powder room, promptly closed the door, and continued on my nosy way.

What I was looking for I didn't know, but I knew that I'd recognize it when I saw it, just as I'd recognized the frozen prepared entrees. I opened a door on the left. Hallelujah! The master suite. I stepped inside and closed the door behind me.

Billy Baldwin's influence was strong in this room as well. White wall-to-wall carpeting strewn with zebra-patterned rugs. Forest green walls, tailored white draperies and bedding. Brass and glass bed tables.

I didn't dare open drawers—even I wouldn't go that far—but contented myself with snooping through the stuff on top of a chest of draw-ers and a dressing table. Very little there: flower arrangements, brush and comb, perfume bottles. Then I recalled that in Woody Allen's movie, *Manhattan Murder Mystery*, Diane Keaton punched the telephone's recall button to learn the number her suspect had last dialed. I walked over to the bed table, and hit the recall button on the phone. A num-ber appeared in the small window. Tearing a page off MaeMae's monogrammed notepad, I scribbled the number on it, then quickly hung up before it rang.

In the same movie, Keaton had hidden under the suspect's bed. At the time, I'd reflected that it was incredibly clean under there. I always have bolts of fabric shoved under my bed. I never have to worry about someone hiding under it, there's no room. Wonder what's under MaeMae's bed? I asked myself.

Glancing back at the door to be sure Mrs. Danvers hadn't crept up on me about to pounce, I bent from the waist and lifted the neat white dust ruffle. There *was* something under the bed. One item. A book. I picked it up. Flower sprigs on a cloth binding.

What a dilemma. Could I stoop to stealing a book? Surely I had more scruples than that. As I weighed the ethics of my situation, one standard stood out: Binkie's entire future depended on my finding the real killer.

Swiftly, I lifted the back of my jacket with one hand, stuffed the book under the waistband of my slacks with the other. Then I fled. I dived into the powder room, flushed the toilet, splashed water in the sink, and dampened a hand towel. As I was closing the door behind me, a chilling, disapproving voice, so close to my ear that I jumped, said, "Miss Wilkes is leaving now."

At the front door, Melanie was tapping the toe of one mossy green suede pump, hand on door knob. MaeMae and Lucy Lou fluttered about nervously, thanking Melanie profusely for our condolence call, but prob-ably just eager to return to their "little drinkies."

Lucy Lou said, "Ashley, we didn't get to visit with you a minute."

"We've got to run," I said, my voice crackling with guilt. I cleared my throat. "Melanie has to show a house. I hope you enjoy the casserole. It's one of Mama's recipes. Thirty minutes at 350 degrees." That's what everyone always says about reheating casseroles, so I didn't feel I'd give anyone food poisoning.

"Well, y'all come back now, you hear," MaeMae trilled.

I walked slowly to my car, back ramrod straight, the crisp edges of MaeMae Mackie's diary digging into my flesh.

12

With the hot diary burning a hole in my passenger seat, I drove west on Oleander, heading for the historic district and home. I couldn't wait to get inside my house, to lock my doors and draw the shades, to get down and dirty with MaeMae Mackie's psyche. But first I wanted to check out the phone number. Using my cell phone I tapped in the number I'd jotted down, while stopped at a red light. A woman at the funeral home answered. Well, shoot, a wild goose chase.

I had two suspects in mind for Sheldon's murder and MaeMae was prime. The second was Earl Flynn. There was no way it was Binkie. Jon's little talk with Binkie on Sunday evening had revealed nothing new. Binkie was sticking to his story: he didn't kill Sheldon, he didn't know who did, and Sheldon had robbed the Atlantic Coast Line's payroll in 1960.

On my "To Do" list was a meeting with Betty and Wayne Matthews. Wayne would possess all the facts about the payroll robbery. But, alas, the Matthews were on a winter holiday in Palm Beach and I'd have to wait two weeks to see them. If Nick hadn't reverted to his pigheaded cop's role again, he could help me. But knowing him, he'd balk at a suggestion that there might be a connection between Sheldon and the robbery, especially if that suggestion came from Binkie and me.

While sitting at the interminable stoplight on College Road, a sporty red Mustang convertible drew up alongside my car on the left. I glanced over. If I'd been fitted with dentures, they'd have dropped in my lap. Earl Flynn. Speak of the devil. And here I was pegging him for Sheldon's murder.

I averted my face and fiddled with the radio dial in case he looked my way. Some instinct told me not to let him see me. The tiny hairs on the back of my neck were saluting, and my adrenalin was pumping like mad. Here was my opportunity to observe Flynn undetected. All those Nancy Drew books I'd consumed in junior high school had made a first rate detective out of me.

The Mustang set off with tires spinning. I let one car follow, then swung in behind it. Flynn was an impatient driver—must be the result of driving those L.A. freeways—for he veered in and out of traffic at every opening, gaining a whole car length each time he did. Then we'd get to a red light and he'd be stuck with the rest of us slow pokes.

After a while I fell back a bit, just keeping a sharp eye on the silver-haired speedster. At Fifth Street, Flynn made a sharp right turn into the historic district. I trailed behind, allowing a pickup truck to drive in between us. Here on Fifth Street, traffic moved slower. This was my turf. I wasn't going to lose Flynn. I knew the district like I knew the inside of my house.

The red car hooked a left on Palace Street. I dogged it. There was no need for me to worry about being seen now. I lived just blocks away; I had every right to be cruising my own neighborhood. But what was Flynn doing here?

Without signalling, he whipped into the curb alongside the four abandoned, derelict bungalows that were for sale. Now I was really curious. There was no place for me to park without being seen so I cruised past Flynn, and he didn't notice me. I drove around the block, pulling into a parking space on the side street. From here I had a good view of the four houses and Flynn's red car.

While I'd been around the block, a black Mercedes had joined Flynn's car at the curb. Flynn and the other driver were nowhere to be seen, but they had to be nearby. I settled in to wait. Within minutes, Flynn and another man appeared from around the side of one of the houses. They stopped, and the other man lifted his arm, pointing skyward.

What a perplexing vignette. What possible interest could Earl Flynn have in four tumbledown houses just outside the historic district? And even more perplexing, why was Joel Fox interested too?

They tramped around in the tall grass, and I pulled out my new cell phone and pressed a button. The female who resides inside my cell phone said, "Name, please." Why does she always sound so irritable? I told her distinctly, "Melanie Cell," and in a nanosecond her cell phone was ringing.

"Melanie Wilkes," she answered smartly, prepared for any client. When she heard my voice, her tone became as irritable as the mechanical voice in my cell phone. "Ashley, it's only been twenty minutes. Can't you do anything without me?"

"Oh, stop having a hissy fit and answer a question for me. What do you know about the four bungalows that are for sale on Palace Street?"

"Palace Street?" Melanie repeated. "Why are you interested in that property?"

"I'm not," I replied, trying to be patient. "And I'm wondering why anyone would be interested. Can't you just answer my question? They've been for sale for almost a year. Are they under contract? Can't you look it up on your MLS thingie?"

"Ashley, I have a policy of not discussing my deals until they're done and the money's in my pocket. You should know that by now."

"What do you mean *your deals*? Are you saying you're representing a buyer?" Why was I feeling sick to my stomach?

"Ashley, if you tell one soul about this, there'll be another murder in your library, and you know who the victim will be. I'm Joel's broker and he's buying the property. We're going to develop it together."

"Hell's fire and damnation!" I cursed, quoting one of Daddy's favorite expletives and venting my frustration on Jon. It was seven in the evening and sweet ole Jon had suggested we get together for dinner the moment he heard the panic in my voice. We were seated on the deck of the Pilot House Restaurant. Here it was December 6th and the day was so balmy that with sweaters we were able to dine *al fresco* in comfort. Jon was doing the honors with a bottle of *Our Dog Blue* from the Chateau Morrisette vineyards.

"Just exactly what did Melanie say?" he asked, trying to understand the situation that had me so upset.

"She said that with so many movie stars and production people coming to town, we needed a luxury hotel. She said it would be a gold mine and she didn't understand why no one had thought of it before." Melanie had waxed lyrical when she'd told me, "Joel is a genius." I wanted to say, yes, and he must be mighty good in bed to separate you from your money, sister dear.

"But exactly what kind of hotel are they planning to build?" Jon asked. "Here, have some more wine." He refilled my glass from the blue bottle.

"Well, according to Melanie, it'll be something tasteful. Something in keeping with the architectural style of the historic district. La-di-da! What does she think? That I just fell off the cabbage truck?"

"You don't trust her?" Jon asked, a concerned look on his earnest face.

I leaned forward and said emphatically, "I don't trust Joel!"

At the savagery in my voice, the waiter who was about to set dinner plates before us backed away from the table. I glanced up at him. He was young, probably a student at UNC-W. "Sorry," I said, smiling to show I didn't have fangs.

He set the plates on the table, did a little kowtow and vanished to the safety of the kitchen. I was starved. I always get hungry when life gets stressful. And before me sat a dinner to die for: baked grouper in a sweet potato crust, mushroom ravioli, and organic greens. I pondered the current use of that term. Organic means derived from living organisms. So aren't all greens organic? They're not cardboard, for pity's sake.

Jon was having backfin crabcakes with Hoppin' John and steamed vegetables.

"Should we confront Joel and Melanie?" I wondered out loud.

"And get into a pissing contest with a skunk!" Jon exclaimed. "Look, whatever they're doing, they'll have to get building permits. I'll check around at the courthouse."

"Oh yes, please do that. Then we'll know what they're up to."

For a few minutes, silence reigned as we feasted.

I said, "We can't expect the National Trust to come to our rescue. Those houses are outside the historic district. And they're not old enough or significant enough for us to apply for landmark protection. I've been worried that something like this might happen to destroy the quality of the historic district."

"The city's skyline is still low but that could change," Jon remarked.

"The 'Carolina Apartments' is six stories tall, but it's in the District and a landmark."

"And the former home of Claude Howell," Jon reminded me.

"And where they filmed *Blue Velvet*," I added. "Located as it is right across the street from the immense Bellamy Mansion, it doesn't appear outsized."

"Look, maybe we're jumping the gun here. Maybe's there's nothing to worry about. Let me do some checking. How about dessert?"

I brightened. "I'll have the Caribbean fudge pie. With ice cream."

For a moment I was transported back to childhood. On hot summer afternoons, we made ice cream in our shady garden, cooled by breezes off the Waterway that rustled the centuries-old live oaks. Melanie and I took turns helping Daddy turn the hand crank, which became less and less yielding as the ice cream hardened, while Mama scooped handfuls of ice cubes into the stainless steel canister. At memories like this, I miss my parents so much the loss feels like a knife slicing through my gut. My daddy died the first Christmas I was in college. Gone to heaven, I tell myself. Mama is with me in body only. But I am grateful for her corporeal self.

13

They tell me I'm an alcoholic but I don't believe them. Sure, Lucy Lou and I like our cocktails. Without them, how could I have put up with Sheldon for all those years? Lu Lou and I can quit anytime we like.

Thus wrote MaeMae Mackie in her last journal entry on Tuesday, December 4th, the day of Sheldon's viewing. I continued reading.

If I hadn't married Sheldon, how different my life would have been. I might have become a successful decorator in my own right. He stole my ideas and took credit for them. I've got more talent in my pinkie finger than that big jerk had in his whole body. Oh, I hate him, hate him, hate him, and I'm glad he's dead!

Whew! This was heavy stuff. I slammed the diary shut. Still she hadn't admitted to killing him. But would she make a written confession?

I was snug in my bed. Then I thought it might be a good idea for me to record my impressions so I jumped out of bed and grabbed a legal pad and pen from my desk. Systematically, I wrote down the information I had gathered.

On the first sheet, I drew the layout of my house. The library—or the crime scene as it had come to be known—is situated on the east side of the house in the rear, off the back hallway. The hallway is connected to the front reception hall, and opens into the dining room on the west side, and the back staircase. The back staircase meets the front staircase on a landing, then a single flight of stairs carries one to the second floor.

The hallway angles around the library and leads to the side door that opens into the porte cochere.

At the far rear of the house is the kitchen. It's set off by a fire wall in a one-story wing. I am grateful for prudent nineteenth-century builders.

The parlor and dining room are both located on the west side of the house and are connected by a large, arched opening.

I marked an "X" in the center of the library where Sheldon's body had lain.

Although the tour route through my house had brought visitors in the front door and exited them out the side door into the porte cochere, with a hundred tourists or more inside my house at any given time, it was entirely possible that the murderer had slipped in through the side door where he mingled with the crowd. Who would have known? Then he'd waited his chance to find Sheldon alone in the library. But no. It was Binkie who'd been posted in the library. Anyone looking for Sheldon would have expected to find him in the dining room.

Don't go jumping to conclusions, Wilkes, I admonished myself. What if the murderer didn't know what Sheldon or Binkie looked like? What if he possessed only a general description? What if, for some unfathomable reason, someone had sneaked into the library to kill Binkie, but finding another mature, gray-haired man there, killed him instead? A case of mistaken identity. Sheldon not the intended victim. But no, that didn't make sense, not even to my overwrought imagination. For who would want to kill dear, gentle Binkie?

Was it mere coincidence that Sheldon was in the library at the time of his murder? Or had he gone there to meet someone? Had he required a private place to speak to someone—MaeMae, for instance—and so they went into the library together to be alone? Something went wrong, and MaeMae killed him.

According to Dr. Banks, the medical examiner, Sheldon's death had been caused by blunt force trauma to his left temple. That meant he'd been facing his killer and the killer was right-handed. Well, that ruled out the lefties, but included a whole lot of other people.

I skimmed through MaeMae's diary, fascinated by her sketches of interiors. She was right. She did possess design talent.

Scanning entries randomly, I perused a litany of slights and offenses committed by Sheldon. Nothing he did pleased her. It was sad to read about all the bickering and mental cruelty they'd inflicted on one another.

I reflected that the murder case was having the unintended consequence of derailing my romance with Nick. I missed him. Our talks. Our walks. Kisses that left me dizzy.

If only we could discuss the case, share our thoughts, trade information. Fox was making money by persuading others—my sister Melanie for one—to invest in his projects. And from what I'd witnessed earlier, possibly Earl Flynn was an investor too. What was the source of Flynn's income, I wondered.

A swank, high-rise hotel located on the outskirts of the historic district would bring in big bucks, but would destroy forever the charming quaintness of the District.

My doorbell rang frantically, as if whoever was out there was leaning against it. Eleven-forty-five. I pulled on my robe, thrust my feet into slippers, and hurried down the stairs to the reception hall, switching on inside and outside lights as I went. I looked out through the sidelight to see Nick.

"I've got to talk to you!" he said when I opened the door. He looked whipped.

Because of the late hour, I feared the worst. "First tell me Melanie hasn't been in an accident."

"Sorry, I didn't mean to scare you. It's not bad news." He stepped inside, his presence filling the space. His eyes traveled over my robe, my nightgown, my slippers. "Were you asleep?"

"Not yet."

There was pain in his eyes, a pinched-quality to his face. Always well dressed, tonight he had on a tailored suit in charcoal brown with a thin white pinstripe. His shirt collar was open at the throat, tie missing.

"Would you like a cup of coffee?"

"Yes. I . . . Ashley. . . ."

I don't know who moved first but I was in his arms, wrapped up tight, held like he'd never let me go. I knew I missed him, but not until that moment did I realize how much. I showed him how glad I was to see him.

When we came up for air, he said, "Ashley, I can't stand it when there's trouble between us."

"Neither can I." But remembering I had a duty to save Binkie, I took a step back. "Why are you gunning for Binkie?"

"I'm not gunning for him, Ashley." With one step, he closed the distance I'd put between us. Lifting his hand to my face, he brushed droopy curls off my forehead. "You look pretty without makeup. We need to talk. I have to work this case, but I don't want to lose you over it."

"Oh? And what about Lisa Hamilton? Hasn't she already replaced me?" I hadn't planned to blurt out such an accusation.

His eyes met mine. "Replaced you? Is that what you think?" He reached for me again. "No one can replace you, Ashley. Lisa? Well, that's just work stuff. She's new here and I have to show her around, show her the ropes."

A mental picture of her dangling at the end of one of those ropes was very satisfying.

He continued, "Besides, you and I . . . we . . ."

"We don't have an exclusive relationship," I finished for him.

He kissed the tip of my nose. "Do you want one?"

The question surprised me. "I . . . I don't know." I pulled away and paced, using my hands to help me talk. "Nick, when you're working a case, you become another person, someone I don't know. You treat me like a stranger. You're suspicious of everything I say and do."

He grabbed my shoulders, anchoring me. "Stand still and I'll try to explain. When I'm working the job I've got to remain objective. I can't allow my judgment to be clouded by people close to me. And you, you're so important to me, Ashley, I'm afraid I'll lose all sense of objectivity. So, well, I'm afraid I go too far, push you away."

His hands slid down my arms. Through the thin fabric of my robe, I felt their heat. My skin tingled. This was hopeless. I wanted to throw my arms around him, bury my face in his neck. Be kissed again. Tell him everything was all right. That anything he did was okay with me.

Instead I gently removed his hands. "Come on back to the kitchen. I'll fix us some coffee."

I brewed a gourmet decaf, one of my few accomplishments in the culinary department. Within seconds, the scent of Chocolate Cherry Kiss filled the room, the suggestive name of the flavor not eluding me. Nick slipped off his jacket, hung it over the back of a chair and sat down. He looked like he hadn't slept in days. While the coffee dripped, I massaged his shoulders. They were stiff and the muscles were in knots. I worked the tension loose.

"What am I going to do with you?" I wondered out loud.

"What do you want to do?"

"You wouldn't consider resigning from the force, would you?" I asked, holding my breath.

"I can't do that. Anymore than you could give up your restoration work."

"We only have problems when you're working a homicide case that somehow involves me," I ventured.

"Ummm, that feels good." He grabbed my hand. "I don't want you anywhere near my cases, Ashley. They're dangerous. There are psychopaths out there who will stop at nothing. I have to keep you safe, separate from that world. But, yes, the rest of the time we get along like . . ." he pulled me into his lap, ". . . like this."

"Yes, we do," I murmured, giving up to the pleasure of having my neck nuzzled. "Famously," I added, remembering the fun times we'd shared. His shoulder holster nudged me back to reality. "Coffee's ready," I announced, jumping clear of temptation's reach.

Over coffee, with the table separating me from his lap, from his arms, from his lips, he explained, "Ashley, I have to follow a case where the evidence leads. And in this case, all the evidence points to Professor Higgins. He has motive, opportunity, and means. Sure I know he's a nice old guy, well-regarded in the community, but we've got a smoking gun — the murder weapon with his prints, and only his prints, on it."

I drew back. "Well, doesn't that tell you something? My prints should be on that poker too! The real murderer wiped the poker or wore gloves."

He grimaced and arched an eyebrow, a sure sign we were headed for a fight. "Or, Ashley, you polished the brass handle when you were cleaning up for the house tour."

That gave me something to think about. It was true, I had polished some brass items the week before the tour. And I hadn't built a fire so the poker hadn't been used. "Even if I did polish it, and I honestly can't remember, I would have returned it to the hearth so my fingerprints should be on it. Binkie said he tripped over it and picked it up. And I believe him." I slammed my coffee mug down. "Nick, Binkie is not a killer!"

He sighed. "Guess I'd better be going. I don't want to fight with you. I thought we could work this out."

"Are you looking at any other suspects?" I asked.

"Of course I am. What kind of detective do you think I am? I'm looking at everyone. We've got a team tracing everyone who bought tour tickets by credit card, and many people did. We're questioning all of them. Most of them have returned to their home towns, so we're interviewing over the telephone."

"And? Did anyone see anything?"

"So far there are no witnesses to the murder."

"Well, at least that's in Binkie's favor. What about Earl Flynn? Did you interrogate him?"

"Interview, Ashley. We don't interrogate, we interview."

"Interview. Interrogate. What's the difference? Sounds like something your little PR girlfriend made up. *Did* you talk to Earl Flynn?"

Nick pushed back his chair, grabbed his jacket. "Thanks for the coffee. Yes, I talked to Flynn. He was nowhere near your house at the time of the murder."

"Does he have a witness?"

"A couple of hundred."

"All he needs is one, Nick. Does he have one witness who will swear he was somewhere else?"

"He was way over on Chestnut Street, Ashley. People saw him."

I slumped in my chair, defeated. "Are they sure it was eight o'clock when they saw him?"

"There was a lot going on that night. The streets were crowded with people. The houses were filled with tourists coming and going. No, no one can say with certainty that Flynn was on Chestnut Street at eight o'clock. What's Flynn's motive? He doesn't have one. He doesn't even know Sheldon Mackie."

"How can you be sure of that? Earl Flynn grew up here. He told Melanie he knew Daddy. Maybe he knew Sheldon too."

"Well, he told us he didn't. And I have no reason to think he's lying. There's nothing to connect him to Mackie. So drop it, Ashley, and let me do my job."

I wanted to show him MaeMae's diary, to prove to him that someone else had a strong motive for murder. But then I'd have to explain how I got it. Still, I needed to implicate her. "You know MaeMae stands to gain from Sheldon's death. I thought the spouse was always the most obvious suspect. You need to look at her closely, Nick."

I could see he was losing patience. "The spouse is not the most obvious suspect when another suspect has threatened the victim, and when that suspect is found standing over the deceased with the murder weapon in his hand!"

"Okay, let's call a truce. Don't leave mad, please. I want to ask you about something else. What do you know about the Atlantic Coast Line payroll robbery?"

14

Nick warmed to the subject of the payroll robbery. In fact, he became so effusive in his recitation of Wilmington's most famous robbery, he forgot to ask me why I was interested.

"July 1, 1960," he said almost reverently. "My dad was a rookie cop back then."

Nick's father had been the chief of Wilmington P.D. for over a decade before his illness and subsequent death.

He continued, "I grew up hearing stories about 'Black Thursday,' December 15, 1955, the day the Atlantic Coast Line announced it was moving its headquarters from Wilmington to Jacksonville. The Coast Line was the largest employer in the area with 13,000 employees. Even though the move wouldn't take place for years, the town was devastated. Not everyone was offered relocation, and many didn't want to move to Florida."

"How much money did the robbers steal?" I asked.

"The total week's payroll amounted to $800,000 dollars, with a half million in cash."

"Cash! Five hundred thousand dollars in cash. Why cash?"

"The Brotherhood of Railroad Workers required the company to pay union members in cash. Not unusual for the fifties. Members of management, who weren't part of the union, got their salaries by check. Every Thursday night, an armored car delivered bags of cash to the railroad's payroll office. Clerks worked through the night, counting the money, depositing the correct amount of cash into each employee's pay envelope. There were three clerks and one armed guard. The office was locked. Plus railroad security officers patrolled the rail yard and the administration complex during the night."

Hanging on his every word, I refilled his coffee mug. He picked it up absently, then set it down to say, "That's why my dad and everyone at the P.D. thought the robbers had help from inside. On July 5, four days after the robbery, the railroad began moving families from Wilmington to the new headquarters in Jacksonville. They moved 950 families in one month. The president's office was the last to go. My dad's theory was that the inside man could have been someone who then left for Jacksonville, putting himself outside our jurisdiction. Or he could have been one of the hundreds who weren't offered relocation, somebody left behind. Maybe he left town right away, on the pretext of looking for a job elsewhere."

"How did they pull it off?" I asked, wiggling forward to the edge of my seat.

"They knew when the security patrol made its rounds, and they timed the robbery between rounds. That left only one guard to disarm. It was July and hot; the office wasn't air conditioned. The clerks weren't supposed to open windows but they did anyway. The robbers skulked around outside, waited for their chance, then shot the guard through an open window. Didn't kill him though so the charge was never murder."

"How did they get inside? Through a window?"

"No. The windows were protected with iron bars. They shot out the lock on the door. The shot was heard by a security officer in the rail yard but by the time he got to the payroll office, the robbers and the bags of cash were gone."

"Did the police think the security officer might have been the inside-man?"

Nick shot me a look of renewed respect. "I remember asking my dad that same question. Yes, they suspected him. But there wasn't any evidence, nothing to link him to the robbery."

I nodded. "Did they shoot the clerks too?"

"No. The clerks weren't armed so they didn't pose a threat. They were too startled or too scared to push the alarm button until the robbers fled. Guess it just happened too fast. The guys knocked them to the floor, grabbed the bags, and were gone in less than a minute. The clerks reported there were three of them and they wore ski masks."

He chuckled. "Ski masks and shorts. They weren't able to give descriptions except to say the men had young, white legs."

He continued, "They must have had a car nearby, possibly with a getaway driver, but not necessarily, and there wasn't a trace of them when the railroad security officers arrived. The police were summoned, but there wasn't a clue. After shooting off the lock, one of them shoved the door in with his shoulder. So they didn't leave fingerprints. They didn't drop anything, or leave anything behind. They vanished without a trace."

"I remember my dad talking about it but I never heard the details before."

Nick reached for the coffee mug. His color was high, his eyes bright. He was as intense as a bloodhound on the trail of an escaped convict. It was clear he admired his quarry. "It was a daring job, that's for sure. And they pulled it off without a hitch. That's why the investigators felt sure it was an inside job."

"And the money was never recovered?"

"Not a cent. The payroll was insured so the railroad didn't stand to lose any money. Guess that's why they didn't press too hard. Besides they were in the middle of the big move. The insurance company wrote it off decades ago. To this day, we don't know who those guys were and what they did with the money."

We were both thoughtful for a moment, mulling over the facts of the case.

"Why are you interested?" he asked, suspicious again.

"Oh, someone mentioned it recently." I couldn't tell him that Binkie had accused Sheldon of being one of the robbers.

Nick got a dreamy look on his face. "What I wouldn't give to crack that case!"

15

On Saturday morning I drove home from Wilmington Architectural Salvage with antique doorknobs rattling around in a box in the back of my van. The Historic Wilmington Foundation runs the salvage shop on Brunswick Street where donated building materials are sold, thus providing funds for the non-profit association and at the same time recycling old materials that would otherwise end up as landfill. Historic preservation is the ultimate recycling effort. My finds this morning were doorknobs made of glass, brass, and porcelain, some of which I planned to use in my house, the rest I would save for future clients' homes.

The van's radio was on. "I Saw Mommy Kissing Santa Claus" played, a song I generally detest, but I was in a super good mood this morning so I sang along as I drove merrily homeward. There's nothing like being kissed to put a girl in a good frame of mind. I had to agree with Nick: my life runs more smoothly when our relationship is running smoothly. Although our major problem—me getting mixed up in his case—didn't get resolved last night, at least when we kissed goodnight, we each had a better understanding of the other.

I pulled into my narrow driveway. Homes in the historic district come on tiny lots. My driveway is a rarity; most residents have to park in the street. Rachel's Jetta sat at the curb in the shade of a live oak. I wondered how she'd managed to get her car away from her foul-mouthed boyfriend.

I parked in the porte cochere — another rarity — and went around to the back of the van to fetch the box of doorknobs.

It was then that I noticed that the side door to my house was standing open. But Rachel was here, I reasoned, so she could have left the door open while she carried in paint supplies. Yet a worry nagged at me: maybe it's that evil Eddie, robbing me blind. How *had* he got in on Monday anyway?

Yesterday I'd called ADT to order the installation of a security system. And I'd called the locksmith to have all the locks changed. The soonest they could get to me was next week. Christmas is a busy season, they explained. Must be all the Christmas presents need protection from the Grinches.

I approached the door but some sixth sense caused me to hesitate. Christmas music from Rachel's portable radio flowed through the house. So she *was* here. "Rachel!" I called, yet still hung back.

Behind me, Nun Street seemed unusually quiet. I glanced up and down the street and saw no one. Every instinct I possessed warned me that something was wrong.

They say when you come home and find your door standing wide open, you should go to a neighbor's house and call the police. But I wasn't about to create further problems with Nick. Yet what if Evil Eddie was in there with Rachel? What if they'd quarreled again and he'd hurt her? I recalled the malice in his eyes when he'd lifted his hand to strike her. If I hadn't stopped him, he would have hit her.

The common sense thing to do, I told myself again, is to call 911 and wait for the police to arrive.

But what if Rachel's hurt? What if she needs me? "Rachel!" My voice sounded strained in my own ears. The house felt odd, giving off strange vibrations. No cars in the street. No neighbors in their gardens. Usually, there's some activity down by The Verandas B&B. Not today. At noon, my neighborhood seemed to be asleep. The innkeepers' car was missing from their driveway. Only a black Mercedes was parked at the curb.

I pulled out my cell phone, punched in 911, gave the dispatcher my name and address, and reported, "My door's standing wide open and I think something's wrong. I know I shouldn't go in there, but my friend's inside, maybe hurt. I've got to check on her. Please, send a police car right away."

The dispatcher repeated what I already knew, "Don't go in the house. Wait for the police. Stay on the line."

I held the phone to my ear and waited. I was about to yell for Rachel again when I thought better of it, decided it was safer to remain silent. If someone *was* in there, let him think I had gone.

Images of Rachel lying bleeding or unconscious changed my mind. Silently, I crept into the back hall, sidling along the wall that adjoins the library.

Out of the corner of my eye I saw something flash toward me. I whirled to face whatever it was, saw a blurred figure flying toward me, arm upraised. I screamed.

From a distance I heard the dispatcher call, "Ms. Wilkes. Ms. . . ." Then nothing.

Someone was in pain. A woman was moaning. Then I remembered. Rachel. Rachel's hurt. Where is she? Why am I lying on the floor? Why is Nick leaning over me, calling my name? Then I realized I was the one who was moaning. Pain in my head split it apart. All I wanted to do was slip back to that blissful place Nick was determined to keep me from.

He wouldn't let me sleep. He slapped my wrists and repeated my name. He sounded desperate. "Hold on, Ashley. Stay with me, baby. Don't close your eyes. Look at me, Ashley. Look at me!"

I tried to do as he instructed, but my eyelids wouldn't cooperate. Through thin slits, his blurry face drifted in and out.

"The ambulance is here, Ashley. Just hold on. You're going to be all right. Stay with us."

How worried he sounds, I thought.

Then another face, a paramedic's, hovered over mine, spoke calmly to me, took charge. I felt a blood pressure cuff being wrapped around my arm. Heard the puff, puff, puff, as it was inflated, felt its squeeze.

"Let's roll," a voice said. "On my count. One, two, three."

Hands lifted me off the floor, and a hard board was pushed under me. Then the board seemed to float through the air with me on it, and people were running with me out through the door, past my van to the ambulance beyond.

Sunlight struck my eyes. The glare knocked me out.

Curtains enclosed my hospital cubicle. Nick and I were alone inside. Doctors and nurses had come and gone; now we waited for test results. So far, no one had told me anything. My head felt like a baseball someone had used for batting practice.

Nick clung to my hand. I wanted to squeeze his but didn't have the strength. Just talking was a great effort. "Rachel? Is she all right?"

His chin dropped onto his chest. He closed his eyes. This was the real Nick. The Nick I loved. "You've got to tell me." Then I realized what I'd just thought.

His eyes locked onto mine. There was pity there and something more. "I'm sorry, baby. She didn't make it."

"She's dead? Murdered?" Like Sheldon?

"The M.E. has to confirm it, but, yes, it looks that way. Head wounds. Sweetheart, please don't cry." He dabbed at my eyes with a tissue. "Try not to cry. You'll only make your head hurt more."

He leaned close. "I wish I could put my arms around you, but I don't want to jostle you."

"It'll be confirmed," I whimpered. "Oh, Nick, what's going on?" Sheldon's dead. Rachel's dead. He tried to kill me too. But I fooled him. I survived. I'm going to get you, I promised. Whoever you are, I'm going to get you for killing my friends. "Tell me. It's hard to talk. Don't make me ask."

He straightened up, wrapped my hand in both of his. "She was struck like you were. We haven't found the weapon yet. It's possible she fell and hit her head, but no one believes that."

I studied him through half-closed eyes. He was suffering. He's a good man, I thought. "Thanks," I whispered.

"She probably surprised a burglar. You too."

I whispered, "No. Eddie."

"Who's Eddie?" His voice became alert, prickly, and he dropped my hand.

"Boyfriend." Shallow breath. "Bad news. Tried to hit her." Deep breath.

Nick pulled out a notebook and scribbled in it. "Does he live with her?"

I blinked. Even that hurt.

At least Binkie's off the hook, I thought. What a way to prove Binkie's innocence, for poor Rachel to have to die.

"I'll find him," Nick promised. "Now, don't worry. Try to stay calm." He lifted my hand and pressed it to his lips.

What a paradox you are, Nick Yost, I thought. He had removed his suit jacket, loosened his tie, rolled up his shirt sleeves. His shoulders were magnificent, but his weapon was an intimidating presence in the small, sterile cubicle.

The curtain swept back and the emergency room doctor stepped inside, a nurse peeping over his shoulder as he read my chart. "How are you feeling, Ms. Wilkes?"

"Awful." Shallow breath. I was nauseated. Earlier I'd had a brief bout with vomiting. "I'm warm."

"That's because your temperature's slightly elevated. But your blood pressure is down and your pulse rate has slowed. All good news." He passed my chart to the nurse, crossed his arms. "Okay. Here's the deal. The CT scan shows only a mild concussion. I want you to lie as quietly as possible, and keep your shoulders and head elevated. I don't want you moved for a while so we're going to keep you here until evening."

"You're not going to admit her?" Nick asked.

The doctor stared at Nick's gun. "She doesn't need to be admitted. Trust me. Besides, we're full up. This is the flu season."

He put a hand on my shoulder that was supposed to make me feel reassured. "The nurse is going to bring you something for the pain and the nausea. Sorry I couldn't give you anything sooner. And keep that ice pack on the bruise. We've stitched you up, so there shouldn't be any more bleeding.

"You're going to have a doozie of a headache for a couple of days. You'll have to take it easy. No driving, not until we check you out again. I'll send you home with a prescription. Now that the CT scan results are in, we can start you on meds. Something very mild. I know your head hurts."

He gave my shoulder a reassuring squeeze. "So, stay calm. Get some rest. I'll be back in about an hour to check on you."

He turned to Nick. "Okay, I know you've got questions for her. You can ask them, but only if she feels like talking. The medication will make her drowsy. She'll drift in and out."

He was gone, disappearing as swiftly as he had come.

"*Do* you feel up to answering a few questions, Ashley?" Nick asked. "Did you see who hit you? Was it this Eddie?" He drew up a chair, his pad and pen ready.

"No, I didn't see him." Shallow breath. "Just movement. A flash."

He scribbled in his notebook. "I was hoping you got a good look at him. The forensic team is collecting evidence at your house now."

Shouldn't you be there too, I wanted to ask.

"Another detective is handling things. It's more important for me to be here with you."

I'm more important than his work, I thought, glimpsing heaven. I tried to smile, couldn't, reached for his hand instead.

"We'll talk later," he said.

A nurse in a pink pants outfit bustled in. She gave me pills from a tiny paper cup. The medication worked quickly and magically. I was fading, the tiny cubicle receding. I drifted off, feeling safe with Nick watching over me.

His angry voice woke me and I blinked back to wakefulness. Through half open eyes I saw him in the corner of the cubicle, back to me, shoulders squared, rigid as a cardboard cutout. His cell phone was pressed to his ear. "I don't care if there are ten thousand fingerprints in her house, I want every one of them lifted and identified! Take a flea comb to that house. I don't want anything overlooked."

Irritably he snapped off the phone. "No one messes with my girl," he growled.

Velvety sleep dragged me down. I felt a goofy smirk play across my lips. *His girl. I was Nick's girl.*

I dozed. The ER doc came and went. Each time he said I was doing fine. "Rest," he advised, the pressure of his hand on my shoulder now a familiar gesture. Had they given me tranquilizers? Something very mild, he'd said. Once when I opened my eyes, I thought I saw Jon and Binkie waving to me through the curtain's flap. The next moment they were gone. I lost all sense of time, falling in and out of light sleep.

The next time I awoke, Melanie and Lisa Hamilton were whispering at the foot of my bed. Nick was gone. Lisa was nodding at something Melanie was saying, all the while studying my face. Seeing me awake, she asked sympathetically, "Hi, Ashley. How are you feeling?"

Melanie pushed past her, her face the picture of concern. "Oh, baby sister, how are you?"

"Groggy," I mumbled. I didn't mind her calling me baby sister. I took her hand. "Thanks for coming."

"Wild horses couldn't keep me away."

Where's Nick, I wondered. And what is Lisa Hamilton doing here?

Melanie fussed over me, straightening the blanket. She reached to adjust the pillow. "Don't touch me!" I cried.

She jumped back, offended. "I was only trying to make you comfortable." She looked like she was going to cry.

"It hurts to move my head," I explained.

Lisa moved in closer, peering at me. I didn't want her here. I started to tell her to leave.

"Lisa has some questions to ask you, shug," Melanie gushed, shooting Lisa a warning glance.

"Where's Nick?" My head was swimming.

"He had to go to your house to supervise the homicide team," Lisa said.

Melanie kissed my cheek. "Look at those awful bruises! How could anyone do that to you?" Tears welled up. Her green eyes shimmered. "You might have been killed."

Poor Melanie. "Guess I have a hard head," I joked feebly. I caught Lisa staring at us, like we were an alien species. An odd expression crossed her face. In the blink of an eye, it was gone. She's jealous of Melanie and me, I realized in a flash. What delicious irony, I thought, for here I am jealous of her and Nick.

"What do you want?" I asked. She was the last person I wanted seeing me like this. I could imagine how I looked: bruised, dopey, flat on my back. My one consolation was that Nick was not here to see us side by side, to compare the difference.

"I know you're feeling badly, Ashley. I'm sorry to put you through this, but there's a press conference scheduled for the evening news. I tried to put them off until tomorrow, but you know how the media are. They're clamoring for information about the murders. Two murders in four days in your house—well, you can understand." Her tone was appropriately sympathetic and professional, but under it I sensed she was being patronizing, as if I had somehow brought this calamity on myself.

Now I noticed that she was dressed for the TV cameras. Serious gray wool suit. Pearl choker necklace. Pearl button earrings. Make-up just so. Every gleaming blonde hair in place. I struggled to concentrate. "What do you want to know?"

"I just wanted to see you for myself, to see how you're doing. So I can report your condition accurately. Nick told me you didn't get a good look at your assailant. But if you remember anything, if you want to talk, well, I'm here to listen. And to help."

Melanie fluttered around the tiny space, distracting me. I wanted them both to leave. I wanted to go back to sleep.

Then I thought of Rachel, who wouldn't be around to paint flowers on my walls ever again, or to decorate Christmas trees with me. And I thought of Sheldon who wouldn't be decorating any more houses. And of Binkie, who was facing a murder charge while the guilty person was getting away with murder!

"Just find the person who did this to me. And who killed Rachel. And Sheldon. That's all I have to say."

16

After Lisa left the hospital for the press conference, Melanie took charge of my nursing duties. Helped me to get up and walk to the bathroom. Grabbed the pill cup out of the nurse's hand, shaking the pills into my palm herself. Even held the water glass to my lips. The nurse started to argue, but Melanie shot her a withering glare. The woman threw up her hands and backed off. She had plenty of other patients to look after. If this red-head wanted to play Florence Nightingale, that was just fine and dandy with her.

On the curb in front of the hospital, Melanie helped me out of the wheelchair and into the back seat of her capacious Lexus. She settled me among the pillows and blankets she'd thoughtfully provided. She wanted to take me to her house but I insisted on going home, telling her I'd rest better in my own bed. She got Nick on the cell phone to verify that the crime scene unit had completed processing my house. Then she drove me home. Once there, she put me to bed, heated broth, fixed Jell-O, and called the pharmacy and had my prescription delivered. She was my perfect big sister.

I was as touched by her devotion as I had been by Nick's. The two of them, they were a couple of walking paradoxes. But I was used to Melanie's personality swings. Nick was an enigma. And then I remembered my unsettling thought about him in the hospital: I loved him.

In the middle of the night I awoke in my own bed. I'd been sleeping for hours, and my internal clock was out of sync. The house was warm and cozy.

Sliding out of bed, I felt mildly dizzy and waited for the spell to pass. My head pain had settled down to a dull ache. I didn't bother with slippers but pulled on my robe. Tiptoeing down the hall, I passed the guest room where Melanie slept. In it, magnolias blossoms covered the walls. Who would finish painting them?

I felt my way to the stairs in the darkness. As woozy as I felt, maybe I shouldn't have been doing this but I was hungry. On the landing, a wave of dizziness hit me, and I sank down on the top step. Suddenly tears were streaming down my checks. Rachel. Rachel, my good friend, was gone. And Sheldon. I'd never see them again.

I dried the tears with the hem of my nightgown, crept quietly down the back stairs. Nick was sleeping in the parlor on the divan in the Turkish corner. He'd let me come back to my house on one condition — that he be allowed to spend the night. "I have to. I wouldn't sleep a wink at home, worrying about you. This way I know you'll be safe."

A light in the kitchen guided me through the back hallway. Some-one had thoughtfully left a lamp on. My stomach had settled. With only broth and jello for dinner, my gnawing appetite drove me toward the refrigerator where I knew there was a pint of hazelnut *gelato*.

Then I made a mistake. I looked over my shoulder in the direction of the open library door. Without warning, I was reliving the attack. A whirling figure came flying at me from out of the shadows. An arm raised threateningly. A long, cylindrical weapon came crashing down. "No," I cried, my arms flying up to protect my face and head.

"Ashley?" Nick rushed from the kitchen to catch me as I fell. I felt his arms go around me, lift me. "I'm here, baby. I'm here."

I was crying. Shivering. My arms and legs trembled, out of control. I was cold—very, very cold.

He carried me into the parlor, lowered me onto the divan, grabbed an afghan and wrapped it around me. I wanted to tell him not to worry, but I couldn't speak. He crawled onto the divan with me, stretched out alongside me, pulled me close. I squeezed into the curve of his body.

"You're okay," he soothed. "I'm here." One arm held me tight. His free hand stroked my hair.

My body shuddered helplessly. "Oh, Nick. I saw him. He was going to attack me again." I buried my face in his chest.

"Shhh. It's okay. It'll go away. It's post-traumatic stress. I thought you were too calm this afternoon. I think you ought to see someone. Right away. Before this gets worse."

"You mean a therapist?"

"Yes. I can give you the name of a good one who works with the force. Take a deep breath. Try to think of something pleasant."

"That's easy," I said lightly. This was the first time we were in bed together. Our amorous encounters had always taken place at my front door, or on moonlit walks on Wrightsville Beach. His body heat warmed me. The shivering stopped. I was conscious of only one thing: Nick and my desire for him.

My voice was steady now, a husky whisper. "You feel wonderful."

"I know." His voice was husky too.

"Oh, you know," I teased, poking him in the ribs.

"I mean I know how good you feel. Ashley. . . ."

"Shhh." I lifted my mouth to be kissed. His mouth met mine, sweetly, hungrily. There was nothing else in the world but the feel of his mouth on mine. My crazy world of murder, my worry about Binkie, everything vanished. We were alone in a private world, just we two.

Our kisses grew deeper, more urgent. My need for him engulfed me, took over. I pressed my face into his neck, inhaling him, wishing I could crawl under his skin, I wanted to be that close. He held me tighter, whispering my name over and over. His breath came in ragged bursts.

Abruptly, he pulled away, rolled onto his back. Blew out his breath. "I can't do this. It's not the right time." His voice hoarse with desire, he coughed.

I moved my head to his chest. "No, Nick, it's right. Very right."

"You're upset, Ashley. You've suffered a shock. I won't take advantage of you. Ashley, I . . ."

"Yes, Nick?" I studied his profile in the faint light.

"Nothing. When we do this, I want it to be right. Now, I'm going to hold you. I want you to go to sleep. I won't let anyone hurt you ever again."

I let myself drift. "This is nice," I whispered.

"Very nice." He pulled the afghan over us.

I yawned. And slipped into the contented sleep of lovers.

I woke at first light, my headache a mere shadow. Sleeping in Nick's arms had been the most delicious experience. Through the night I'd been aware of him yet I'd slept soundly and peacefully. But with the coming of dawn, I feared the return of "Nick, the Cop." I cherished my memory of "Nick, the Lover" and wanted to hold on to it. Plus, if Melanie saw us together, I'd never hear the end of it. For right now, I wanted to hug this beautiful new feeling all to myself.

Reluctantly, I slipped out from under Nick's arm and tiptoed upstairs. Back in my own bed, I dozed, feeling luxurious and marvelously content. If it feels this good to sleep together like innocent babes, I thought, how wonderful will it be to sleep together as lovers? With that happy image playing across my brain, I slumbered.

At seven Melanie brought a breakfast tray, remarking that Dick Tracy had gotten up early and was gone. I felt disappointed that I didn't have a chance to say good morning, to send him off with a kiss. As I sipped sweet tea and nibbled toast, she added the finishing touches to her outfit. "At least he had the good sense to assign a squad car to this house."

"Where?" I threw back the covers and crossed to the window.

"Right out front where everyone can see it."

A blue and white Wilmington P.D. cruiser was parked at the curb in front of my house. Looking down, I could see a uniformed officer at the wheel.

Melanie gave her luxurious auburn hair a toss. "I'm off to meet Lisa."

"You two have sure become tight," I said, returning to bed and the breakfast tray.

"She's such a sweetie pie. You know, she's led a truly wretched life. She's practically an orphan. What that poor girl . . ."

"Mel. Not now. My head hurts." The last person I wanted to hear about was Lisa.

Melanie rushed to my bedside. "Oh, baby sister, I'm so sorry. Let me get you a pain pill before I leave." She fussed over me, fetching pills and water.

"Thanks for being so good to me," I said, ashamed of myself for lying and for all the times I questioned the depth of her love and loyalty.

She picked up her handbag. "All we have is each other. Well, I'm off. Wish me luck. She's going to commit to a house today, I just know it."

"*Merde*," I said, and blew her a kiss.

17

A few hours later, Jon was unrolling blueprints on my dining room table. I floated to his side, my feet barely touching the floor. I was happy, oh so happy. I knew I was wearing a silly grin on my face; I'd seen it when I was brushing my hair, examining the stitches. Love changed everything, turned my world upside-down. Distraught as I was about Rachel's death, fearful as I was that her murderer had tried to kill me too, my secret love for Nick buoyed my spirits and gave me wings.

Yet, I was being practical too. A locksmith was expected later to change all the locks. When he called for an appointment he told me that Detective Yost said it was urgent police business. Even ADT responded without delay when called by a homicide detective. The alarm system would be installed this afternoon. Nick, God bless him, was looking out for "his girl."

"Are you sure you feel up to this?" Jon asked. "You're acting kind of goofy. Must be the medication."

"I'm okay," I said. "A little tired. Now let's put 'Operation Treasure Hunt' into effect. By the way, did you and Binkie come to the hospital yesterday? I thought I saw you."

"Sure we did. We were worried about you, but when we looked in, you were asleep."

"That was sweet of you."

"Binkie thought a treasure hunt for Suzanna O'Day's hidden gold would cheer you up and take your mind off the murders."

"If there's gold here, why didn't we find it when we were remodeling? We were all over this house."

"Maybe because we weren't looking for it. Binkie says it's here and that's good enough for me." He strolled over to the windows and drew back the lace curtains. "Let's check out the gazebo too. It's as old as the house."

I joined him at the window and clapped him on the back. "Good thinking. We haven't touched that."

The gazebo: a pretty structure in the garden, covered with Carolina jessamine vines. "A perfect hiding place."

I headed toward the back hall. "Let's start down in the cellar, get that over with. We'll tackle the gazebo later when the dew's burnt off."

"You go on down. I'll get the metal detector from my car and join you."

I unbolted the cellar door and snapped on the light switch. Reaching the bottom of the steps, I heard the telephone ring upstairs. It had been ringing off the hook all morning: the newspaper, the local TV stations. According to a perky anchorwoman, there was an All Points Bulletin out for Eddie Parker.

I scanned the basement, taking in the foundation that had been constructed of ballast when the house was built in 1840. In the antebellum period, English ships crossed the Atlantic with ballast for weight, which they'd off-load in Wilmington to make room for lumber and turpentine, our leading exports. In those days, fires had taken a toll on the town, destroying most of the wood structures. This house had been lucky. Originally, it had served as the manse for Reverend Israel and Hannah Barton and their nine children. How had they ever raised nine children in three bedrooms?

I heard Jon's footsteps cross overhead then he appeared on the stairs, carrying the metal detector.

"How about we imagine there's a grid overlay on the floor, then we'll work it square by square," he suggested. The floor was made of dirt with a top layer of sand and crushed shells.

"Sounds good to me. Can I help?"

"No, you just sit over there on the steps and rest."

He turned on the metal detector and paced the width of the cellar, guiding the piece of equipment inches above the floor, like a divining rod in search of water. We made a hit right away. The detector started to click, and I told him where to find a shovel. But his labor netted us only a bag of rusted nails.

"Are you sure you're up to this?" Jon asked.

"Sure. I'll just sit over here and watch."

He picked up the metal detector again, marched back and forth, back and forth. The machine remained mute. He was nudging the device into the last corner when it suddenly went berserk.

He began digging next to the foundation. I crossed the room to watch. About a foot down, his shovel clanked on something metal. He knelt over the hole, dusting the dirt away with his hand. "Well, la-di-da, Miss Scarlett, I think we struck gold." He leaned into the hole, humming under his breath. Then, using both hands, he pulled a heavy metal box out of the dirt.

I pressed my knuckles against my teeth. This was too easy. "Oh, it's padlocked."

"Let's take it upstairs where the light is good. I'll find something to break that lock. I've got a tire iron in my van. That'll do it."

I followed him up the steps on a cloud of anticipation. A treasure. A box full of gold coins. Binkie did know what he was talking about!

I spread newspaper on the dining room table and Jon plunked the box down. While he went to get the tire iron, I examined the box closely. The lid was embossed with a pattern that looked like a coat of arms and was caked with dirt. Rust flaked off the bottom and corners.

"Okay, you hold it steady while I break the lock," he said when he returned. The padlock flew apart with a loud retort.

"Here we go," he said. "Ready?"

"Yes. No. Wait." My eyes met his. "Fifty-fifty. We'll split it fifty-fifty. Okay?"

"Deal." He raised his hand and we slapped palms in a high five. "Now, you take that side, I'll take this. One, two, three! Open sesame!"

The lid was tight but finally gave. "What in the world? Old photographs!" he cried, clearly disappointed as he pulled out a sheaf of vintage photos. "And hair!"

I clapped my hands. "It's a time capsule! Look at this stuff. Look at these pictures of Wilmington from a hundred years ago."

But Jon wasn't happy. "Aren't you disappointed? You act like this junk is as good as gold."

I stopped pawing through the box and gave him a hug. "Oh, Jon, I know it's a let down. Sure, I wanted it to be gold, but this stuff is priceless. In its own way, it's treasure too."

"What? Bits of hair? As good as gold?" He shook his head. "I'll never understand women."

"It's hair jewelry. The Victorian women, with their abundant hair, used to cut locks and braid them into hair jewelry." I held up a sample. "See, a brooch. It's sweet. But these photos, they're really something. Oh look, here's one of my house from the turn of the century. And here's a picture of a family standing out front. This must have been their house then." I laughed. "Obviously, before it became a bordello."

I turned the photo over. In fancy script on the back, the words "Gerard Family" and then the date, "1899" were written.

"The Gerards. Jon, this is too spooky. I just realized who the Gerards were."

He gave me a speculative look. "Who?"

"In my research of the house's background, I remember discovering that the Gerards were former owners. But I just now made the connection. MaeMae Mackie was a Gerard. These are her ancestors. How weird is it that the Gerards once owned the house where Sheldon was murdered?"

Later when I checked my answering machine, a features writer for the *Star-News* had called and left his number. WWAY-TV-3 had called, and so had WECT. There was a rushed message from Melanie. "I'll be over at twelve-thirty to take you to lunch." But no Nick. Not a word from Detective Nick Yost, my midnight lover. Disappointment stabbed my heart like a knife wound. He's busy, I told myself, working two murder cases, trying to find my assailant. I've got to be patient. And whatever you do, Ashley Wilkes, don't you dare call him. Don't you dare become one of those women who can't give a man a little breathing room.

I poured coffee for myself and Jon, and we talked about the attack yesterday. "There was no sign of forced entry, so the police think Rachel must have let the killer in. Probably Eddie." I filled him in on Evil Eddie.

Jon set his coffee mug down on the kitchen counter. "What else do you know about him?"

"Only that he lived with her. And that he's scary. She never talked about him. I didn't know until he barged in here on Monday morning that she had a boyfriend.

"He was the second person to come on the tour on Saturday afternoon. I thought he was with Earl Flynn. Eddie is good looking, except for the mouth. Nasty mouth. Kind of sneering, you know. Like he's a superior being, and Rachel's supposed to provide for him. On Saturday, when he came on the tour, Rachel acted like she was thrilled to see him. That was when I had to go back to the library to stop Sheldon and Binkie's quarrel from escalating into fisticuffs. So if Rachel was introducing him around, I missed it."

"I don't want you staying alone here anymore," he said, "even with new locks and an alarm. If Melanie can't sleep over, call me, I'll stay with you."

I was touched by his concern. "It's a deal. I don't like the idea of being alone in the house either, not as long as this killer is on the loose."

"Oh, by the way," he said, "I did a check at the courthouse on those four lots on Palace Street, but didn't get anywhere. The files had been checked out by someone on the City Council. But, you know how I'm friendly with Bonnie, one of the clerks over there?"

"Yes," I said, dragging the word out thoughtfully. What had Jon discovered?

"Well, you'll never guess who checked out the file before the Councilman."

My heart skipped a beat. "I think I know, but tell me."

"Sheldon."

"Sheldon," I repeated. "So Sheldon, being on the Historic Preservation Commission, was interested in the activity on the Palace Street property. And he cared enough to check it out. Wonder why he didn't mention it to me?"

"We won't know that until we know what's in the file. Could be something as innocent as a permit for a construction dumpster." Jon stood up. "Now, let's take this thing out to the gazebo and get started." He lifted the metal detector and was already making for the kitchen door.

I grabbed a jacket and caught up. The sun was shining, the sky true Carolina blue. "I can't believe Christmas is just two weeks away." I lifted my face to the sun. I'm going to keep busy working on these murder cases in my own way, I told myself, and that'll keep me centered. My preservation work usually kept me grounded, but at this time of year, no one wanted to start a remodeling project. After the first of the year, I'd be as busy as a tick in a tar bucket.

Jon circled the gazebo, the metal detector leading the way. About midway between the gazebo and the neighbor's fence, the device started to click. "There's something here," he called. "Probably another bag of rusty nails. But let's give it a try."

I brought the shovel and he began to dig. "Good thing the ground's not frozen," he said, "or this would be impossible."

"The ground here is softer than in the cellar, that's for sure," I agreed. As I watched him turn over sod, I mulled over what he'd learned about the Palace Street property. Shortly before he was murdered, Sheldon had been interested in Joel Fox's project.

Jon took a rest, leaned on the shovel handle and sucked in air. "I don't want to find any more Victorian relics. Just gold, good old whore's gold."

I sat down on the ground, suddenly exhausted, my headache returning. What was that smell? Yesterday's attack was catching up with me.

After a pyramid of earth had been piled up on the side of a hole, I asked, "Is that thing reliable? There's nothing down there."

"Well, let's try it again and see." He held the metal detector over the hole. This time the clicking was more rapid and louder than before. "There is something. Let's try another six inches. You're fading. We'll quit after that."

"Let me try," I said. "I'll get my second wind." The shovel met mild resistance. "Okay, I've hit something."

Jon took the shovel from me. "I'll do it." He stepped down on the shovel. "Well, there's something there but it shifts when I put pressure on it."

"It felt that way to me too." An unpleasant memory floated just out of reach. Something about a time when I was a little girl helping Daddy in the garden.

Jon got down on his knees and scooped dirt out with his gloved hands. Eyeing me over his shoulder, he groaned, "Another bust. Just an old belt buckle."

I peered into the hole. "Yes, it is. Brush some of the dirt out of the way, so we can see it better. Maybe it's a Civil War artifact."

Jon scooped and pushed at the dirt, tossing handfuls aside as he complained, "I'm not doing this for Civil War artifacts." Then, "Wait a minute!"

"Oh, no," I cried. "I see it too. This can't be happening." The ground under my feet tilted wildly. The sky grew black. I remembered what I'd been trying to recall about helping Daddy in the garden. I'd dug up a dead animal. Except this was no dead animal. This was a dead human.

18

It was *deja vu* all over again with me lying flat on my back on the ground and Nick patting my wrists and calling my name. I opened my eyes and looked up into his terrified face.

"I'm okay. Help me sit up." The ground was cold under my back.

"How's your head? Does it hurt?" he asked.

A half dozen uniformed cops and technicians leaned over the grave. Out of the corner of my eye, I saw Jon talking to two officers. He was waving his hands in the air, excited.

"Yes, it hurts. Not like yesterday." I hugged my knees for comfort. "Did you see it, Nick? What's going on? I can't take any more of this." Dammit, I couldn't help myself, I started to cry.

He knelt beside me, put his arm around my shoulders in a brotherly sort of way. Too many cops around for a real embrace, I realized. "Think you can stand up? I want to get you inside, away from this crowd. Here, let me help you."

I leaned into him as he walked me to the kitchen door. Jon followed our progress with his eyes. I couldn't read the message he was sending me.

At the kitchen table, I sank into a chair and rested my head in my hands.

"Where're your pills?"

"Right over there with my vitamins." I pointed to a basket on the kitchen counter.

Nick shook out a capsule and filled a glass with water from the tap. I swallowed, then laid my head on my arms on the table. When I looked up, he was filling the coffee maker carafe with water. "Where do you keep your coffee beans?" he asked, surveying the room helplessly. Another lost soul in the kitchen.

"In the freezer."

As the coffee dripped, he pulled out a chair across from me. "Ashley, I don't know why you're always in the middle of trouble. You're supposed to be recuperating from a head injury; you're supposed to be resting." His voice went up a decibel. "Then I find out you're digging up the backyard. What's wrong with you? Why can't you act like a normal woman?"

"A normal woman? What does that mean, Nick?" Hot tears stung my eyes. In a moment I was going to shake. He's doing it again, I thought. His mother must have been one perfect wife and mother. And I'm what?

I lost it. Tears streamed down my cheeks and I couldn't stop them. "And if I'd been a normal woman, Nick?" I gulped between sobs. "If I'd been up there in my boudoir, lolling around all day, who would have found that body out there? You've got another corpse on your hands. Another murder. Or would you prefer not to know? Let sleeping dogs lie? Let murder victims remain buried in their unhallowed graves?"

Nick's face turned beet red. "You're out of control. You're talking like an idiot."

"Give me another pill, will you," I said. "My head is killing me. Crying makes my head ache."

He got up, yanked me out of my chair, wrapped his arms around me and held me tight. "What am I going to do with you? Don't cry, baby. I can't stand to see you cry."

Voices coming from the front of the house caused him to spring away from me so fast you'd think I'd stuck him with an upholstery tack. I dabbed at my eyes with a soggy tissue. One of the uniformed cops trudged into the kitchen. "Miss Hamilton is here." He spoke directly to Nick, as if Nick was the only person in the room and owned my house. I might as well have been invisible. "And this other woman says she's related to the woman who dug up the body."

At this point I wanted to jump up and down and wave my arms. Hey, I'm standing right here in front of you, you big dopey bubba. And I have a name. I'm not "the woman."

Instead, I grabbed a roll of paper towels and pulled off a sheet. It scratched my cheeks.

Lisa came in first with Melanie barking up her shins. Lisa gave me a cool appraising stare from head to toe. Why was she always around when I looked my worst? Face swollen, muddy jeans, grass stuck in my hair. While the incomparable Lisa looked as sleek as polished platinum. She had on a jade green outfit that made her eyes shine like emeralds.

"Hi, Nick," she said in a low, seductive tone, turning her back on me and rendering me invisible.

Nick nodded. "Lisa." His voice was husky. He coughed.

Uh oh. Something's going on between those two. Before I could analyze the chemistry sizzling between them, Melanie charged into the center of the kitchen.

"I thought you were going to take care of my little sister," she cried. "You and your homicides! Leave her out of your messes!"

Nick's eyes widened. His homicides? This was crazy. He blamed me for the homicides. Melanie blamed him.

She wrapped an arm around me and lowered me gently into a chair. She pulled a bundle of clean soft tissues from her purse, handed them to me, and removed the paper towel from my hand. "Come on, shug, buck up. I'll take care of this. Lucky for you Lisa and I were in my car when she got the call." She cast Lisa a fond glance. "We were shopping. Lisa has such divine taste."

Divine taste? Who cares, I wanted to scream. How tasteful is it to dig up a body in your backyard?

Lisa had her hand on Nick's arm. Their eyes were locked in silent communication. Without exchanging a word, she motioned for him to follow her out of the kitchen and into the hall. And, damnation, if he didn't follow along like a trained puppy dog. No protests. No, I can't leave Ashley, she needs me. He just allowed himself to be silently drawn into the clutches of that blonde vixen.

Melanie moved to the coffee pot and poured coffee into a clean mug. "Thank goodness someone made coffee. I need this."

I could hear the undertone of Lisa and Nick's conversation coming from the hall.

"Oh, would you like a refill?" Melanie asked.

I was mute. Too stung to speak. I nodded my aching head up and down, which only made it hurt worse. Maybe a swallow of hot coffee would restore me to speech.

I longed to escape, to open the door and run outside. To dismiss Nick and Lisa and their furtive whispering, to slip away from Melanie's theatrics. But when I looked out the window, my garden offered less respite. A knot of uniformed cops and crime scene technicians blocked the grave from my view. I couldn't see it or the remains they were carefully removing. It didn't matter. A picture of the soft earth, the belt buckle, the fragments of clothing, the bones, tissue that looked like parchment, were engraved on my brain. Where was Jon?

Melanie pulled out a chair and sank down beside me. "I know what we've got to do. As soon as the holidays are over, we're putting this house on the market."

I opened my mouth to protest, shock restoring my speech, but Melanie's raised palm stopped me. "You'll have to take your lumps. You'll lose money, but we'll recoup it later on another house. This house is a jinx. We'll be lucky to get a buyer. But we'll mark it down cheap, and I'll show it to out-of-towners."

"But . . ."

"Now I don't want to hear another word. I'll take care of everything." She gave me a pleased-with-herself smile. "I'll even waive my commission."

I grabbed my coffee cup and stood up. "I'm going to bed. My head is splitting."

"Oh, baby sister, here, let me help you."

"No," I said, new tears dashing against my lashes. "Stay here with your precious Lisa."

Before I could push past Melanie, the cop was back, outside the door with Nick and Lisa. "There's an old guy who insists on coming in here. I told him no one was allowed inside, that this was a crime scene, but he says he's the lady's father."

Daddy? My knees buckled and I grabbed the chair for support.

Binkie pushed past the cop. "Ashley dear, are you all right? I saw all the police cars outside. I thought you were hurt again." He moved in close to me and whispered. "I told them I was your father so they'd let me in."

I dropped down in the chair and cradled my head in my hands. They all meant well, but they were too much for me. I wanted to sprout wings and fly away. I know, I thought to myself, a light bulb going off in my aching head. Tomorrow I'm getting on a plane and flying to New York. I'll check into the Plaza Hotel. I'll have high tea in the Palm Court every afternoon from now till Christmas, scones dripping in clotted cream, tea cakes, peppermint tea in silver pots. I'll take long walks around the city to clear away the cobwebs. Sure, I'll encounter some street crazies, but compared to this bunch, dealing with them will be a cakewalk.

19

Jon slept in the big rice bed in the guest room on Sunday night. Nick was off somewhere, playing cops and robbers. Melanie couldn't sleep over because she and the divinely tasteful Lisa had tickets for *A Christmas Carol* at Thalian Hall.

"This house is ruined for me," I told Jon over Monday morning coffee. "I might as well sell it like Melanie says. I can't bear to go into the library. I see Sheldon lying on the floor and a boogie man ready to leap from the shadows. Now, I'm can't even go outside."

I glanced out the kitchen window at the garden where a plastic tarp covered the empty grave. The police had strung crime-scene tape around my property, mostly as a favor to me, to keep reporters from tramping around outside or taking pictures of me through the windows.

"Nick made me promise to mind my own business and 'to keep my pretty little nose out of his murder case.' Work-wise, everything's on hold until after the first of the year. I don't have enough energy to tackle the jobs around here that need doing, and besides, working on the house will just remind me of Rachel. We did most of the decorating together. So how am I going to get through the holidays?" I was building a case for telling the folks in my world that I was taking off for New York and wouldn't return until after New Year's.

"How about Christmas shopping?" Jon suggested. "Women love to shop." He had that pink-cheeked scrubbed look men get from their morning shave. Golden hair slightly damp, pink shirt sleeves rolled up over downy-haired forearms. Brown eyes friendly and wanting to help. Smelling of aftershave, spicy and clean. The girl who gets him is going to be lucky, I thought.

"Christmas shopping? I know I have to, but I can't bring myself to begin. Christmas was ruined for me when Daddy died on Christmas Eve." I'd been hoping that having my house on the candlelight tour would restore my delight in Christmas, but now I had one more tragedy to burden future winter holidays.

During my freshman year at Parsons, Daddy drove into a live oak tree on Airlie Road on Christmas Eve while swerving to avoid a golden retriever. For the longest time, I was unaware of the role the retriever had played. I'd thought the accident had been the result of Daddy's drinking too much. I'd been angry with him for years. Finally, learning the truth, I'd been able to let go of that anger. How like Daddy to save the dog. But the Christmas season still depressed me. Now, I had the loss of Sheldon and Rachel to bear.

The morning papers were stacked at the end of my scrubbed-pine kitchen table. Once again, the macabre goings-on at my house were front page news.

Jon had gone out early for the papers and bagels. I'd made coffee, the real thing, not decaffeinated, and the caffeine snapped through my synapses like a rubber band. I sat tall in my chair.

"Did you see the notice in the 'City' section?" Jon asked.

"No. What notice?"

"Joel Fox is making a presentation to the City Council and the Historic Preservation Commission. Tonight. Seven-thirty. That's why Binkie was here last night. To warn us. He told me about it after you locked yourself in your room."

"But this can't be an official hearing. They have to give notice."

"No, it's not official, but get this, Joel and his supporters hope to persuade the public to back him."

"That's impossible."

"Maybe not so impossible. The developers love it. A lot of the local businesses are for it. People are putting the old pocketbook first."

Maybe the caffeine had put some starch in my backbone, because I said with determination, "I'm not going to let him ruin my town. And that goes for Melanie. I know what we can do."

"Uh oh, why does that worry me?"

"Stay right here. Let me get my laptop." The beguiling dream of escape to New York evaporated.

In minutes I was back, lugging my laptop computer, setting it up on the table. The batteries were charged, and in a "hotmail" minute I was sending an e-mail. Jon pulled up a chair to look over my shoulder.

"We're in luck. He's online," I said.

"Who's online?"

"Jay Trusdale. Remember him? He's an Online Contact."

Jon draped an arm over my shoulder. Cheek to cheek we viewed the screen. "Sure I remember Jay. The lawyer in the Trust's Public Policy Department."

We'd met Jay at the National Trust for Historic Preservation's spring conference. Hitting it off, the three of us had palled around Reston Town Center together, going out for drinks and dinner, playing hooky from a workshop to go skating on the Center's rink.

I typed a message.

Dear Jay,

We've got a problem here in Wilmington. Four lots just outside the historic district are about to be developed into a high-rise hotel. On the surface, the property doesn't appear to qualify for Trust protection. I can't recall the specifics of historic designation. I do remember that it's a complicated list. Refresh my memory. What are the guidelines for historic designation? What should we be looking for to save it?

Best regards,

Ashley

P.S. Jon says hello.

By the time I poured a third cup of coffee and ate half a bagel, my computer dinged and up popped a message informing me I was engaged in conversation with Jay Trusdale. Clicking on it, I read aloud to Jon:

Ashley- Great to hear from you. Merry Christmas to you and Jon. The information you requested is attached. Let me know if I can help.

Yours, Jay

I clicked on the attachment. "We're going to need to print this out. Do you mind bringing the printer from the library?"

We hooked up the cable, then watched as the printer ejected text-covered pages. I passed a couple to Jon, and read through the remainder myself.

"Structures must be at least fifty years old," I read to Jon. "I knew that. I think those houses were built in the Seventies, but we can verify that."

Jon paraphrased from the text, "If a structure is less than fifty years old, it can qualify if it is of exceptional importance."

"But those houses are not of exceptional importance," I said. I read on, "'A birthplace or grave of a historical figure' … Well, that's not likely."

"Wait," Jon said, "Here's something. 'Associated with events that have made a significant contribution to the broad patterns of our history.'"

"And," I interjected, "'may be likely to yield information important in prehistory or history.' You know what I think? I think we've got our work cut out for us. We've got to thoroughly research that property." My juices were bubbling again. "Who knows, maybe it was a campsite for Union soldiers. I'm not giving up."

"Me, neither. Why don't we take a walk over there? Walk around the property. Look around. Who knows? We might see something that'll spark an idea."

"I'm game. Let me get a sweater."

"I don't remember any 'No Trespassing' signs," Jon commented.

So what, I thought to myself. Sometimes Jon is a regular wuss. I wouldn't let any little ole "No Trespassing" sign stop me.

I turned off the computer. "What did we do before the Internet?"

We left my house and strolled toward the river. When the wind is just right, a brackish odor permeates the area. Smelling it I am reminded of crab pots and egret nests, tall grasses and the knobby knees of Cypress trees.

We turned the corner at The Verandas and walked south toward

Palace Street. Hands jammed in pockets, I told Jon, "Nick wants me to talk to a therapist. I had a panic attack the other night. He says it's post-traumatic stress disorder."

Jon stopped, inclined his head to give me a worried look. "You didn't tell me about this."

"No, I haven't told anyone."

"You told Nick."

"Well, no, actually Nick witnessed the—whatever it was. It happened Saturday night after I was attacked. He slept downstairs, remember?" I related the details of reliving the attack, leaving out the part where Nick and I got all lovey-dovey on the divan.

"And *are* you going to consult a therapist?"

"I don't know. Probably. If things ever slow down long enough for me to catch my breath. A vacation might be just as therapeutic." New York beckoned.

"Well, I agree with Nick. And this might be connected to the depression you're experiencing. Have you ever talked to someone, you know, a professional, about your dad's death?"

"No. Just Melanie."

Jon gave me a quick squeeze around the shoulders. "Think about it. It might do you good."

"I will," I promised as we arrived at Palace Street. The four lots and houses were quiet, no one around. "At least there's not a bulldozer here knocking these houses down." In the distance, Memorial Bridge sang with traffic.

"Yet," Jon said. "No bulldozers *yet*."

The houses looked like four boxes lined up in a row, all the same style: one-level bungalows with tiny front porches and, at the backs, short flights of steps leading to an abandoned lot. Paint was peeling, windows were boarded over with plywood, and one roof was sagging around the chimney.

We walked around each house, plowing through long grasses and knee-high weeds. Turning a corner, I spotted movement under a short flight of back steps. I grabbed Jon's sleeve. "There's something under there."

He backed up, pulling me with him. "Don't get any closer. Could be a rat."

"Oh, yuck." But my eyesight was keener than his. "It's not a rat. Too small." I leaned forward, peering hard. "Jon, it's a kitten."

We both heard a tiny meow, a feeble cry for help. Jon got down on his hands and knees, stretched both arms between the steps. "I think I can just reach it."

I knelt beside him, meowing all the while so the kitten wouldn't be frightened. Jon lifted the tiny ball of black fur out from under the steps. "It's really young. Not much more than newborn."

"Let me," I said, taking it with both hands. It felt incredibly soft and fragile.

The kitten didn't have the strength to fight a stranger's hands. In fact, he nestled in my palms. "You're okay, kitty. We're not going to hurt you. Jon, we've got to get him home. He's shivering."

Jon stroked the tiny head with a fingertip. "Yeah, but maybe we'd better take a minute to look around. There might be others, if this one is part of a litter."

Jon is so smart sometimes.

My sweater had large patch pockets and I slipped the kitten into one. We broke up to explore the foundations of each house, looking under steps and porches, behind bushes, while making puckered-up kissy noises. From time to time I reached into my pocket to reassure the kitten that dinner was coming soon.

"This one seems to be on his own. I'm just going to walk over and take a look around those stones. Then we'll get this little one straight home."

I headed for a pile of stones under some trees, part of a fallen wall, or the remainder of the foundation of a former structure. "Here, kitty, kitty," I called softly, walking hunched over, searching the ground for another small kitten or the mama cat. I saw nothing but weeds growing out of pockets in the stones. Dry grasses reached my thighs.

I turned around, about to start back, when suddenly soft ground under my feet yielded and caved in, taking me with it. "Help! Jon!"

As I slid down what felt like a giant rabbit hole, I heard Jon's panicked voice shout my name and the pounding of his feet as he ran toward me.

I landed on a layer of river sand at the bottom of a small underground room of some sort. I wasn't hurt, but the bruises I'd have tomorrow would be beauts. Instinctively, I'd held on to my sweater pocket and the kitten while I was falling. Light filtered in from the hole above, so at least I wasn't trapped in total darkness.

Then the patch of light above grew dim as Jon leaned over the hole. "Ashley! For godsakes, are you all right?"

"I'm okay," I called. "Nothing's broken." But the kitten hadn't even meowed and I wondered if it was dead. I slipped my hand into my pocket, so relieved to feel a heartbeat.

"Ashley, I'm calling 911. The firemen will get you out!"

"Jon! No! Don't! If you call 911, Nick will find out and he'll be here making a fuss. He already thinks I haven't got any more sense than this kitten."

"Well, I've got to get you out of there, and I can't reach you."

I could see his face looking down at me. He must have flattened out on the ground.

"Don't go to any of the neighbors either," I instructed. "They'll just call the police. My house is five minutes away. There's rope in the basement. Get it and come back. I'll be perfectly all right while you're gone."

"There's just one thing wrong with that scenario, Ashley."

"What's that?"

"I don't have a key to your house."

"Oh. That's right. Okay, well, stand back and I'll throw the keys up to you."

I didn't want to jostle the kitten, so I took him out of my pocket and hugged him against my breast with my left arm. It took several tries for me to throw the keys directly through the ceiling hole.

"I'll be right back," Jon called. "Don't go anywhere."

I knew he was trying to cheer me up. "Very funny," I shouted. "Hurry."

Overhead, the thuds of Jon's racing feet grew fainter as he ran to Palace Street.

With his head not blocking the hole, a shaft of sunlight penetrated my prison. The underground room was dry and small. River rocks lined the walls. On shelves made of juniper logs, what once had been heaps of root vegetables—potatoes, onions, turnips, rutabagas—had decomposed into pyramids of dust.

I moved around, exploring. In one corner, a flight of stone steps started up, then ended at a solid wall of tumbled stones. Someone had sealed the entrance to the root cellar. But over the years the ceiling timbers had rotted under their layer of earth. Then I happened along, and stepped on the most vulnerable spot. I sat down to wait, my sore rump pressed against the cold ground.

The kitten was very still. I hugged him to my chest, crooning, "Please don't die, little kitty, please don't die." Tears filled my eyes. "You can't die," I whispered. "Everyone around me is dying. You can't. Just hang on. Please hang on. I'll get you home soon, and we'll manage to get some milk into you somehow." I stroked him with my fingertips, remembering that I'd heard somewhere that mama cats lick their newborns vigorously to instill life into them.

Jon returned very quickly. He lowered a rope, yelling instructions for me to tie it under my arms. "Be sure the knot is tight."

Soon, my feet were dangling above the floor as I twisted on the rope. Jon was lying on the ground again, struggling to haul me out. "You're going on a diet," he said when I emerged into daylight. I grabbed the ground and pulled my leg up and over.

Kissing Jon's cheek, I said, "You were fast."

"I drove back," he said, leading me to his van. "On the way, I called a vet who makes house calls. She's on her way to your house now with emergency supplies. She'll show us how to take care of our little friend here."

"What would I ever do with you?" I asked, and kissed his cheek again.

He smiled at me. "You'll never have to find out. Oh, and we've got to report that cave-in to the police. I'll do it anonymously from my cell phone. We don't want anyone else tumbling down in there."

On my lap, the kitten stretched out his paws and kneaded my denim jeans. Instinctively, he was trying to nurse. I rubbed his back and he purred.

20

"Rachel's parents were here this afternoon," I said. Nick, Jon, Binkie and I were gathered around my kitchen table to share Thai takeout. "They came to Wilmington to arrange to have Rachel's body sent to Greensboro for burial. Talking to them was one of the hardest things I ever had to do."

Little Spunky, for that is what I named the kitten, was asleep on a heating pad in a basket at my feet. Nick was still clueless about my fall into the root cellar that morning. I told him the kitten had turned up at my back door. I reflected that if I'd gone to New York as I'd planned, this little guy would have starved to death. Sometimes things work out the way they're meant to.

"Rachel's home is in Greensboro," Nick told Jon and Binkie.

The Thai food was fragrantly spicy. We had See Ew—noodles with black soy sauce, broccoli, and shrimp—and chicken Gra Prao, plus Gang Ped, red curry with fresh vegetables. I was working on my salad. Peanut dressing, I was addicted.

I swallowed quickly. "Oh, the Jacobs told me something interesting. Evil Eddie is from Greensboro too. Rachel and Eddie met at UNC-G. Mr. and Mrs. Jacobs never liked him. Well, I can sure understand why."

Nick said, "The Greensboro police are working with us. They went to Eddie's parents' home with a search warrant but he wasn't there.

And they claim they haven't heard from him."

Well, I should have known that Sherlock Yost would be one jump ahead of Ashley Watson.

"You'll get him," Jon said. "I'll bet he's hiding somewhere here in town. He doesn't strike me as a man with many resources."

"He hinted that he was about to come into big money," I said. "He's probably involved in drugs."

"He's got a rap sheet," Nick told us. "Dealing."

That didn't surprise me.

"Is Eddie now your prime suspect?" Binkie asked Nick, inserting the knife and giving it a twist. Not that I blamed him.

Nick blanched. "Professor, you aren't a suspect in Rachel's murder. We know you didn't kill her."

"I didn't kill Sheldon either. Lord knows I hated him enough, but I'm not a killer."

"I know you're not, Professor. It's just that all the evidence points to you."

Well, that got my attention. Just when I think I've got him pegged, Nick surprises me. "Circumstantial evidence, Nick," I argued. "No witnesses."

"True. But the D.A. has won cases with less. I shouldn't even be sitting here talking to you about the case, Professor."

Binkie gave Nick a half-smile. "But you are. You wanted to see Ashley. And I'm not feeling kindly toward you so I'm not bowing out. I was here first. Besides, you know I didn't kill him, no matter how much evidence points to me. If you had any sense you'd be asking for my help. But you young people, you think you know it all."

Jon choked on his food and got up and went to the refrigerator for a bottle of iced tea. He stood leaning into the refrigerator for a long while, his hunched shoulders shaking. He's trying not to laugh out loud, I thought. I wasn't inclined to come to Nick's rescue. Besides, I reminded myself, he's not mine to rescue.

Nick defended himself with, "Look, Professor, when Rachel was killed on Saturday morning, you were conducting the Ghost Walk tour. Dozens of people saw you. It's different with Mackie's murder. You have no alibi. You were found alone with him in the room where he was killed. Ashley found you with the murder weapon in your hand. You understand how it looks."

"Don't drag me into this," I said. "You ought to take him up on his offer, Nick. He can help. He's got the low-down on everything that's ever happened in this town. Maybe he can help you identify the corpse."

"We've already identified him," Nick announced.

Jon, who'd rejoined us and had just picked up his chopsticks, dropped them. "Well, why didn't you tell us, man? I'm having nightmares about digging up that body. Who was he?"

I gave Nick a hard stare. Any other man would have blurted out the news the moment he hit the door. But Nick was first and foremost a cop. The way he operated confused me. I'd never understand him. My love for him was hopeless. This is not going to work, I told myself. I laid down my fork. The sweet basil chicken turned sour in my mouth.

"Who was he?" I asked.

"His name was Jimmy Weaver. There was a wallet with identification in his pocket. The medical examiner says he's been buried in your yard for about forty years. He . . ."

"Nineteen-sixty. The Atlantic Coast Line payroll robbery," Binkie interrupted, looking smug.

"He was involved!" I exclaimed. "Ohmygosh, that means Mrs. Penry's son must have been involved too."

Nick leaned back in his chair, clasped his arms behind his head. "Why don't I deputize all of you?" There was a twinkle in his eyes and his dimples looked adorable.

"Well, Nick, you told me the other night that the robbery was pulled off by three young men. And this is where Mrs. Penry's son lived in nineteen-sixty."

"Might have been four if there was a getaway driver," he speculated.

"But where is Mrs. Penry's son now?" I asked. "The nursing home manager told me no one ever comes to visit her."

"We're looking into that," Nick replied.

"Wait a minute," Jon interjected, "just because this Jimmy Weaver was killed forty years ago doesn't prove he robbed the Coast Line."

Nick was chuckling. "Civilians," he muttered under his breath.

I heard him. "Oh, and what is so funny about civilians?"

He threw up his hands. "Nothing. Just the old blind pig theory."

Binkie laughed. "Even a blind pig can dig up an acorn once in a while."

"And what's that supposed to mean?" Jon asked.

Nick said, "It means that for amateurs you've come to the correct conclusion. Jimmy Weaver was a security officer for the Atlantic Coast Line. He disappeared several months after the robbery. The Coast Line had already moved to Jacksonville, but their employee records show that Weaver did not relocate with them. I guess the investigators back then assumed he left Wilmington to find work elsewhere. He was never charged with anything. He was free to leave town if he wanted to."

"So with his body turning up dead forty years later," I said, "you've got to assume he was the inside man. And one of his confederates killed him for the money. Maybe Penry."

"Looks that way," Nick said, enjoying himself.

I remembered him saying he'd give anything to crack the old case. So he'd come to my house and thrown down the bait, and we'd all swallowed it.

Accustomed to being in charge in the classroom, Binkie took over. "Let's review what we know. Well, let me rephrase that, what I know."

He started to tick off items on his fingers. "One. I know that I did not kill Sheldon Mackie. Therefore, it had to be someone who slipped in with the other tourists. Ashley recognized many of the guests, as did I. And you, Nick, have got a partial list of names."

I jumped in. "Number two. Only Binkie's fingerprints were on the poker handle, when mine should have been there as well."

Jon smacked his forehead. "Poker handle! Hold on a minute, I just remembered something. Rachel's fingerprints should have been on that poker handle too. I was over here the day before the tour. Rachel was adding holly berries to the mantel greenery. I distinctly remember seeing her pick up that poker and move it out of the way. She moved the other fireplace equipment too. Then she set it all back in place."

"See, Nick!" I cried. "I told you."

"Thus," Binkie said, "the murderer either wiped off the poker handle or wore gloves that smudged Ashley's and Rachel's prints."

Nick looked at Jon. "I wish you'd told me that sooner."

Jon arched his eyebrows. Don't blame me, he seemed to be saying. "Well, you didn't ask me. I wish I'd remembered sooner too."

"Let's remain focused," Binkie said. "The next thing that happened was Rachel was murdered in the same manner as Sheldon. We don't have that murder weapon. And Ashley was attacked, also by a blow to the head. We don't have that murder weapon. So if Eddie killed Rachel, and tried to kill Ashley because he feared she'd identify him, what we've got to figure out is, why did Eddie kill Sheldon? What was his motive? He was here that night. Ashley says he was the second guest on the tour."

"I thought he was with Earl Flynn," I said again. "I can't say why. I just got that impression. So if they were together, how does Flynn fit into this?"

Nick was still leaning back in his chair, his arms clasped behind his head. He seemed to be deep in thought.

"Well, we can't connect Eddie to that corpse buried by the gazebo. Eddie wasn't born when that guy bit the dust," Jon said.

The front legs of Nick's chair hit the floor with a thud and the kitten jumped. "Be careful," I warned. "You're scaring Spunky."

"Oh, sorry. It's too much of a stretch to think that the current murders, and Jimmy Weaver's, were committed by the same person. There's too much time in between. It's a coincidence."

Binkie crossed his arms across his chest. "I don't believe in coincidences."

"Neither do I," Jon said.

I chimed in, "Ditto for me."

21

The City Council chambers was jam-packed. During the day, word of the meeting had spread through town, bringing at least two hundred Wilmingtonians to City Hall. The mayor and the five council members presided over the chambers. At a table up front sat eight members of the Historic Preservation Commission. The ninth chair, Sheldon's, was empty. Binkie, a member, chatted with fellow commissioner Betty Matthews. The Matthewses had cut short their winter vacation to return for the emergency meeting. It was so typical of Betty; she was as dedicated to our town as Binkie.

I spotted the city manager and the city engineer and various members of the Planning Commission in front rows. Members from the Historic Wilmington Foundation, the Lower Cape Fear Historical Society, and the Historic Preservation Society milled about, voices excited, body language militant.

A model of the proposed hotel was exhibited under spotlights. "I want to get a good look at that," Jon said. Making our way to the dais was slow progress. Everyone wanted to talk to us. They wanted to hear the latest news on the murders. When we said we didn't know any more than was in the papers, the topic changed to: "Don't you think this hotel business is ghastly, Ashley?"

Well, yes, I did. And to think my own sister was at the heart of it. "Dreadful," I responded.

The model of the hotel and its environs was built to scale. There was the towering hotel itself, a parking deck, the grounds, even a swimming pool made from a small mirror. Tiny green plastic trees and shrubs dotted miniature astro-turf.

"Twenty stories!" I exclaimed. "That's more than was quoted in the paper. It'll distort the skyline."

Jon shook his head, disgusted with the whole project. "Let's find some seats." In reverse order we bucked the same agitated crowd, squeezing into the sixth row and settling down to wait for the gavel to fall. Someone up front waved a sign in the air. "REMEMBER LUMINA," it read, referring to the destruction of the historic Lumina ballroom, a turn of the century landmark on Wrightsville Beach.

"Joel's added a penthouse tower," Jon groused as the mayor called the meeting to order.

He asked for quiet. He asked everyone to find seats. Eventually everyone settled down but they never did get quiet. He explained that this was an informal meeting, that Mr. Joel Fox and his associates had requested an opportunity to make a presentation. Mr. Fox, he explained, was reimbursing the city for all costs associated with this unscheduled meeting. The tax payers would not be charged. Mr. Fox was merely asking for an opportunity to show how his resort hotel would benefit the community. Some members of the business community, he added, believed the hotel complex would bolster economic growth for the city.

He was about to turn the mike over to Joel when Betty Matthews claimed it. She said she was sick and tired of responding to emergencies. "Preservationists are not bein' apprised of zoning requests in a timely manner. We're always bein' forced into rushin' in at the eleventh hour to stay the wrecking ball!"

"Hear! Hear!" roared the crowd.

She sat back down amid cheers and whistles. Binkie patted her on the back.

Joel strode out onto the platform and introduced himself as if we didn't know the name of the trouble maker in our midst. He did not fit in with our down-home Southern style. Boooos erupted from the rear of the auditorium. Undaunted, he stepped to the podium. What does

Melanie see in him, I wondered again.

He reminded us that he'd turned down offers from big cities like Charlotte and Atlanta to relocate his development company to little Wilmington. He got overly sentimental when he talked about our small-town atmosphere and sense of community. He called it a wholesome place where he'd like to settle down and raise a family.

"I think I'm going to be sick," I told Jon. "What a lot of phony baloney."

Joel told us how he believed we could all work together for our mutual profit. If only we'd do things his way.

"He thought we wouldn't fight back, is what he thought," Jon said.

At this point, a heckler in the back of the auditorium shouted that Fox should pack up his development plans and take them and himself back to L.A.

The mayor tapped his gavel and cried, "Order! Order!" But he didn't have the heckler removed.

"He's on our side," Jon said.

Thrown off stride, Joel smoothed back his slicked-down hair. He leaned into the microphone to explain how his commercial enterprise would provide direct and indirect revenues to the city. He then introduced Murray Caulfield of the Los Angeles law firm of Caulfield, Zimmer, and Zeiss who would make the presentation for him.

More booos, joined by a few hoots.

Joel Fox and Murray Caulfield could have been twins. Or else their hair stylists were twins. Same long slicked-back hair, same black on black outfits, same arrogant stance and haughty way of speaking down to us "backwoods" North Carolinians.

"Bet he thinks we all left school in the eighth grade and that we're sitting here with bare feet," I said.

Caulfield had slides and one of those telescopic pointers with a light on the tip that he waved around over bargraphs. He had a graph for revenues, and a graph for taxes, and a graph for traffic flow, and another graph that predicted how the influx of hotel guests would boost business for local restaurants and retail establishments.

One of the downtown restauranteurs leapt to his feet. "I'm not falling for this crap. You'll have your own restaurants in that hotel. This is just a ploy to get us to go along with you. I oppose your hotel on the grounds it'll destroy the quaintness and charm that brings tourists to Wilmington and into my restaurant in the first place!"

The auditorium erupted in cheers.

Caulfield's grin was toothy.

"He looks like the wolf in 'Little Red Riding Hood,'" I told Jon. There was no need to lower my voice. The noise level around us was escalating.

Then I saw why. Melanie had just slipped in through a side door. She was vivid in a red suit. Wrong choice of color, sister, I telegraphed.

An irate woman headed her off as she started down the aisle to join Joel.

On the dais, Caulfield was saying, "We do plan to have a restaurant, but it will not be large enough to accommodate all our hotel guests. Many will seek out local establishments." A flash of wolf teeth. "There'll be more than enough business for all of us. And a fresh supply of money will pour into Wilmington. We'll all profit. And with our luxury resort hotel, the famous stars who come here to make movies will have a quality place to stay."

Someone yelled, "They already got quality places to stay. I rent 'em my beach houses!"

The woman cornered Melanie in the side aisle and pressed her against the wall. Melanie cast about frantically, seeking a way out. "How can you consort with the enemy?" the woman roared. "You're one of us. Why, my folks played bridge with your mama and daddy."

A commotion in the center aisle diverted attention away from Melanie and her predicament. I recognized the man who was charging down the aisle to stick his face in Caulfield's. He owned a popular downtown nightclub. "I don't buy none of this." He turned to the audience. "And if the rest of you do, you're bigger fools that I thought."

A man joined the woman who was rebuking Melanie, shouting, "You'll never sell another house in this town!"

An elderly woman sprang to her feet. She was near hysteria. "I own a gift shop and hardly make ends meet. I can't afford to retire. Those hotel people will be good for my business. What's wrong with you knuckleheads?"

Melanie spotted me and waved, a big smile plastered on her face as if this was all a huge misunderstanding. "Ashley, sugah! Thanks for saving me a seat." She waded through the angry mob toward me. I could see her mentally calculating her choices. She turned to the threatening mob and smiled prettily. "My sister and I are opposed to this hotel. We're for historic preservation. For keeping our town small and quaint."

On the dais, Murray Caulfield was tapping his telescopic pointer on yet another graph. He grabbed the microphone off the stand and held it to his lips as he paced. His was the only voice heard over the din. "Thank you, madam, for that excellent observation. You are so right. Our accountants project that sales at gift shops and boutiques will triple."

The mayor rapped his gavel and called for order, but the decibel level was so high no one heard him.

The lady who owned the gift shop whipped out an umbrella and started whacking it across the shoulders of the nightclub owner. "You wanta see an old woman starve to death!"

His arms raised defensively, he screamed at her, "You old fool, they'll have gift shops in the lobby. Are you insane? Get away from me!"

At the head table, a dignified Binkie rose to his feet, seized the microphone from a startled Caulfield, and asked everyone to please remember our Southern heritage of courtesy to strangers and to one another. He launched into a lecture about how we'd overcome the Yankee carpetbaggers, and how we'd overcome the Hollywood carpetbaggers as well.

Just when I thought nothing more could go wrong, thuds, punches and loud shouts erupted at the rear of the auditorium. One man pulled back his fist, about to punch the daylights out of another man. Someone behind him grabbed his arm, and the man who was about to be hit let go with a punch of his own. The first man dropped against the man who was clutching his right arm and they both went down for the count.

"FIGHT, FIGHT," came loud, testosterone-driven cheers.

Melanie's eyes blazed. "Who are those rednecks? I'll bet you arranged this. You and your culture-vulture historic society friends, turning this meeting into mayhem so we'll never get a fair hearing."

Up front, in a seat far off to the right, Joel Fox held his moussed head in his hands. It was the one sight in the room that restored my faith in the democratic process. Joel was getting a good lesson in how things got done in rebel territory. He was just lucky no one had pulled a pistol on him.

22

On Tuesday, the day after the disastrous City Council meeting, Jon and I walked to Joel's office on Market Street. When we'd parted last night—after the cops had broken up the fights—Melanie had insisted that we meet her and Joel for lunch the next day. If only we'd get to know Joel better, she'd said, we'd see what a great guy he was, and we'd trust his judgment about the resort hotel being good for Wilmington. With two of the town's leading preservationists on his side, she'd argued, referring to Jon and me, Joel might stand a better chance of rallying support for the project.

I argued and argued, said no again and again. But when Melanie started to cry, Jon patted her arm and said we'd come. "What can it hurt?" he'd told me later. "There's nothing Joel can say that'll change our minds."

Joel's receptionist stood up to greet us, and Jon did a double take. I've never seen him so enthralled with any woman, but this young woman was a beauty, glossy long brown hair, big brown eyes, a voluptuous figure.

"Hi," she said warmly, giving Jon a big smile. "You must be Mr. Campbell. They're expecting you. You too, Ms. Wilkes." But she only had eyes for Jon, and I felt redundant.

She led us down a hallway to Joel's office. Jon eyes were rivetted on her walk. I was tempted to snap my fingers in front of his face, but then

I thought, why not? Why shouldn't he take an interest in a pretty young woman? Am I so petty I'm jealous of dear Jon? Didn't he deserve to find someone he liked? What a *putz* you are, Wilkes, I thought.

Christine Brooks—that's what the name plate on her desk said—showed us into the office and left. Melanie, Joel, and Earl Flynn were waiting for us.

"Hi, you found us. Hi, Jon." Melanie gave us both loving hugs. She was in her Southern belle mode.

Jon shook hands with Joel and Flynn. It's a man thing. I slipped my hand inside my pocket. I only shake hands with people I respect.

The model of the hotel was set up on a table in the center of the room. Automatically, we gravitated to it. "We'll have a health club," Joel said proudly. "And swimming pools, of course, indoor and outdoor." He shot me a shrewd look. "The folks here are going to love it. Once they get used to the idea."

"I've got a lot of money riding on this deal," Earl Flynn said.

"Is that right?" I said, not knowing what else to say.

"Joel's got a limo outside," Melanie gushed. "We're driving down to Southport, to a great seafood restaurant."

So that explained the white limo I'd seen out front that had taken up half the block.

Joel led the way past the receptionist's desk, with Flynn trotting faithfully at his heels like a devoted dog. "Bring you back something, Honey?" Joel asked Christine.

"Oh, would you, Mr. Fox? Some fried shrimp. That'd be sweet of you."

"Why does he call her Honey?" I asked Melanie in a whisper as we stepped through the door.

"Because that's her nickname. Everyone calls her that. Even me. Oh, shoot. Don't they ever give up?"

"Damn," Joel said. "Those bitches are back."

The white limo was surrounded by a circle of demonstrators, all women. They didn't look like bitches to me. In fact, they looked like my former Sunday School teachers, with their flowered hats and white gloves.

"Those awful women. They're picketing us again, sweet cakes," Melanie said.

Joel's driver was a big husky man he called Frank, who looked like a body guard. He pushed through the picket line in a menacing kind of way so that the ladies parted, and escorted us to the car. He held the door open for us and shielded us as we got in. I recognized some of the women, and felt ashamed to be seen with Fox.

"This is a big mistake," I whispered to Jon as I slide in beside him. We got to ride backward.

The driver got in behind the wheel and was so far away, Joel had to speak to him through an intercom. "Go on, Frank. Get us out of here. Drive straight through the old biddies if you have to."

Joel's expression grew as dark as the tinted windows. Studying him, I reminded myself that Joel Fox was a dangerous man. I'd recognized the sinister element in his makeup the first time I'd met him, last year when he'd escorted Melanie to a benefit at Thalian Hall. Living in New York had given me some street smarts and sharpened my instincts; I was a better judge of character than Melanie. Melanie has lived her whole life in Wilmington among familiar folk. Joel Fox came across as an exotic specimen compared to the men she was used to dating. The number of good men she'd cast aside to take up with someone as sleazy as Fox amazed me. And she was blind to his faults, maybe even found them attractive. This time, was she really in love?

"Those narrow-minded church women! Dried up spinsters, all of 'em," Flynn said.

When the limo pulled away from the curb sharply, the women jumped to either side of the car. "Didn't know those old broads could move so fast," Flynn snickered.

But the women were determined and moved in swiftly to surround the limo. The driver had no choice but to slow to a crawl. They crowded up to the windows, tapping the roof with the stick handles of their placards. Inside, it sounded like hail raining on us. I read the messages on the placards: *Just Say No to Ho-tels* and *Reject Resorts.* My favorite was *There's a Fox in our Henhouse.* Clever.

The women pressed up against the windows, yelling and tapping the glass with their purses. The driver saw an opening in the crowd, leaned on the horn, stepped on the gas, and shot through.

I looked out the back window. No bodies littered the ground. Only flowered hats.

"Those hypocrites just don't understand progress," Melanie complained as we pulled away. "And their 'holier than thou' attitudes! Poor baby," she crooned to Joel, laying her head on his five thousand dollar suit.

"Fix us a drink, will you, Earl?" Joel snapped, as we sped across Memorial Bridge.

Earl Flynn sat nearest the bar. He got out a crystal decanter and offered drinks all around. I declined.

I caught Jon's eye. I wondered if he was thinking the same thing I was. I was reminded of Binkie's story about the Ladies Temperance League and how they'd cleaned up the town when Woodrow Wilson was expected to visit. The history buffs of New Hanover County weren't going to stand for the desecration of their beloved historic district. They'd struggled too long and too hard to preserve it. Joel was a fool to underestimate them. But then maybe he didn't.

We made the thirty minute drive to Southport in gloomy silence with Melanie dozing on Joel's shoulder, and Joel drinking and brooding. If this trip was supposed to be a time when he persuaded Jon and me to join forces with him, he was failing miserably. Flynn drank too and stared glumly out the window at the passing live oaks that lined the road. Jon looked like he was wondering what he'd got us into, like he'd rather be back at Joel's office, helping "Honey" answer the phone.

Surreptitiously I studied Joel. His bones were good but he always had a five o'clock shadow. Must be rough kissing him, I thought. Right now he was thinking hard, like he was putting plan B into effect. Joel wouldn't let any small-town preservationist women prevent him from building his hotel. What was it Melanie had called them last night? Culture vultures? Cute.

We arrived at Southport in foul moods, cruising through the quaint business district to the waterfront where majestic white clapboard residences stood watch over the harbor.

"*The Jackal* was filmed here," Earl Flynn commented. "And that other movie, what was it? With Diane Keaton."

"*Crimes of the Heart*," I offered.

"Yeah, that's it," Flynn said.

I didn't tell him that Southport was the birthplace of Robert Ruark. I didn't think Flynn knew who Robert Ruark was, and Mama had taught us not to embarrass others.

Parking the limo in front of a rustic seafood restaurant that loomed over the pier where fishing boats unloaded their catch, the driver got out and opened all doors. Joel detained me with a hand on my arm as Melanie, Jon, and Flynn moved toward the restaurant's entrance. Frank got back in behind the wheel and closed the car door.

"A moment alone, Ashley," Joel requested, pleasantly enough. "I'm hoping I can count on your cooperation with the hotel." His grip on my arm tightened.

I tried to pull away, but his grasp was too strong.

"You're hurting me, Joel. Now let go."

"Not until you hear me out. This project is very important to me and my West Coast associates. Anyone who gets in the way is going to get hurt."

"Is this how you plan to persuade me? By threatening to hurt me? Well, you don't know me very well if you think that'll work."

"Not you, Ashley. I know you're sleeping with a cop." He gave me a leer but there was no lechery behind the leer, no feeling at all, only bone-chilling evil. His eyes were as flat and cold as a dead fish's.

He twisted the skin on my forearm and I winced. Lucky for me I was dressed in my "construction-wear chic" steel-toed boots. I stomped down hard on his soft Italian loafer.

"Shit!" he yelled, jumping up and down and grabbing his foot.

I turned away and started for the restaurant. The menace in his words stopped me. "Melanie's a beautiful girl. It'd be a shame if something happened to her face. She's vain. Not like you. She'd be nothing without her looks. It'd destroy her if . . . well, say some punk slashed her face."

I whirled around to face him. "You slime!" I screeched. "I'll tell her!

Then she'll be through with you."

Fox's chuckle was smug. "She won't believe you. She'll think you made it up because you're jealous."

Inside the restaurant, a tired waitress brought two baskets of hot hush puppies to our table. There were small tubs of cinnamon butter for dipping the hot hush puppies. Then you popped the warm, buttery hush puppy in your mouth, let it melt, and thought you'd died and gone to heaven.

Everyone reached into the baskets but me. I held my hands under the table so no one could see how badly they were shaking. I was upset and near tears. I excused myself, got up, and left for the rest room. "Do you want me to go with you, shug?" Melanie called.

"No," I said, my voice falsely cheerful. "I'll be right back."

Fox ignored me, as if the grotesque scene outside hadn't occurred.

I went into a stall and threw up. When I came out I was trembling. I rinsed out my mouth then splashed cold water on my face. I ran water over the red streak on my forearm until the stinging subsided, all the while staring at my frightened face in the mirror. My eyes were red too, smarting with hot tears. How was I going to sit through an entire meal with that scumbag Joel Fox? Maybe I should just march back in there and tell everyone how he'd threatened Melanie.

But no, I thought, I've got to be smart about this. Seeing how desperate he was, I was beginning to wonder if Joel Fox might have had something to do with the murders and the attack on me. He was certainly capable of it. I had to be very careful. Melanie trusted him and that made her vulnerable. I knew I'd have to tell Nick, yet what could the police do? It would be my word against his. I had to think this through. Devise a plan.

Maybe I could get Melanie out of town, take her to New York with me. Jon would take care of Spunky for me. But no, Melanie wouldn't leave Joel at the holidays.

I patted my cheeks with paper towels, rolled my sleeve down over the red welt, put on lipstick and combed my hair. When I got back to the table, I caught Joel's eye. I stared him down and didn't bat an eyelash. Instead, I gave him a knowing look. I've got your number now, that look was meant to say. You've started something and there's no turning back. You've revealed your true self to me.

I wasn't afraid of him now, and that surprised me. Somehow, seeing into his heart, seeing the evil there, had prepared me. I was forewarned. I would be on guard. And I'd take care of Melanie too.

"Fried fish platter," I told the waitress. Let Joel see that I wasn't going to shrivel up and fade away. Let him see that he had made an enemy, and that he had to deal with that enemy from now on.

I didn't hear the conversation going on around me. I was too caught up in my own thoughts. There *was* something I could accomplish while sitting through this detestable luncheon. I'd wanted to learn more about Earl Flynn. He was sitting next to me.

As I was wondering what to say first, he opened the conversation with, "That's some house you've got, Ashley. And what a great job you did fixing it up. You see, me and Joel, we're not against old houses and historic preservation. We just think there's room for both, the old and the new."

"I'm glad you like my house," I said pleasantly, peeling the paper from a straw and sticking the straw into my glass of iced tea, keeping my hands busy as my mind raced.

Flynn continued, "It's a shame about those murders though. Aren't you afraid to live there?"

The waitress and a helper set our platters in front of us. Fried shrimp and clam strips, thin fillets of flounder, french fries, cole slaw. Down the table, Joel was watching me. Defiantly, I broke a hush puppy in half, dipped it in butter, and popped it in my mouth. Scrumptious! I swallowed. It would take more than a rat like Joel Fox to spoil my healthy appetite.

"Right now I'm feeling a little uncomfortable about my house," I said to Flynn, "but when the murderer is caught, I think that'll close the chapter and I'll love my house the way I used to."

"Do you think they'll catch whoever did it? They're looking for the boyfriend, aren't they?"

"Yes, I think Nick Yost and his detectives will catch the murderer. By the boyfriend you must mean Eddie Parker. He was with you the night of the house tour. Do you know him well?"

Flynn, who had just speared a shrimp, stopped, fork poised mid-air. "Know him? No, I don't know him at all. We may have exchanged a few words while we were waiting in line that day. I had no idea he was the dead girl's boyfriend until I read it in the papers. What made you think I knew him?"

"Oh, just a hunch. You two looked like you were together. That's all. By the way, I admired the handsome cane you were carrying that day. Ebony with a silver handle. I notice you don't have it today. Your leg must be better."

Flynn sniffed. "I have a touch of gout. There are times when I need the assistance of a cane. Today, I'm feeling fine."

I munched on coleslaw for a while. "Melanie said you grew up in Wilmington."

"Yes, I was born and raised here. Left for Hollywood when I was nineteen. I'd wanted to be an actor since my first part in a school play." He smiled. "As it turned out, I was one of the lucky ones. I got a screen test right away. They said the camera loved me. I got better and better roles. I had more work than I could handle."

"What movies were you in? Maybe I've seen some of them."

Flynn dabbed at his mouth with a paper napkin, then gave me a wry smile. "I don't think you're old enough."

I faked a smile of my own. "Yes, but they're always running the old movies on TV. I could have."

"They don't run my old movies on TV."

"Hmmm. You must have left Wilmington in about nineteen-sixty. Is that right?"

"About then," Flynn replied. He pushed his plate away. "I don't remember the exact year."

"Then you must have been around when the big railroad robbery happened," I suggested.

"I don't recall, Miss Wilkes."

"Funny, Mr. Flynn, everyone else your age sure remembers it and what they were doing when it happened. Kind of like when they talk about where they were and what they were doing when JFK got shot.

It's something you don't forget."

Flynn pushed back his chair. "Well, it's something *I* forgot." He signaled Joel. "We'd better get back to the office."

23

"I'll have the Super Duper Grouper," I told the waitress at The Oceanic Restaurant. The entree description made me drool: fresh grouper, pan-seared in a crust of cashew nuts and sesame seeds, layered over celery mashed potatoes with roasted red pepper butter. Watching out for Melanie was turning into a superb culinary experience. Whoever said good deeds went unrewarded?

"A simple salad with balsamic vinaigrette on the side," Melanie said with distaste. "And unsweetened iced tea."

In answer to my inquiring look, she explained, "Joel says I'm putting on weight."

"Weight? You? You never gain weight. You've got the most enviable metabolism of anyone I know. Besides, you look fabulous." She was wearing a pistachio green sweater set over chocolate brown capri pants and bronze-colored high-heeled slides. Long legs crossed at the ankles stretched out from under the table.

At one o'clock on Wednesday afternoon we were relaxing on The Oceanic's pier. The sky was blue with marshmallow swirls, pierced through periodically by pelicans and sea gulls as they knifed into the surf for their own lunches. Sea foam bubbled under the pier like soap suds. Further out, surfers rode the waves. On the horizon, a shrimp boat trolled.

Melanie had charged ahead to a table under an umbrella, saying, "I've got to watch my skin. I can't afford blotches."

"What are you worried about? You're beautiful."

She pulled a mirror out of her purse and admired her cameo face. Tossing loose coppery curls, she said, "You're right," and dropped the mirror into her soft leather shoulder bag. "But in California Joel dated Hollywood starlets."

I gave her a good, long, hard look. What had happened to my sister Melanie? Who was this "Stepford Wife" person? This was worse than I'd imagined.

I'd rehearsed my pitch on the drive over to Wrightsville Beach. In an effort to win her cooperation, I'd forsaken my khaki shorts and construction boots in favor of black silk pants with a belted pink jacket. It had been necessary to advance the buckle into a new notch, but what the heck? I like food. Maybe if I got sex regularly the way Melanie did, I wouldn't sublimate by eating so much. I had on my Holly Golightly sunglasses which lent me an air of sophistication. Melanie scoffs if I meet her for lunch dressed in my work clothes. She claims it's embarrassing to be seen with me. Well, I didn't want to embarrass her today. I had her safety to consider; I was setting my plan in motion.

"I have a favor to ask of you," I began.

She gave me a megawatt smile. "And I've got one to ask of you."

I had a pretty good idea of what was coming, so I said, "You go first."

"Baby sister, my career is on the line." Our iced tea arrived. We waited till the waitress was out of ear shot. Melanie busied herself with tearing open tiny pink packets of artificial sweetener.

"Those people at that meeting on Monday night were vicious. They'll stop at nothing to ruin me. They'll spread lies and innuendo until I'm destroyed. And I need my real estate commissions."

"What do you want me to do?"

"Well, until this furor blows over, I'm going to have to keep a low profile. I can't be seen speaking out in public in support of the resort hotel. I'll lose real estate listings if I do."

"But don't people already know you're invested in the project?"

"No, how could they? Oh, a few people know I date Joel. But they don't know we're business associates. There's no paper trail."

"Are you telling me you gave Joel cash!"

"That's exactly what I'm telling you." She got the same defiant look on her face she used to get when Daddy told her to go back upstairs and put on something decent.

"You mean you're not listed as a part owner of the Palace Street property?" This was so unlike Melanie I was appalled. Normally, she's the most astute business woman I know.

"That's it. And good thing too. Otherwise I'd be connected to the project, and that would surely damage my standing in the real estate community."

I couldn't believe my ears. Joel Fox had mesmerized my sister as surely as if he was one of those cobras in a basket, swaying back and forth until you're hypnotized, then it strikes, and you gulp your last breath.

The waitress brought my entrée and Melanie's pathetic salad. I dug in with gusto. She picked at her salad.

I asked, "What do you know about Joel, really? His background in L.A., for instance."

She set her fork down. "Why, he's the best thing that ever happened to me, Ashley. He makes me feel like a real woman."

Unconsciously, she arched her back and thrust out her bosoms. A man on his way to a nearby table caught sight of her and lost his footing. Thank goodness for the guard rail; without it, he would have toppled into the sea.

"I'm not getting through to you," I said. "I'm not talking about his performance in bed, I'm talking about his business performance. Surely you saw financial statements before you invested."

Splayed fingers crossed her heart. "Check up on Joel! Don't be a donkey. Why that'd be like investigating Mama and Daddy." She leaned across the table. "Let me tell you one thing. I trust Joel. I'd trust him with my life."

You may, but I sure don't, I thought. I took a deep breath and dared to ask, "He ever get rough with you? You know, when you're . . ."

"Are you daft? Joel is the sweetest, most tender lover I've ever had. And by far the most fascinatin', with his Hollywood connections and all. Why, I'm basking in the glow of his celebrity. For the first time in my life I know what it feels like to be with a real man."

She leaned a few inches closer. "Let me tell you something else, baby sister. I love him. And I won't hear a word against him." She got a smug smile on her face. "Don't be surprised if he's your brother-in-law someday."

I threw up my hands. Brother-in-law? That snake. But Joel was right about one thing. She'd never believe he'd threatened her. "What do you want me to do?" I asked, defeated.

"Oh, you *are* precious." She gave me a smile so dazzling, the radiant sky paled by comparison. "Nothing too difficult. Just drop a word here and there among your preservation friends that a luxury resort hotel will raise little ole Wilmington out of the dark ages and into the twenty-first century. Tell them how impressed the famous actors and actresses will be when they come here, and that word will spread and soon we'll be right up there with Atlanta."

Hot-lanta, I thought. Who wanted to be like them? But right now I had a more urgent agenda so I simply agreed, saying, "I'll see what I can do." Under the table top, I crossed my fingers.

"Oh, you are divine, shug. Now what can I do for you?"

Instantly, she frowned, then turned and snapped her fingers. Our waitress trotted over on the double.

"Melanie!" Who's embarrassing whom? I asked myself.

"I'm starving," she complained to the waitress as if the poor girl had forced field greens on her. "Haven't you got some rolls to go with this measly salad?"

The waitress scurried back to the kitchen. This arrogant behavior is Joel's doing, I thought.

"Mel," I said, getting back to pressing matters, "I know it'll be hard for you to understand, you're so brave and all, but, well, I'm having trouble sleeping. Even with the new locks and security system, it's really scary in my house at night. You know how old houses creak and stuff."

She covered my hand with hers. "Oh, you poor thing. 'Course you're having trouble sleeping with all that's gone on in that drafty old barn you live in. I say the sooner we put that place on the market, the better. Right after the first of the year."

I ignored that part. "Do you think you could sleep over for a few nights? I really need you."

"Sure thing. I'll pack some things and be over tonight." She gave me a self-satisfied smirk. "This works out real well. Poor Joel's had to work nights lately. He's been real worried about me, afraid that I'm lonely. Now I'll be able to put his mind at ease. Don't expect me till around ten tonight though. The local realtors association is holding its annual Christmas party. We're taking over the Bridge Tender Restaurant."

As I drove out Waynick Boulevard on my way back to the mainland, two Wrightsville P.D. cruisers sped past me toward the south end of the island. Then on the bridge, a convoy of Wilmington P.D. blue-and-whites roared toward Wrightsville. Now what? I wondered. It had to be mighty important for Wrightsville P.D. to invite Wilmington P.D. onto their turf. Should I turn around? Follow?

More immediate concerns crowded out the image of speeding blue-and-whites and flashing lights. I vowed to destroy Joel Fox's face, his career, and if I could manage it, his ability to sire children.

At home I played my answering machine. I'd left several messages for Nick to call me. His reply was curt. He was up to his eyeballs with the murders and would call when he could. I'd planned to tell him about Joel's threat. "Oh, what's the use?" I muttered. He's acting true to form. When will I ever learn?

There was a message from Binkie. "Ashley dear, an assistant district attorney called to tell me that at Detective Yost's recommendation, they're dropping the charges against me. But he instructed me not to leave town. I'm feeling rather kindly toward your friend Nick right now."

I smiled. And so am I, Binkie.

Next I fixed formula for little Spunky, held him in my lap, and fed him from a bottle like a baby. He was soon asleep and I returned him to his basket.

At the library table, I turned on my laptop. Like climbing back on a horse after you've been thrown, I was determined to conquer my fear of the library. With Melanie insisting I sell, I realized how much my home meant to me. I argued with myself that good people had lived here, good people had done good things here, and didn't that compensate for the evil? Maybe when all this was over I'd ask Father Andrew to bless my house.

The library was cozy and warm, the heart of the house. We'd painted the walls with red paint and Rachel had stenciled Dutch metal-leaf designs to suggest tooled leather. Heavy velvet draperies, tied back on either side of lace curtains, allowed a fair amount of sunlight to seep in. Shoulder-high built-in cherrywood bookcases flanked the fireplace, and there was a compartment for firewood.

The floor was temporarily bare. The police had not yet returned the rug on which Sheldon had drawn his last breath. Don't dwell on that, I chastised myself. You've got to get past it.

The red light on my new security panel glowed with holiday cheer. The new locks, although not period pieces, twinkled with a polished brass patina. I wasn't giving a key to anyone, although I would have to lend one to Melanie. But I planned to be at home each night when she returned so I could personally reset the alarm system and not have to give her the code. How our relationship has changed, I mused. While we were growing up, she'd been my protector. Now I was hers.

During the previous night, as I tossed and turned and mulled over all the horrific events that had occurred since December 1st—a mere twelve-day span—I'd come to the conclusion that either Rachel had given Eddie a key to my house, or more likely, he'd "borrowed" hers and made a copy. That's how he got in that Monday morning a week ago, not knowing that I'd be here too. And if it turned out he was the murderer—and I thought it would—that's how he got in when he killed her and attacked me.

Without Nick to fill me in on the latest developments in the murder cases, I was forced to rely on newspapers and television. So far, there'd been no report of the police apprehending Evil Eddie.

Not expecting much, I went to the Google search engine and typed in "Earl Flynn." To my astonishment, up popped a website. I clapped my hand over my mouth in astonishment when I saw what it was. Flynn had been a porn star, called "Eros" Flynn. The site had been set up by an unabashed fan who called herself, or himself, Psyche, the mythological wife of the mythological Eros. I figured she, or he, must be as old as Mama because the last movie Flynn starred in was made in 1975.

"Oh, shoot," I complained out loud. The web-site was rather graphic. I scrolled through it quickly. Finally, I got to what I was looking for. Earl Flynn was born in March 1941 in Wilmington. He was older than I'd thought, and certainly older than he looked. He'd graduated from high school in 1960. The next year was unaccounted for. In 1961 he turned up in Hollywood as a stunt car driver. He'd got his first minor role in a skin flick in 1962. Quickly Flynn rose to stardom in what Psyche referred to as "the Hollywood meat locker." He'd racked up twenty-five acting credits over the next thirteen years. Flynn had been a busy boy.

Psyche had posted headshots of Flynn from age twenty to thirty-four. I studied them. Good-looking, with the golden-boy looks of a Leonardo DiCaprio. Over the years, he'd aged well.

My instincts told me that Flynn had been living in Wilmington during the Atlantic Coast Line's payroll robbery and that he'd been involved. Perhaps he'd used his share of the loot to set himself up in Hollywood. But then why, I asked myself, did he have to get work as a stunt car driver? Wouldn't that indicate he needed money?

Stunt car driver? Had he been the driver of the getaway car? Maybe Earl Flynn and Jimmy Weaver, the dead man in my garden, were part of the robbery team. Possibly Mrs. Penry's son Russell was involved as well. Weaver was the inside man and Flynn drove the car. That left the three who'd broken into the payroll office and made off with the money bags. So if Flynn waited in the getaway car, there were two robbers unaccounted for.

I mulled over the situation. Did Flynn have a hidden motive for relocating to Wilmington? Or was it simply that he was an investor in Joel's resort scheme?

I typed in Joel Fox's name and clicked on Search. Zilch.

The telephone rang and I grabbed it, hoping it was Nick so I could share what I'd learned about Flynn. As soon as I heard Jon's voice, I said, "I just found Earl Flynn on the net."

"Forget about him. Turn on your TV. They found a body washed up on Wrightsville Beach."

24

Jon picked me up in his sporty black Beamer, and we sped out Oleander Drive to Wrightsville Beach with the top down. Sunshine baked the tops of our heads. Perfect beach weather made the Christmas decorations I spotted along the way appear incongruous. Yet we had not set out for a beach outing but were on a mission. The traffic light gods smiled down, blessing us with green lights. We made good time.

I brought Jon up to speed on how I'd persuaded Melanie to start sleeping overnight at my house so I could keep an eye on her. He'd gotten an earful yesterday about how Joel had threatened to disfigure her.

"Nick's giving Binkie a break," I reported. Jon replied that Nick was a good cop.

I also told him what I'd learned about Earl Flynn, and about my theory that he might have driven the getaway car during the railroad robbery.

The bridge over the Waterway was open to traffic. "How about that?" Jon said. "I didn't think they'd let us across."

I've noticed that men have a way of expecting things not to work out.

We tore straight down the middle of Harbour Island, then zoomed across the bridge over Banks Channel. Still no squad cars blocked our way. A few people fished off the bridge. Bikers and skaters rolled along at a leisurely clip on quiet streets.

"Things sure look normal. Are you sure you heard the news right?" I asked.

"Yes. Maybe these folks haven't heard yet."

We took Waynick Boulevard south past beach houses and the Blockade Runner Motel. Then we hooked a left and dead-ended into Lumina Avenue. Right past the Surf Motel, we hit a police barricade.

"No one's allowed in," a uniformed officer said flatly. "You'll have to turn around."

"What's going on, officer?" I asked cordially.

"Just turn around, ma'am," he said, short of patience and no doubt resentful that the fun stuff was going on down on the beach and here he was stuck out in the road dealing with nosy tourists.

I saluted his mirrored sunglasses as Jon executed a smart three-point turn.

"Pull into the Surf Motel's parking lot," I told him as he doubled back.

"But their lot is for guests only. I don't want to get towed."

"With all the excitement, no one's going to pay any attention to us. Come on. They're not going to bother with tow trucks."

"You'd better be right because I don't want anything happening to my car." He patted the hood affectionately, then scampered to follow me through the motel's covered walkway that led to the ocean side of the island.

Guests crowded the motel's balconies, staring and pointing toward the south end of the island. Abandoned lounge chairs and umbrellas littered the beach. I glanced over my shoulder at the skeletal frame of the Oceanic pier and reflected that less than two hours earlier Melanie and I had lunched there. On the ocean side of the Blockade Runner, a live cam mounted on a tower scanned the beach, transmitting real-time pictures over their website. I wondered if a similar camera had been mounted at the south end of the island where all the excitement was taking place.

Down the beach a ways, a group of curiosity seekers in swim suits and shorts, plus a few wet-suit figures hugging surf boards, pressed against police barricades. Jon and I infiltrated their ranks. A uniformed officer prevented the boldest among us from slipping around the barricades. Unable to see over other people's heads, I squeezed and wiggled and soon I'd wormed my way up to the front of the crowd.

A knot of uniforms, plain clothes detectives, and forensic technicians were gathered around something on the ground, presumably the body. I spotted Nick but he didn't see me, and that was just as well. Wrightsville was not Nick's turf. I wondered why he'd been called in, then figured that the understaffed, small, beach community police department needed extra help when a big case broke. The most demanding cases they handled were empty-house break-ins and joy-riding teenagers.

A shrill beep, beep, beep pierced the soothing whoosh of the surf. I looked up to see an ambulance backing out onto the beach. Nick broke ranks and the knot unraveled. For a split second, I caught a glimpse of a body lying face down in the sand, right at the water's edge. It looked kind of bloated. By the shirt and pants on it, I thought it was a man.

"I need a drink," Jon said when we got back in his car, which was right where he left it, safe and sound and unsullied by a tow truck's hook.

I checked my watch. Three-forty-five. A mite early for me but these were trying times and I aim to be a good sport. "Sure, but I can't leave Spunky for too long. He's got to be fed every few hours."

We drove back over the Waterway, straight to Landfall Center and the Hampton Inn. We went in through the side door, and were headed for the lobby when Jon stopped so abruptly I had outdistanced him by several paces before I realized I was on my own. I strolled back, wondering what was up. I followed his stare across the hallway to the elevator bank.

A man and woman waited for an elevator.

"It's her," Jon said in wonderment. His eyes zeroed in on a young woman in a brief tank top.

"And look who she's with," I gasped.

We scarcely breathed, not wanting to be caught in the act of spying. But the couple were so wrapped up in each other, we could have set off firecrackers and they wouldn't have noticed. The guy was standing slightly behind the woman, stroking her bare upper arms, massaging her shoulders.

"What does a beautiful woman like her see in him?" Jon pondered aloud, clearly disappointed in Christine Brooks' taste in men.

The elevator doors enfolded them, not a moment too soon. I trotted off furiously toward the bar, Jon loping along behind me. "Ashley, wait up!"

I turned so fast we almost collided. "What does any woman see in Joel Fox?" I demanded.

I got home feeling slightly drunk. Two Margueritas in goblets the size of soup bowls will do me in. But I was sober enough to feed Spunky.

As soon as the sun went down, the temperature began to drop, plunging steadily. Finally, seasonable winter weather. It was December 12th and there were only thirteen shopping days left.

Spunky, full and drowsy, slept in my lap as I relaxed from the day's adventures, and I confided my worries into his little ears. "Your aunt Melanie is the most complex person I know. She's been dumping men since she was twelve. Cheating on them, too. Now someone's doing to her what she's done to others so often. And the scoundrel's threatened to have her pretty face slashed. Yet, she's behaving like a slavish fool where he's concerned. Giving him money. Giving him permission to treat her like dirt."

Spunky's ears twitched and he looked up at me and yawned. I noticed then that his eyes looked just like Melanie's. These were the things I longed to say to her, but could I? And would she believe me? She'd go on the defensive, make excuses for Joel. Maybe say he was working late with his receptionist. That I'd misinterpreted what I'd seen. Sure, he was massaging her shoulders, she'd say. Why not? She was worn out, poor baby. All that typing. But she was just an employee. Simple as that. She meant nothing to Joel. Then Melanie would get into one of her snits and stomp out, return to her own home where Joel was free to come and go as he pleased. Not a safe place for her to be.

No, I had to keep her here with me. Stay as close to her as she'd let me. The slow holiday season suited my plans. My restoration projects were dead until after the first of the year. So was Melanie's real estate business. People were settled in for the holidays and waiting for the new year to arrive before proceeding with restorations or the sale of their homes.

Where was Nick, I wondered. What was he doing right now? Where was he having dinner? Was he in danger? We were dealing with a ruthless killer. Somewhere out there in the night, Evil Eddie lurked. I'd seen for myself the cruelty in his eyes, how menacing he could be, how evil. And today another dead body had surfaced, no pun intended. But was the man on the beach a victim of a drowning accident? Or was it murder?

I went into the kitchen and drank a full glass of water. Spunky followed me, sniffed at my fuzzy slippers and puffed up like a dandelion. I laughed out loud at the sight of that tiny creature posturing like a lion. He waddled to the safety of his basket. He was getting positively plump.

I returned to the front parlor and looked out into the street. Somehow the murders were tied to the Atlantic Coast Line payroll robbery. I just knew it. But how? Four or five young men had robbed the payroll office in 1960. Today those men would be in their early sixties, like Earl Flynn, and Mrs. Penry's missing son, Russell. Jimmy Weaver, whose remains we'd found buried in the garden. And Sheldon Mackie, I thought with a start. I wondered if Sheldon knew the other men.

Joel Fox was too young, around forty. I had no idea where he'd grown up, or where he'd gone to school.

On Thursday morning, the local anchorwoman reported that the man washed up on the beach was still unidentified. Then Lisa Hamilton's pretty face filled my TV screen. The public information officer said that Wilmington P.D. and Wrightsville P.D. were working together with the medical examiner to establish the dead man's identity. Lisa conducted herself in a highly professional manner during the interview, smoothly deflecting a question about whether the man's death was attributable to drowning or another cause. Bet she doesn't frustrate Nick the way I do, I thought.

It was three days since I'd last seen him and he wasn't returning my calls. "Just goes to show how important I am to him," I muttered as I wandered from room to room, giving my five Christmas trees big healthy drinks of water.

Jon hadn't called either. I filled a spray bottle with water and spritzed evergreen swags and mantelpiece arrangements. "I really must do something about Christmas shopping," I told Spunky as I fixed us both lunch. Warm formula for him, Progresso's basil tomato soup for me. My culinary skills were reaching an all time high. Last night in honor of our nippy weather I'd made hot cocoa for Melanie and myself by stirring the powdered contents of individual packets into boiling water. Move over, Julia Child!

I'd carried the steaming mugs up to the guest bedroom and sat on the foot of the rice bed while Melanie changed into a nightie. I wanted to tell her about the provocative scene I'd witnessed between Joel and his receptionist, but the words just wouldn't come out. Each time I opened my mouth to say them, I got a queasy feeling in my stomach that prevented me from telling her that the man she loved was doin' her wrong. Instead, I told her all about the body being washed up on the beach.

She shrugged her white shoulders and said, "Probably a surfer. They're daredevils. What can you expect? Every couple of months one of them drowns."

"But that's different," I said. "Their buddies are usually around when they go under. And there are people waiting on the beach who know who they are. So far, no one's got any idea who this guy is. Besides, he wasn't wearing a wet suit. Looked like street clothes to me."

Melanie hung her suit in the armoire. "Why don't you ask your detective?"

"I haven't heard from him all week, Mel. He's probably being led around by the nose by your new best friend Lisa."

Melanie plopped down beside me on the bed and picked up her hot chocolate. "Don't be so hard on her, Ashley. She didn't have advantages growing up like we did. She was shuffled around from one foster home to another. Lucky for her she was smart so she got a full scholarship to the University of Georgia. But she had to wait tables for pocket money."

"Sorry," I muttered, and called myself a petty louse. Jealous of

Melanie's friendship with Lisa. Jealous of Nick and Lisa's business relationship. Lord, I must be insecure. Get a grip on your emotions, girl, I chastised myself. All these murders are making you lose your perspective.

"Joel's throwing a party at the office on Saturday night. He especially wants you to be there. You will come, won't you?"

Go to a party with Joel Fox? No way. "I'd rather not. You know how I feel about parties. Besides, I'm partied out."

"Partied out? What parties have you been to, I'd like to know?" She massaged lotion on her hands and arms.

"Well, lots," I said.

"Name one."

She was making me cross. "Well, I'm fixin' to have one tomorrow night. Binkie and Jon are coming over and we're having eggnog." What I didn't tell her was that the three of us had plans to spend the day researching the Palace Street property to try to find a good reason to prevent her and Joel from developing it.

She hooted. "Whoop-ti-do! How can you bear the excitement? What are you going to do for entertainment, play 'Old Maid' cards? Or maybe get out the Ouija board and ask it who the murderer is?"

At that I flounced out of the room, wondering why I was bothering to protect her when she was always trying her best to make me look silly. Because she's your sister and you love her, a voice inside me replied. Even if she's the silly one, foolishly dotty over that sleaze Joel Fox. Still I've got to stick with her. "I've got to be around to pick up the pieces when somebody breaks her heart," I sang under my breath.

Melanie stepped out into the hall. "Ashley, don't be mad. I was just playing with you. Please say you'll come to the party. Joel is trying so hard to be friends with you, won't you meet him half way?"

I came to a dead halt, then turned to face her. "Joel Fox is a turd, Melanie. Someday you're gonna wise up. But for your sake I'll try to come to the party."

She clasped hands with mine. "Oh good, sweetie. Joel'll be so pleased. Seven o'clock, Saturday night, don't forget."

Now, finished with watering the Christmas trees, spritzing the greenery, and calling in an order for a half-cord of firewood, I snuggled up on the library couch with MaeMae Mackie's diary. Someday I'm going to have to get a life. Other women go to holiday parties and shopping with friends but here I am reading the ramblings of a woman with a drinking problem who hated her husband.

MaeMae had written in her diary sporadically. There'd be entries for a few days in a row, then nothing for months, and even years. I thumbed through, looking for some juicy tidbit to catch my fancy. And catch it she did. The word "secret" jumped right up off the page.

Sheldon doesn't know I'm onto his secret. He talks in his sleep. I was about to suggest that he move into the guest room because of one too many torturous nights listening to him groan and mumble. Sometimes he even shouts. It's a wonder he doesn't wake himself, but he sleeps right through it, while I jump so hard, my heart just about stops. Anyway, I was on the brink of moving him out when the mumbling turned downright fascinating. I listened intently and was able to discern certain phrases that led me to believe Sheldon was not the man he wanted the community to think he was. He's got a sordid past. I've told no one but Lucy Lou, and she's sworn to secrecy. I experimented and asked Sheldon questions while he was in his sleep-talking stage and, sure enough, he answered me. Now I know his secret. I'm not sure how I'll use this information, but knowledge is power. Lucy Lou and I are thinking hard on it.

I read all the following entries, but couldn't find another reference to the secret. What had MaeMae discovered? Frustrated, I slammed the diary shut. I was sure of one thing: Sheldon was a good person at heart. Whatever secret he'd been harboring must have been a source of shame for him.

My mind wandered to the prospect of Joel's Christmas party. How could I get out of going? Maybe I should go, I argued with myself. Then I could keep an eye on him. If my stomach didn't turn over in the process. Besides, Melanie will be safe enough with all those people around, I told myself.

I wondered if Joel was connected with the crimes that were plaguing us. I wondered if he too was hiding some deep, dark secret. Maybe he'd committed some evil deed that he was covering up. Some event that linked him to Sheldon's and Rachel's murders and caused him to attack me. Something that connected him to Jimmy Weaver's body being buried in my garden.

Maybe he was a member of the Mafia. Maybe he was a front man for organized crime and it was they, not he, who were behind the resort hotel. He did threaten me that his associates would be unhappy if the hotel was not built. Just who were these associates? Melanie had said the hotel would feature internet gambling lounges. What if organized crime was now controlling internet gambling?

I had to find out more about Joel. A plan was starting to take shape in my devious little brain.

Out of the corner of my eye I saw movement. Panic punched me squarely in the chest and knocked the breath out of me. At the window, the draperies flapped. Was someone behind them, causing them to flutter? I forced myself to look.

"Spunky, you little devil," I cried. I picked up the black and white kitten who now felt secure enough to play. He'd been batting the bullion fringe with his paw.

25

"This is hopeless," Jon said.

We were at City Hall poring over files. "The records only go back to 1974 when those rental houses were constructed. Prior to that, the property seems not to exist. I don't get it."

Jon, Binkie, and I had spent hours at City Hall, looking up old maps and deeds, old tax records. "Wonder if the street had another name at one time?" I mused aloud.

Binkie slapped a bound ledger of old tax cards shut. "I'm beginning to wonder if the records have disappeared. Accidentally on purpose."

"You mean stolen?".I asked.

"That's precisely what I mean. Someone's been bribed to misplace the records. Then after the hotel is under construction, they'll turn up in the wrong file. Innocent mistake. Everyone knows young people don't know how to alphabetize."

Jon stared at Binkie thoughtfully. "Well, that's one explanation. They sure seem to have vanished without a trace."

Our luck didn't get any better at the Historic Wilmington Foundation. Their archives included property that had been presented with a plaque, and the Palace Street houses did not qualify for plaque status.

Back at my house, I served eggnog lethally spiced with Southern Comfort. If I continued with this trend of culinary expertise, I could soon go into the catering business.

"Why is preserving our past always such an uphill battle?" Binkie asked. He was sitting near the fireplace. "When are you going to light a fire?"

"Help me lay one, Jon, and I'll light it right now. You sure you're comfortable with us being in the library?" I asked Binkie. "I'm making a conscientious effort to use this room. But it's not easy."

"My memories of that night make me shudder, Ashley dear. Finding Sheldon like that. But this is your home and you can't let ghosts take possession of it."

"Have you got kindling?" Jon asked.

"I've been saving twigs," I replied. "They're out on the kitchen porch. I'll get them."

"And get some newspaper too," Jon called after me.

Outside my kitchen door, the night was cold and as I exhaled, my breath formed a miniature cloud. When I returned with twigs and old newspapers, Jon had the door to the firewood box open and was carefully selecting logs. "You're almost out of firewood. Did you phone in an order?"

I twisted sheets of newspaper into rope-like lengths. "I took care of that yesterday morning. That bit was left behind by Mrs. Penry. I don't think she had a fire in here in decades, not with her asthma."

"Well, a tin-lined firewood box is a handy feature," Jon said. "Wish I had one. Saves running outside on a cold night for wood." He knelt before the hearth, leaned in and opened the flue. I'd had the chimneys cleaned and inspected over the summer so I knew it was safe to build a fire.

I handed him the waded newspaper and a bundle of twigs. He arranged three logs atop the kindling like a tepee, then flicked the lighter and the kindling burst into flames.

Spunky, who was curled in a ball on Binkie's lap, lifted his face to the glow.

"Thank God we found him that day," I said. "He'd never have survived out there. It's turned cold." I reached over and rubbed his back.

"What a loud motor you've got, Spunky," Binkie chuckled.

Jon stood with his back to the now blazing fire. "Draws well. You know, it amazes me how divided the City Council is over historic preservation issues. Even when we demonstrate the economic benefits to the city from tourism, there are still the diehards who think new is better."

"Don't forget the money the film industry brings in because they use our historic settings," I added.

"And," Jon continued, "the federal grants we're eligible for that'll defray restoration costs. Some of those guys still act like 'smart growth' is a passing fad. One fella even suggested we tear down old buildings and put up new, because in the future the new buildings will be our history!"

"This is all well and good, Jon, but where does it leave us? We don't want a monster resort hotel looming over our historic district."

"Well, we've got some time," Binkie said. "Nothing's going to happen till after the first of the year. And then it'll take a couple of weeks for folks to get back into the swing of things. So let's say we've got until mid-January till the City Council takes this up."

I poured him a second eggnog from the pitcher. "We'll just have to keep pushing. We'll all make phone calls, we'll write letters to the editor, and see if we can drum up more media attention. Joel Fox and his associates aren't going to look good in the spotlight. Maybe we can arouse enough public indignation to help us with our cause."

"I hate to throw cold water, Ashley dear," Binkie said, "but the holidays work against us in that regard. Folks are thinking about Christmas shopping and Christmas parties, plum pudding and roasted goose, family and friends. They're not going to start a crusade at this time of year."

Later, as I was saying good night to Jon at my door, I asked, "Where were you yesterday? You didn't return my calls."

He shrugged. "Just busy. You know. Stuff."

Now what is he up to? I asked myself as I locked the door and reset the alarm. Jon's got a transparent face. He's not good at keeping secrets from me, and he was hiding something, of that I was sure. Maybe it's as innocent as buying my Christmas present, I told myself as I carried the tray of eggnog things back to the kitchen.

With the water running I almost failed to hear the doorbell ringing. I wiped my hands and headed for the front door. Looking out I saw Nick. I couldn't help it, I felt a surge of delight, yet it was coupled with resentment that he felt he could drop by at any hour he pleased.

Still, one look at him and I melted, a fluttery feeling tickling my heart. "Nick."

"Hi, baby."

"What's that?" I asked. Standing at the curb in front of my house was the Springbrook Farms horse and carriage. The carriage was decorated with sleigh bells and holly. The placid white horse wore a red and green blanket and reindeer antlers.

"Grab your coat, honey, we're going for a ride."

Up and down Nun Street, candles glowed in windows and trees glittered with fairy lights. Nick handed me up into the carriage as the driver looked on approvingly from under his top hat. I snuggled close to Nick under the carriage blanket.

Why had I ever thought Nick was not romantic? When the first delicate snowflakes began to fall, everything was perfect. I leaned my head on his shoulder and was lulled by the horse's gentle gait. We crisscrossed the historic district, the Christmas lights a feast for the eyes, the smell of wood smoke so homey. There was no other place I'd rather be, I realized. Not New York and the Plaza Hotel. This was home. I couldn't help wondering if someday I'd share a home here with Nick.

We kissed and nuzzled and when he left me at my front door saying he hadn't slept in twenty hours and had to catch some *zzzz*'s, I had a hard time tearing myself out of his arms. And he had a hard time taking his hands off me. I slipped up the stairs and into my own room without waking Melanie. To discuss the evening with her would dispel the magic. My dreams were filled with Nick, his warmth and strength, his smell, his incredibly sexy voice whispering words of love.

The next morning I sipped coffee, feeling happy and purposeful. Today's assignment was to investigate Joel Fox: to find irrefutable proof that he was unworthy of Melanie's love so she'd ditch him. Something tangible that she couldn't easily explain away. And I knew just where to look.

With Melanie out of the house early, I breakfasted on toasted English muffins with butter and orange marmalade. Then I showered, dressed, and did some household chores, like cleaning out Spunky's litter box. Yuk!

Grateful to be driving again, I got in my sporty little Aurora and ran a few errands, picking up the things I needed for Joel's party. My first stop was A-1 Rentals where they had my costume all ready and hanging in a plastic bag. "We've had a run on these things," the clerk said. "Lucky you called ahead. You got the last one."

At the ABC store I filled my cart with those miniature bottles like they serve on airplanes. Scotch, gin, bourbon, you name it, I bought it. If it was liquid and had "proof" printed on the label, it went into my basket. The cashier looked at me oddly but didn't say a word.

"Christmas presents," I muttered.

"Sure," she said. "This year's hottest item."

For my last purchase I had to drive out to Castle Hayne. Our light snowfall had melted and the roads were clear. The old man behind the counter at the grain and seed store sold me a single burlap sack. "What'cha gonna do, little lady? Trap yourself a squirrel?"

"No," I replied, handing him the money. "A fox."

On my way home I stopped at an old-fashioned barbecue diner, the kind where all the cars pull into slots with microphones. I placed my order, then a teenage car hop brought a bag out to my car. The aromas emanating from the bag on the passenger seat got to be more than I could bear, so I reached in and ate the first barbecue sandwich as I drove home. What with the costume I was wearing tonight, a few extra inches around my middle wouldn't be inappropriate.

I spread my costume out on one side of the bed and was about to spread myself out on the other side for a nap when my doorbell rang. I was pleased to see Betty and Wayne Matthews even if I wasn't expecting them. I invited them inside, hugged and kissed them, and served them my potent eggnog. This stuff sure had a kick. And the calorie count was probably equal to three square meals.

The conversation naturally centered around preservation issues. Betty brought good news that all the historic organizations were banding together to wage a take-no-prisoners war against Joel Fox and his plans. Any member of the City Council who voted in favor of the resort hotel could count on not being re-elected. I pointed out that might be too late.

Mindful of Binkie's accusation that Sheldon had robbed the Atlantic Coast Line of its payroll and used the money to set himself up in the decorating business, I worked the conversation around to Sheldon and got Betty and Wayne to reminisce about the good old days in Wilmington when a trained decorator was a novelty.

"How did Sheldon get his start?" I asked. "Was there family money?"

"Oh, no," Betty replied, "Sheldon's kin were poor as church mice. Respectable, but poor."

"I know firsthand that it takes start-up money," I said. "I used the money Daddy left me to pay for my education and to set myself up in business. How'd Sheldon manage?"

"I lent him the money," Wayne declared.

"You did?" This was not what I expected.

"Sure," Wayne said, "I know a good investment when I see one. I got all my money back and a percentage of his business. I knew as soon as Betty started hounding me that we had to have Sheldon Mackie, who had apprenticed with Billy Baldwin in New York, 'do' our living room, that all the ladies in town would be after him. And my hunch paid off."

"Sheldon was good, wasn't he?" I couldn't think of anything else to say.

"Very talented," Wayne said. "And he needed the money to get him started. That was back when he was married to Beverly Higgins, Binkie's sister. And the Higgins family, although highly educated, were not very well off. But when Sheldon married MaeMae Gerard, he hit the jackpot. 'Course, by then, he didn't need her money. His career had taken off."

"Back in the Seventies, he set this town on its ear," Betty declared.

26

Jon wasn't at home when I called to tell him what I had learned from Wayne Matthews. I ordered a pizza, and after eating half of it, went upstairs to get ready for the party. I was allowing myself plenty of time because I didn't know how long it would take to dress.

After I stripped down to my underwear, I taped a feather pillow to my middle by wrapping three-inch duct tape around my waist and over the pillow. Then I did the same thing around my back. Now I was pear shaped. Fortunately my shoulders are broad so I didn't have to add any padding up top, and Santa doesn't have breasts and neither do I. The way I enjoy food though, soon I'd have his waistline for sure.

I stepped into wide red velour pants, pulling the waistband's drawstring until it was tight and I was confident I wouldn't be dropping my drawers at the party. I slipped my arms into the white-fur-trimmed red velour jacket and buttoned up shiny brass buttons. Then I buckled a six-inch wide black patent leather belt around my middle. Luckily there were belt loops in the side seams of the jacket or the belt would have slipped down around my knees.

At the bathroom mirror I affixed a flowing white beard to my chin with gum spirits. There were wing-like fluffy white eyebrows and a handle-bar mustache and I glued them on as well. I stuffed my short dark curls under a white wavy wig. A fur-trimmed red stocking hat went on top of the wig.

Wow! This was great. Finally, I was getting into the Christmas spirit. And a good thing too if you're Santa. Nobody wants a Santa who vacillates about whether he does or does not like Christmas.

Back in my room, I slipped my feet into black boots. Studying myself in my cheval looking glass, I slung the burlap bag over my shoulder. There was a tinkle and clatter as all the tiny bottles rolled against each other. "Easy, Santa," I told myself. "You don't want to break the kiddies' toys."

Something was missing. I scrutinized my outfit. What was it? Gingerly, I lowered my gift sack to the floor and went to rummage around in a lower dresser drawer until I found Daddy's reading glasses that I'd sentimentally held onto for all these years. I slipped them down onto the tip of my nose. Never mind that they blurred my vision, I wouldn't be looking through them but over them. The frames were silver wires just like Santa's.

Now when I looked in the mirror I saw a perfect Old Saint Nick. I didn't think anyone would recognize him as Ashley.

"Ho, ho, ho." I perfected a belly laugh.

Thirty minutes later, I waddled into the party popping "Ho, Ho's" and "Merry Christmases" right and left. The party was in full swing, loud music, loud voices, low hanging cigarette and cigar clouds. I loved being incognito. I could identify faces at a glance. They'd have a hard time identifying mine. In particular, I didn't want Joel Fox to know I was on board. My mission tonight was to do a little undercover work, and if Santa Claus can slide down a chimney undetected, this Santa surely ought to be able to slip into Joel Fox's office with no one the wiser. Once there, I hoped to find proof of his perfidy to show to Melanie. And maybe, just maybe, some bit of evidence to destroy his credibility as a resort developer.

The first familiar face I encountered was Jon Campbell's. This came as a shock because I had no idea he'd been invited. And I was further shocked that he'd accepted. I'd assumed he shared my revulsion for Mr. Fox. Jon was deep in conversation with a woman. She was almost as tall as he. Her brown hair was long and shiny and made a nice contrast with his golden head. Her pretty face was clean and devoid of makeup. She had on gray slacks and a red sweater set.

Christine Brooks, Joel's receptionist. So that's where he'd been this week. His hand was lightly but firmly attached to the nape of her neck. Uh oh. That was the male sex's signal to each other that this female was taken. A sure sign of ownership. I don't know what man thought it up, but every man I've ever known has used this device at one time or another to lay claim to a woman.

I sidled up to Jon. "Merry Christmas, little feller," I said, mimicking Santa's deep, cheery boom.

Jon gave me a quick take, turned back to Christine, had second thoughts and turned his head slowly toward me. "Same to you," he said, not quite sure what he was seeing.

I moved closer. "Lose the babe," I said in his ear.

His eyes grew wide as he stared at me. "Ashley?" he mouthed.

I gave him one of St. Nick's most knowing nods.

"Would you excuse me a moment, Christine. I promised to help Santa distribute presents. Don't go away now. I'll be right back."

Translation: Don't talk to other men. Hah! Fat chance. A man who can't see a dirty plate sitting right in front of his face can spot a chesty brunette across a football field. It was only a matter of seconds before Christine was surrounded.

I pulled Jon into a corner. "What are you doing here? And what are you doing here with her?" I recalled how evasive he'd been recently when I'd asked him about how he'd been spending his time.

He did have the good grace to look slightly embarrassed. "She's not what you think, Ashley. She's really a nice girl."

I arched my thick white eyebrows.

He countered, "What are you doing here in that get-up?"

"I don't want anyone knowing I'm here. I'm going to have a look around Joel's office. I figured the Santa suit would be a good disguise. No one will suspect me of anything."

He shook his head like I was crazy.

"Okay, now you. What are you doing here with Joel's receptionist?"

"Well, ah, we've been seeing each other. She's a graduate student at UNC-W. She's really smart, Ashley. She's just working for Joel because she needs the money for grad school."

"Uh huh. And what about that lusty little scene we saw between her and Joel at the Hampton Inn? Or have you, in your delirium of being up close to her, forgotten all about that?"

"No. She explained all that. She detests Joel. She said as soon as the elevator doors closed, she let him have it."

"Have what, pray tell?"

"Ashley, don't! She told him to keep his paws off her. She would have told him that in the lobby but she didn't want to make a scene."

"And you believed her?"

"I believe her. She dislikes Fox as much as we do." Jon looked back to where she was being swallowed up by admirers. "I've got to get back."

"Isn't she a little young for you?"

"Not so young. She's an older student. And you'll never guess what she's majoring in?"

"Do tell," I said sarcastically. Why was my stomach feeling queasy? Was it the pizza and barbecue sandwiches?

"Marine biology. She's getting a Ph.D. in marine biology. I tell you, Ashley, this woman's got substance."

"That she does," I agreed. She was top heavy with substance. "Now help me pass out these little bottles and get me over to that hallway that leads to the offices."

"Ashley, I've really got to get back to her."

"It'll just take a minute. Come on."

With my reluctant elf in tow, I worked the room, ho-ho-ing, pressing bottles into willing hands. "Hey, thanks, Santa," someone said. I even gave one to Melanie who was hanging onto Joel's arm, gorgeous in a black, sequined dress that fit like a stocking, her auburn hair bouncing on her shoulders as she laughed at his jokes. She scarcely gave me a glance. Fox didn't notice me either. He must have thought—if he gave it any thought—that one of his lackeys had arranged for the Santa. Who is more ubiquitous in December than Santa Claus?

Finally, we worked our way to the far side of the room where a hallway led off back toward the offices.

"Okay, you can go," I said to Jon.

He was already fighting his way to Christine's side. "Merry Christmas, Santa," he called over his shoulder, grinning broadly.

Looking up and down the hall and seeing no one, I tried the door knob of Joel's office. It turned easily in my hand. I opened the door a few inches and peeked in. Empty. I pushed the door open wider and squeezed my ample girth through.

A small lamp burned on a sleek chrome and birch desk. The office was nicely furnished with leather chairs and a leather sofa. Paintings of lighthouses decorated the paneled walls.

I didn't have time to admire the decor. Quickly, I shuffled through the few papers on the desk, not knowing what I was looking for but hoping that something relevant would catch my eye. Daddy's reading glasses distorted my vision so I slipped them lower and rested them on my mustache.

There was nothing on Joel's desk that you'd expect to find: no correspondence about building permits, no lists of materials, nothing relating to the hotel. I was dumbfounded.

I pulled open the deep bottom drawer expecting to find file folders. A whiskey bottle nestled in the front corner. Shoved in behind the bottle was a roll of blueprints bound with a rubberband. I slipped the rubberband off the roll and spread the blueprints out on the desk top in the lamp light, expecting to see plans for the hotel. These were drawings of a house. A very familiar house. My house! What was Joel doing with blueprints of my house? And how had he gotten them?

Jon was the only person who had a set of blueprints to my house besides myself. I flashed back to that terrible day when we found the body buried in the garden. Jon had been reading the blueprints on my dining room table. That was the last time I saw them. But Jon would never give Joel the prints to my house.

Voices carried through the door. Someone was coming, two somebodies from the sound of it. I lifted my hand from the blueprints and they wound up in a tight roll. I threw the roll into the bottom drawer and kicked it shut with my shiny black boot.

Scooping a bottle from the burlap sack, I unscrewed the top and doused bourbon on the front of my red velour suit. At the same time, I flung myself onto the leather sofa. I sprawled there, head thrown back, mouth open and eyes shut, glasses pushed up across the bridge of my nose. I even managed a gentle snore. The small bottle in my hand dripped bourbon on the carpet.

The door opened and two people stepped inside.

"What the hell!" Joel's voice.

"Santa's had one too many," Earl Flynn commented.

"Get that drunken Santa out of here!" Joel cried.

"Oh, come on Joel, where's your Christmas spirit? Let the old guy sleep it off."

27

The next morning, I met Melanie at St. James Episcopal Church for the eleven o'clock service. I didn't know where she'd spent the night, but it wasn't at my house. I figured she and Joel had done a little private partying of their own. The image made my stomach churn. She slipped into the pew with a swish, dressed in a royal blue suit and looking, for the first time I've ever observed, haggard. Melanie always wakes up looking miraculously fresh and dewy, even after partying into the wee small hours. I had to find a way to show her how ruthless the real Joel Fox really was.

We had shared this pew every Sunday morning since we were little girls and Mama and Daddy brought us to church. This was our family pew, where Mama and Daddy had always sat, and where Grandma and Grandpa Wilkes had sat before them. St. James is that kind of church. It's old, one of the oldest Episcopal congregations in the New World, established in 1729.

I relish the peacefulness that descends over the congregation before the service begins, just the chords of the organ and the rustle of worshippers taking their seats and shushing each other. For me it is a time for reflection, a time to hold myself apart from the busy world. I thought about how things were when Daddy was alive, before Mama got sick. I never doubted that I was loved. At times like this I miss the family we used to be. I reached over and squeezed Melanie's hand. She squeezed mine back. There's a corny expression that blood is thicker than water. It doesn't make much sense, but I agree with its meaning.

This morning, I had much to ask forgiveness for and a lot to seek guidance about. I stifled a chuckle as I recalled my drunken Santa act of last night. Joel had taken me by one elbow, Earl the other, and they'd marched me to a side exit while I pretended to stumble. Pushing me out into an alley, they'd slammed the door behind me, not caring if I was fit to drive or not. I headed for my car where I pulled off my cap and wig, then peeled off the beard and eyebrows. In their haste to hustle me outside, Joel and Earl had confiscated my goody bag.

Jon was lost to me, smitten with Christine Brooks, the gal with boobs and a brain and a Ph.D. in marine biology. I pictured her swimming with the whales. Bet she didn't have any trouble floating. My reflections in church are not always reverent.

The man washed up on Wrightsville Beach never had a chance to float or swim or try to save himself from drowning. According to the *Sunday Star-News*, he was already dead when he fell or was dumped in the ocean. A sharp blow to the skull had caused his death. The police had identified the dead man as Melvin Cox, an itinerant handy-man who whiled away his days hanging around Johnnie Mercer pier on Wrightsville Beach. It was speculated that Cox might have fallen off the pier, struck his head on a piling, then floated in and out with the tide.

For a small town, we sure were experiencing more than our share of deaths by misadventure. I whispered prayers for the souls of the departed, those unknown to me, and for my friends Sheldon and Rachel. I missed Rachel, her talent, her sunny spirit. Why do smart, talented women get involved with the Eddies of this world?

Daddy had always given me sound advice. I wished he were here with me now, to listen to my problems, to counsel me on how to get Melanie away from Joel. And prior to her illness, Mama was always there to go home to. Now strangers live in our family home.

The service began. I glanced across the aisle to see MaeMae Mackie and Lucy Lou Upchurch occupying the Gerard family pew. Seeing them reminded me of Sheldon's diary. Was there some way I might pry his secret out of MaeMae? My instincts told me that knowledge of the secret might help us solve his murder. I decided to pay another condolence call on the widow, and to take her the metal box Jon and I had found in the basement. By rights, MaeMae was the owner of the Gerard family time capsule. I would place it in her hands with my own.

The priest's sermon touched on the recent murders, for he retold the story of Cain and Abel, pointing out that throughout the history of mankind jealousy and greed were most often the motives for murder.

As we left the church, Melanie paused to give Lisa Hamilton a hug. "I'm so glad you came," Melanie gushed. "But why didn't you join us up front?"

"I didn't want to intrude," Lisa replied humbly.

"Isn't she nice?" Melanie said as we got in my car.

Melanie was distracted during brunch and as we drove to Mama's nursing home. Was there trouble in paradise? I surely hoped so.

"You seem tired," I'd said from behind the wheel.

"You would be too if you had three closings in three days," she groaned. "Three crazy buyers who insisted on getting into their houses before Christmas, to put up the trees and all. So, yes, I'm tired and not in a good mood. Stop pushing."

"Sorry," I said. "We won't stay long with Mama. Then we can go back to my house and I'll tuck you in. I won't let anyone wake you." Especially not Joel, I thought.

Melanie mellowed. "You always know just what to do, baby sister."

Ms. Miller, the manager of Magnolia Manor, met us as we passed between Corinthian columns with their bell-shaped capitals and acanthus-leaf ornamentation. No expense had been spared on the faux-antebellum mansion. The columns were painted a dazzling white, as was the main building and the living quarters that winged out at the back.

Ms. Miller was dressed conservatively in a forest green wool suit that set off her prematurely white hair. She shook hands with Melanie and me and greeted us warmly. I liked her and sensed she was a good person who had her patients' well-being at heart. I returned her warm greeting, but Melanie scarcely acknowledged her.

"A word with you before you see your mother," she said.

I was about to ask if Mama's Alzheimer's was getting worse, but the look of encouragement on her face stopped me. Still clasping her hand, I waited expectantly for what she had to tell us.

"You'll see a marked improvement in your mother, Ashley, Melanie. The medication she's on seems to be slowing the progression of her Alzheimer's disease. We don't have a drug that reverses the degeneration, not yet anyway. Someday we will. But you'll be pleased to see how well she's expressing herself."

"Are you saying she doesn't need to be here anymore?" Melanie asked with the most enthusiasm she'd displayed all morning.

"No, no, that's not what I'm saying," Ms. Miller hastened to explain. "She has trouble with short-term memory. And she has lapses when she doesn't know where she is and is unable to recognize the people around her, but those lapses are occurring with less frequency."

She spread her hands, palms up. "Go see for yourselves. She's very excited about the mock wedding ceremony and talks about little else. If you feel the need to speak to me further, stop in my office on your way out. Your mother is waiting for you in the conservatory. We'll serve tea and cookies there at two."

Mama looked much the way she used to before the awful disease struck. From whom else had Melanie inherited her fashion genes? My line of work prevents me from dressing up, but today I had on my Sunday best. Mama looked stunning in a long black skirt and a Christmas sweater with bright red poinsettias embroidered in silk thread, seed pearls, and silver beads. Her hair was cut in a sleek, flattering bob and her nails were manicured. In the past I'd encouraged her to make appointments with the hair stylists and manicurists who came to Magnolia Manor weekly, but she'd just shook her head and mumbled. It had been clear that she was afraid. But now, what a difference. Admiring her outfit, I realized she'd obviously been on a chaperoned shopping trip to a stylish boutique.

Over sugar cookies and tea, which Mama poured graciously, I asked, "Mama, do you remember MaeMae Mackie?"

"'Course I remember MaeMae. She and Lucy Lou were in my bridge group when we were young." She bit daintily into a cookie. "It's the things that happened yesterday that I can't remember."

"Well, what do you remember about MaeMae? What was she like? You know, her kin, the Gerards, once owned and lived in my house, after Reverend Barton and before Miss O'Day."

Melanie leaned her head back in a white wicker chair and closed her eyes.

"Tired, dear?" Mama asked, patting Melanie's knee.

"Ummm. You all just go on talking. I'll listen. I'm just resting my eyes." The wicker chair was surrounded by flowers and palm plants.

"You go ahead and rest, hon. You look like a picture with those flowers all around you. Doesn't she, Ashley?

"Now let's see. MaeMae was from a good family, like you say. They weren't too pleased when she married Sheldon. Not that there was anything wrong with Sheldon Mackie, he just wasn't society and the Gerards were.

"The Gerards were rich too. Now your daddy and I were what you call 'comfortable.' But the Gerards were filthy rich. You know how rich people get their money, don't you, Ashley-honey?"

"Inherit it?" I guessed.

"That might be part of it. The rich acquire wealth because money is important to them. I'm not talking about the luxury money buys, I mean the love of money for itself, the bank accounts, the stocks and bonds. And they are willing to do just about anything to get it. The saying 'the rich are different from you and me' is true. They're not like the rest of us. While you and I would shy away from doing certain despicable things, like paying workers substandard wages or not providing health insurance, rich people don't see anything wrong with that. Then they bribe the politicians to pass big tax write-offs so they can keep what they've made."

I threw my arms around her. "Mama, you're your old self." She and Daddy used to have these political discussions when I was growing up. On the exploitation of working people, they saw eye to eye.

"Why, 'course I am, darlin'." She leaned closer and said, "It's the hormones, you know.

"Now back to MaeMae Mackie. I remember one time, MaeMae went to New York on a shopping spree. Well, she had all these gorgeous new clothes and she was parading around town in them."

Melanie opened her eyes, waking up for a story about fashion and shopping.

"Well, what was she to do with her old clothes, which were nice things too? Now you and I, we'd maybe place the better things with a consignment shop, and take the rest to the Goodwill. But not MaeMae. She invited all her girlfriends, me included, over to her house for a party. Served some cheap jug wine and tacky hors d'oeuvres. Laid the clothes out on the furniture and the beds. And they all had little price tags dangling from the sleeves. And do you know, those silly women bought those used garments. They were just so impressed with MaeMae and her money. I just turned up my nose, and said 'thank you kindly but they are not my size.'"

She spotted someone behind me and waved. "Yoo hoo, Maurice-honey, over here! Come say hello to my girls."

Mr. Dorfsman was a very nice man, quiet and polite, and it was obvious he adored Mama. Mama did all the talking. "Maurice's grandson and granddaughter are arriving on...." She stopped and got a bitter look on her face. "Dang it all, I can't remember a thing. Which day is it, Maurice-sugar?"

"Thursday," he said. "Thursday at noon. US Air from New York City."

"Thanks, sugar. Now I want you girls to go out to the airport and meet Maurice's grandchildren. Show them some Southern hospitality. Lord knows, with what they've been through in New York, they could do with some of our gracious Southern ways."

Melanie groaned under her breath.

"What, sweetie?" Mama asked.

"We'll go, Mama," I said, giving Melanie a warning glare. "How will we know them?"

"Oh, they'll know you. Maurice has told them all about my beautiful girls and described you to a T, haven't you, sugar?"

Mr. Dorfsman nodded and smiled. Mama could do no wrong.

"His grandson is tall and they call him Wizard," Mama added as if that was all we needed to know.

28

The closer it got to Christmas, the faster the days flew by. True to their word, Betty and Wayne Matthews organized the various historic preservation organizations into one cohesive unit. Letters opposing the resort hotel were printed in the newspapers, and local talk radio dedicated programs to Joel's proposed hotel. The consensus seemed to be that the city would be better off without a high-rise hotel, but every once in a while one of those "you're thwarting progress" idiots called in to argue.

Betty was planning a cocktail party for all the members of the city council for right after New Year's. I wanted to offer my house, but then Joel would see that I was thwarting his project and Melanie would be in danger. I told Betty that I couldn't host the party because the scene of the crime would distract the very people we were attempting to influence. We left it that I would co-host the party at her house.

On Tuesday I braved the traffic, and drove out to Lumina Station with all its charming boutiques and cafes to do my Christmas shopping.

My first stop was Bristol Books where I bought Anne Rice's latest book for Jon. He was addicted to the vampire series. I've never read them myself. Right now, I felt like I had enough ghouls in my life. For Mama I selected two pretty picture books, one on roses, the other on lighthouses. An armload of history books for Binkie. Before leaving, I ducked into the mystery section and grabbed a handful of paperbacks for myself.

At R. Bryan Collections, I arranged for a Wardrobe Consultant to visit Mama at Magnolia Manor to assist with the purchase of her spring and summer clothing.

I stowed my books in the trunk of the car and strolled into Centro Cafe for a large glass of juice and a California wrap. Sunshine beckoned me out of doors. I carried my food packets to one of the many porches where I settled in a white rocker. Sheltered from the wind in my cozy corner, I watched the fountain play in the sunshine.

Stiff breezes from the coast whipped skirts and ruffled hair in the parking lot. A woman getting out of her SUV held down her bright auburn hair. Melanie. I waved to her but she didn't see me. Her companion got out of the passenger side. Lisa Hamilton. Were those two joined at the hip? Lisa's platinum hair blew away from her face, then swung back into place perfectly.

I waved again and called to Melanie but she was busy fighting the wind and perhaps its noise prevented her from hearing me. I couldn't very well get up and go to her with my hands full of food.

I watched as she and Lisa went into Fathom's Bistro. Those two were becoming as thick as thieves. You're just being petty, Wilkes, I scolded myself. So Melanie has a friend, so what? Be happy for her for once in your life.

Finishing my lunch, I debated whether I should go into Fathom's to seek them out, but it seemed like it might be awkward, even if she was my sister. They'd feel they had to invite me to join them. I deposited my paper wrappings in a trash barrel and walked over to the Fountainside Fine Art Gallery. The gallery was beautifully appointed with pale blue walls and light hardwood floors. Original paintings by local artists were prominently displayed. A lovely watercolor of a Banks Channel scene attracted my attention. I wanted to buy it, but who would I give it to? Melanie and I usually give each other scarves and sweaters. Feeling I was making a mistake, I left the gallery without it.

At Jennifer's I found a beautifully beaded soft white cashmere sweater for Melanie, and a super-soft cream-colored shawl for Mama. At that point, I and my charge card were worn out, so I returned to my car. Melanie's Lexus was gone.

After locking my packages in the truck, I hesitated a moment. I still hadn't bought a present for Nick. I returned to the Fountainside Art Gallery. The watercolor seemed to say, "Buy me for Nick." I did. He'd once confided that it was his dream to live on a houseboat on the Waterway. Until he could make that dream a reality, he'd have the painting to look at.

Back in the historic district, I drove past Palace Street and saw something that caused me to hit my brakes. Luckily, the driver behind me had good brakes too and didn't rear-end me. His horn was in proper working order as well. I powered down my window to apologize, but he whizzed by, horn blaring, middle finger pointing skyward.

Driving around the corner, I pulled over to the curb. Looking like futuristic beasts, two yellow bulldozers lazed in the sun next to the rental houses. No one was around. The machines were unmanned, just sitting there, waiting for Joel to get the zoning variance he seemed to think was assured. Then they'd start up with a roar.

"Over my dead body!" I vowed.

The next day, I drove to the airport to pick up Mr. Dorfsman's grandchildren. I was happy for Mama. Mr. Dorfsman was a nice man and could provide the male companionship that had been missing in her life since Daddy's death.

I've never been pinned, or engaged, or involved in a torrid love affair. I wasn't even sure that I loved Nick, but my feelings for him were the closest I'd ever come to being in love. Surely, in this great big world, there was someone meant for me.

Melanie arrived in a whirl, dressed in tight faded jeans with soft suede butterscotch boots and a matching suede jacket. Her hair was bound back at the nape of her neck. I was wearing boots too with my long tube skirt because we'd had a hard freeze last night and the ground was cold.

"Am I late?" she asked.

"No. They haven't announced the plane's arrival yet."

"Why do I always let you get me involved in these crazy schemes? Here we are meeting people we don't even know and they don't know us. What are we supposed to do? Hold up one of those cardboard signs that says 'Mr. Dorfsman's Grandchildren'? Why do I always feel like I'm playing 'Ethel' to your 'Lucy'?"

I gave her a long look. "Melanie, you sure are cranky these days. You're not pregnant, are you?"

Her creamy complexion turned stark white. I thought she was going to drop. "Pregnant?" She blinked, then starting counting on her fingers. "No. Can't be." She punched my arm. "Don't ever scare me like that again, Ashley Wilkes, you hear."

The passengers from New York must have arrived while we were sharing this intimate moment, because all at once I heard a loud screech, "Ashley Wilkes! It can't be you!"

I'd know that voice anywhere. I whirled around to see a large woman bearing down on me.

"Kiki? Kiki, is that you?"

"We're here to meet—oh, no, it can't be—you're Scarlett's daughter?"

"You're Mr. Dorfsman's granddaughter?"

She was laughing, doubled over. "If you mean 'Rhett,' he's my mother's father. We're here for the wedding. I can't believe this. Your mother is marrying my grandfather in a mock wedding ceremony. And we're all going to be the little bridesmaids. Ain't life grand?" She threw her arms around me and hugged me to her oversized bosom.

Everything about my former college roommate Delores "Kiki" Piccolomini is over the top. She's almost six feet tall. She's big-boned, and there's a lot of meat on those bones. She's got the biggest brown eyes I've ever seen, and the fullest red lips. Her clothes stand out, colorful and flamboyant, but they suit her. For four years she'd been my best friend. I love her.

I wiggled out of her grip. Melanie was staring at Kiki like she was an alien from outer space. They had never met. The few times Melanie and Mama had come to see me in New York, Kiki had been out in New Jersey. Oh my gosh, visiting her grandfather!

I introduced them and Kiki grabbed a startled Melanie in a bear hug. "Any sister of Ashley's is a sister of mine," she said, her voice raspy and New Yorkish.

Melanie was speechless.

Behind Kiki, a man cleared his throat. Kiki reached around and pulled him forward. "You remember Ray, don't cha, Ashley?"

I extended my hand, feeling pleasantly surprised. Ray was Kiki's brother, older by one year. Melanie was watching us, as fascinated as if we were live theatre. I was eighteen when I'd met Ray. Throughout my years at Parsons, I hadn't seen much of him, he'd been studying at Stanford. I do remember Kiki telling me that he had applied to the Wharton School of Business. After graduation I returned South, and despite my best intentions, Kiki and I lost touch.

Melanie was sizing up Ray. I could see the wheels spinning in her brain. I knew just what she was thinking because I was thinking the same thing: Ray was a hunk. Ray was a male version of Kiki. The features that made Kiki exotic made Ray extraordinarily handsome. He was an inch or two taller than Kiki. His eyes were just as large and liquid, his lips just as full and sensuous. He exuded the same warmth and *joie de vivre*.

"What have you been doing? We've got to catch up," I said to Kiki.

"Haven't you heard? I'm the decorator to the stars."

"Oh no, you're *that* Delores!" *Delores, Decorator to the Stars*, the trade magazines called her. I never made the connection. "You're the one who decorates all those houses in Hollywood for famous movie stars, like Angelina and Brad."

She spread a hand over her large bosom. "In person. I even give them readings." Kiki was the mistress of Tarot card readings.

"You're famous. She's famous, Melanie. Surely, even you've heard of her."

For once Melanie was flustered. "I can't say that I have."

"Now wait a minute here," I said. "Mama kept referring to Ray as 'Wizard.' What's that all about?"

Kiki snorted. Her loud peels of laughter rang through the atrium. People stopped to stare at this larger-than-life woman, dressed in flowing garments of brilliant purple and gold, in the throes of a fit of wild humor. She grabbed her belly.

Ray too got caught up in the merriment—when he wasn't pounding Kiki on the back.

After a coughing spell, Kiki cleared her throat and said, "They call Ray the 'Wizard of Wall Street.' He's the youngest futures trader to have his own seat on the Stock Exchange. What did your mother think, that he was some kind of Harry Potter?" She was off and giggling again.

Melanie, on the other hand, was quivering from the top of her auburn head to the tip of her butterscotch boots. A twenty-six year old member of the New York Stock Exchange who was also incredibly handsome? This was so much better than a forty-year old real estate developer who had to borrow money from her.

She smiled at them, and her dazzling smile disarmed the Piccolominis. Reaching up a hand, she unloosened her hair, and shook it so that it swirled around her shoulders. An arm looped through Ray's, she led him from the terminal, her voice pouring over him as warm as syrup left out in the sun. "Mama said to show you some Southern hospitality, Ray honey, and I always do what my mama says."

29

The first card up was The Tower, the picture of a tall stone edifice on a rocky coastline above a boiling sea. The sky behind the tower was black and ominous. Poseidon was rising from the water, his tail whipping the waves into a froth. In his outstretched hand, a trident was aimed directly at the tower.

"I think the tower represents Joel's hotel," I said.

"You see in the cards what you need to see," Kiki replied.

Kiki is the mistress of the Tarot so I was in expert hands. If anyone could get to the root of the tragic events occurring in my life, it was Kiki and her Tarot cards.

Melanie had whisked Ray away from the airport in her Lexus. I'd driven Kiki into town to The Verandas where they'd stay until the day after Christmas when the bed and breakfast closed for a few days.

"You and Ray can move into my house then," I'd offered. "I have plenty of room."

Ray had arranged to have a rental car delivered to the B&B and it awaited us when we arrived. Melanie and Ray were parked in front of the Italianate mansion. "I'm taking Ray to lunch and for a drive around town," Melanie informed me through her lowered window. To Ray she said, "We've got one of the finest historic districts you'll see anywhere."

"Why don't you take Ray over to Palace Street and show him the bulldozers?" I quipped.

For an instant Melanie's smile faded but she recovered quickly. "Oh, pooh, you are such a silly. We'll meet you back here in a couple of hours so Ray can drive Kiki out to Magnolia Manor." Turning to Ray, she explained, "Ashley loves to tease. You must be so anxious to see your dear grandfather." They were off.

I helped Kiki carry her bags inside and get registered. Then we went to my house. On the drive in from the airport, I'd told Kiki all about the murders in my library. How Rachel's murderer had attacked me as he fled. She'd cringed when I told her about digging up the body in the backyard.

"What I need is a house blessing."

"I can do that," she declared.

"You?"

"Yes, me. I'm a Wiccan high priestess."

"You're a what?"

"A Wiccan high priestess. A witch, but only in the best sense. Some call us goddesses."

"You mean you cast spells, stuff like that?"

"I cast spells. I make charms and magical potions."

"Can you make a love potion?" I asked, scarcely breathing.

"Is there someone you want to fall in love with you?"

"Oh yes. If I could be sure of him, then maybe I could let go with him." I told her about Nick, how he threw himself into his work, how we quarreled when one of his cases involved me. "Can you do it?"

"Yes," she said thoughtfully. "But I want you to think carefully about this and be sure it's what you really want."

"I will. I'll give it a lot of thought. Are you saying you can't undo a spell once it's been cast?"

"It can be reversed, but it ain't easy, kid." From a tote bag at her feet she withdrew a small object wrapped in tissue paper and dropped it in my lap. "I want you to wear this for protection."

"What is it?" I asked suspiciously.

She laughed. "Nothing that will hurt you. It's an amulet. It'll protect you. Here I'll show you."

She took the gift from my lap and unwrapped the tissue paper. I glanced over to see a tiny blue cloth pouch stitched together with blue thread, attached to a long blue cord.

"It smells like herbs," I said.

"That's because there's herbs in it, silly. Here, let me." She fastened the cord around my neck so that the amulet hung over my heart.

At the next stop light she said, "Now repeat after me. 'I call upon the powers of the mighty Goddess Artemis, Lady of the Wild Things. Charge and bless this amulet of protection and empowerment. Shield me from harm. Strengthen and empower me. So mote it be.'"

Feeling ridiculous, I repeated the chant.

"As soon as we get to your house, I'll give you a reading. The cards will tell us what evil is at work here."

So she performed the reading in my library, scene of horrible violence, as we sat on either side of the library table on which randomly selected tarot cards were spread before us in the Celtic cross pattern. The tower card was on top.

Kiki explained, "The tower is the famous Labyrinth of King Minos. A shameful secret was hidden in its core. The secret was the seed of the tower's destruction. In your case, there's a secret that will prevent this resort from being built."

"A secret hidden at its core," I repeated thoughtfully. Should I call Jon and suggest we explore the four bungalows right away?

Kiki turned selected cards face up. "Here we have the chariot which augers conflict and struggle. You will come face to face with naked aggression, and you will discover that you too harbor aggression in your nature. The amulet I gave you will protect you from others' aggressive acts, but only you can control your own aggressive impulses."

Quickly Kiki flipped cards. "Ah, the lovers. They signify you will have to choose between *your* lovers."

What lovers, I wanted to ask, but remained silent.

She continued, "And here's Zeus, meaning that you'll be forced to rely on your own inner resources, something you haven't had to do since living in this close-knit community. A powerful, evil force has insinuated itself into your life and the showdown's coming!"

"And what's the final card, Kiki? What's does my future hold?"

She turned over the last card.

"The Hermit!" we shouted together.

"I don't want to be a hermit."

"You're not interpreting this card accurately, Ashley. Yes, there will be a period of solitude and withdrawal, but it will, if you embrace it, bring you wisdom and patience. All the great figures in history, even Christ, benefitted from a period of withdrawal. You'll build a solid foundation. You'll be a better person for it."

"Do I have a choice?"

"You always have a choice."

"Okay, who's responsible for these murders? You haven't told me that."

"The answer is here in The Devil card. The Satyr. Half-man half-goat. Precisely who this person is, I don't know. But bear in mind, Ashley, the goat is also the scapegoat, as much a victim as those he victimizes."

30

Late Saturday afternoon Melanie pushed through the front door carrying two lush, velvety poinsettias. "Drive out to MaeMae's with me, will you?" she requested. "I want to give these to the girls."

I tipped my head from side to side as if to drain water from my ears. "Huh?"

Melanie repeated her request with good humor and infinite patience. I *had* heard correctly, I just couldn't believe my ears. The girls? When did MaeMae and Lucy Lou get to be 'the girls?' And how come Melanie cared enough to take them Christmas plants? And why was she in such a good mood?

Except for last Saturday night, Melanie had been sleeping at my house every night. Spunky, now eating on his own, was true to his feline genetic makeup and quickly mastered the skill of stair climbing. One day he must have gazed long and hard into Melanie's feline eyes and—bingo!—discovered a soul mate. Now Spunky spent his nights at the foot of Melanie's bed, forsaking the sister who had saved him from a life of cold and misery. Honestly, cats are either short on memory or long on ingratitude.

Next Wednesday, the day after Christmas, Kiki and Ray would come to stay at my house. I'd have to think up an excuse for Melanie to stay too. I couldn't follow her around during the day, but I figured she wouldn't be alone at her office or at Joel's office. Although it was hard not to speak out, I was staying behind the scenes in the battle that was being fought over Joel's resort hotel. He didn't know I had taken sides against him and I wanted to keep it that way.

"Okay," I told Melanie, "I'll drive with you to MaeMae's. I have something to give her anyway. Are we expected?"

"Why, of course, shug. MaeMae called and invited us herself. I'll drive. Your car is way too small for us, these plants, and that awful looking rusty box you're taking. What is that anyway?"

"A time capsule," I replied.

She made a face. "I don't want to know."

Driving with Melanie is an adventure not for the faint of heart. "What did Ray think of your driving?" I asked as we sailed through a red light on Oleander Drive. Horns blared and drivers cursed, but Melanie only turned up the volume on Elvis singing "Blue, Blue Christmas."

"What?" she asked absently. "Ray? Oh, that reminds me. I invited Ray and his sister . . ."

"Kiki," I prompted.

". . . Kiki to my annual Christmas Day party. Oh, and I won't be able to sleep over at your house tomorrow night because I've got to get everything ready and decorated. Ask Jon to stay with you."

"Is Joel going to help you get things organized for the party?" I asked, fishing. In the past, she had relied on hired professional help for her parties.

"Joel had to make a quick trip to L.A. Some pressing business matters with his associates. But he'll be back on Christmas Eve. Naturally, we want to spend Christmas Eve together. You can find someone else to stay with you, can't you?"

"Don't worry about it. I'll find someone." So Joel was out in L.A., answering to his associates. I was convinced they were underworld figures. As an investor in Joel's enterprises, might Melanie be indirectly and unknowingly consorting with the mafia?

"Maybe Kiki can move into your house for a while. I must say, she is rather strange. I didn't know you'd shared an apartment with such an odd woman."

"Don't worry about it. I'll find someone. And Kiki isn't strange." I reconsidered. Actually, she was odd. "Well, if she is odd, she's a lovable oddity. I took her and Ray out to Port City Chop House for dinner last night. They were mighty impressed. Weren't expecting such a sophisticated restaurant in our little town. You know, people from New York and California must think we eat squirrels and dirt, because they act so surprised when they see we have elegant restaurants."

"Isn't that Ray something," Melanie crooned, as we skidded onto Greenville Loop Road. "He's accomplished so much for someone so young."

He's got big bucks is what you really mean, I thought. I was trying to think of how to maneuver the conversation around to my blueprints being in Joel's desk drawer without giving myself away when we arrived at MaeMae's white French Provincial house. A blustery wind blew off the Intracoastal Waterway and I pulled my jacket tighter around me.

"Okay, Melanie, what is this little visit really about?" As she scooped up poinsettias into her arms, I hefted the memory box off the backseat.

"Why whatever do you mean? Do you think I'm incapable of simple Christian charity? Don't you think I have a heart?" She gave me a stricken look, then pressed the doorbell.

"Good afternoon, Velma. My, doesn't your hair look lovely today. You must have spent the morning with the finest hair stylist in town."

Velma patted her perfectly coiffed hair. "As a matter of fact, I did, Miss Wilkes. Please come in and I'll let Mrs. Mackie and Miss Upchurch know you're here."

With an unpracticed smile, Velma took the poinsettias from Melanie, but I refused to relinquish the box. Again we were left to cool our heels in the Seventies-era foyer.

"You know it's the cocktail hour," I whispered to Melanie. "They'll be drunk as skunks."

"Shush, they might hear you."

Since when do you care, I wanted to ask.

A very sober MaeMae Mackie came into the foyer to welcome us graciously and thank us for the beautiful poinsettias. She hugged Melanie like they were the oldest and dearest of friends. Then she hugged me. What was going on here?

Lucy Lou greeted us from the white living room sofa. An enormous Christmas tree, beautifully decorated with silver ornaments, towered over the hearth where gas fire logs blazed. The room was cozy and warm, and our hostesses seemed genuinely happy to see us.

I swept the room with a curious eye. Not a cocktail shaker or liquor bottle in sight. After dispensing with the niceties, MaeMae told us all about their transformation.

"We're so glad you could come, Melanie. You too Ashley. We've got some good news to share. We've come out of the closet." She clasped Lucy Lou's hand. "We're in love. We've always been in love. And we want the whole world to know. We've become 'life partners.'" Wrinkling her nose, she confided, "We don't like that other term."

Lucy Lou explained further, "Now that we don't have to worry about keeping our relationship secret, we don't feel compelled to drink." The look of adoration she bestowed on MaeMae would have melted the heart of a snowman.

"Oh, it's so wonderful to be free," MaeMae sang.

Melanie jumped up from her chair and reached for 'the girls,' embracing them in a great hug. "I'm so proud of you two. That took courage. How I admire women who have the courage to live their convictions."

"And how we admire you, Melanie," Lucy Lou said. "We were just saying so before you arrived. You've been our heroine for many years. We've always wanted to be able to embrace life openly and fearlessly as you do. You do exactly what you please and don't give a hoot what people say."

"I'm so glad you see it that way. Most people are so narrow minded, don't you think? Now, tell me, what will your living arrangements be? Who's moving in with whom?"

"Melanie, dear, aren't you the practical one? No wonder you're such a success in business."

Melanie returned to her seat next to mine where I sat with my eyes popping and my mouth hanging open.

MaeMae looked to Lucy Lou for approval. "Excuse us for a moment. We don't mean to be rude." She whispered something into Lucy Lou's ear. Lucy Lou nodded and whispered back. They grinned broadly.

"We both have nice homes," MaeMae said. "We'd like you to appraise them for us, then sell the one that will bring the most money."

Melanie's splayed fingers crossed her heart. "What a surprise. Why, I'd be honored."

To further add to my confusion, we were invited to dinner. Melanie quickly accepted. Velma was a wonderful cook, serving home-style food: roast chicken and mashed potatoes, steamed green beans, apple pie. Melanie skillfully maneuvered MaeMae and Lucy Lou into revealing their assets. Now why doesn't she practice those ferreting techniques on Joel, I asked myself. You'd have thought shrewd Velma would have caught on, but Melanie had won her over too. She served Melanie the white meat and the first slice of pie.

As they discussed the values of Gerard family holdings in rental property and office parks, my mind skipped to the obvious. Now I knew why MaeMae resented Sheldon, and it wasn't even poor Sheldon's fault. There was nothing he could have done short of a sex-change operation that would have won MaeMae over. She'd exclaimed how wonderful it felt to be free, but was she referring to freedom from Sheldon, or freedom from the "secret"? And what about Sheldon's secret? So many secrets. If only Melanie would take an interest in solving the murders, she'd have these two pouring their hearts out.

As we carried our pie and coffee back to the living room, I tried to think of how I might worm Sheldon's secret out of MaeMae. Finishing off the pie, which was very sweet and moist, I got up and wandered to the Christmas tree to admire the silver ornaments.

"Those ornaments were passed down through my family," MaeMae said.

I was about to offer the memory box to MaeMae when a row of books on a bookshelf near the tree brought me up short. "High school yearbooks!" I squealed.

All eyes turned to me and conversation stopped.

MaeMae said, "Those were Sheldon's yearbooks. I should do something with them. I'd donate them to his old high school but the city tore it down in the late Sixties before people here started to value our heritage."

"May I?" I asked.

"Why, of course, help yourself. But whatever do you want with those musty old things? I have no idea why Sheldon insisted on keeping them in here but sometimes late at night I'd find him poring over those old things. Lost youth, I 'spect."

Fixing me with a glare of disapproval, Melanie said, "My sister has eclectic tastes. You never know what will catch her fancy."

I extracted the 1959 and 1960 volumes. Carrying them to my chair, I started to thumb through them.

"Ashley!" Melanie hissed. "Mind your manners."

I looked up. "Oh, sorry. May I borrow these?"

MaeMae blinked. "Why, sure 'nuff, if you want to." A sudden idea brightened her expression. "Perhaps, Ashley, with your contacts, you know a collector who might want to buy the entire set."

As we were saying goodnight and thanking them for a lovely dinner, I offered MaeMae the metal box. "This is rightfully yours. I found it in my basement." I didn't tell her I'd been digging for buried treasure when I found it. "It's a time capsule your ancestors assembled over a hundred years ago."

MaeMae's eyes misted. Her hand went to her mouth and she was momentarily speechless. She reached for the box and cradled it to her breast as if it was a newborn babe. "The memory box. I remember my mama telling me about it. I thought it was lost forever and I'd never see it." She kissed me on the cheek. "You're a thoughtful and generous person, Ashley, just like your dear mother."

As we started off, with much fluttering of hands and blowing of kisses, I wondered if MaeMae would soon be offering her ancestors' Victorian hair jewelry to a collector. I made a mental note to find out how much Sheldon was worth.

31

On Sunday after church, Melanie and I took her car and drove out to Magnolia Manor. Wearing our bridesmaid's dresses with their circular tulle skirts spreading out a mile, we needed every extra inch her capacious SUV offered.

"I hate these dresses. Did you have any idea Mama was going to make us wear these clownish outfits?"

"None," I replied. "I couldn't believe my eyes when they arrived. At least yours is a pretty peach color. Mine looks like lime sherbet."

"It's not peach. It's orange. And all these gathers make me look fat."

"Melanie, you look just like you always do. You are not getting fat no matter what Joel says."

She glanced down at her stomach. "You're right. It's just the gathers. I can't wait till this stupid wedding is over."

"It's not stupid. It's making Mama happy. You'd better not let your foul mood spoil this day for her. She's better than she's been in years."

"See, I told you she'd be better off in assisted living. Yet you argued and argued with me about keeping her at home. Anyway, Ray's the best man and I don't want him to see me looking like . . . like a squashed pumpkin. You know, he is the sweetest thing. He came over last night to help me put up the tree and all."

Put up the tree? Melanie has a professional florist who selects, delivers, and decorates her tree. How interesting that Ray stopped by to give her a hand on the very night Joel was three thousand miles away. Was she developing a crush on young Ray? I sure 'nuff hoped so. Anything to distract her from Joel.

"Is Joel really thinking of making his home here?" I probed.

"Yes, sweetie, he is. Isn't that good news? Because I could never live anywhere else. When I told him your house was coming on the market, he was very interested."

"My house is not coming on the market."

She turned to give me a confused stare.

"Keep your eyes on the road," I warned.

"Why, certainly we're selling your house. We agreed that you can't live there. It's been ruined for you. But Joel doesn't seem to mind about the murders. And he's become quite fond of the historic district. You're really lucky he wants to take it off your hands. We'd have a hard time finding a buyer. No one wants to live in a house where people were recently murdered. Joel wants it because it'll put him close to the site while the hotel is going up and he can walk over and check on the progress."

"That'll never hap . . . wait a minute. You didn't show Joel my house when I wasn't at home, did you?"

"Not yet. He saw it briefly the night of the candlelight tour. I did intend to show it to him, but we've been so busy planning the hotel, we haven't had time. I did have a copy of your blueprints run off for him, and he likes the layout."

So that explained the presence of my blueprints in his desk drawer. "Melanie, please don't bring anyone inside my house when I'm not at home. I mean it. Promise me."

"Well, 'course not, shug. Don't get your knickers in a knot."

Kiki was waiting for us inside the main entrance to Magnolia Manor.

"Where's your bridesmaid's dress?" I asked.

She looked me up and down, taunting me with a smirk. "You look like Kermit the frog in that dress. I wouldn't be caught dead in the dress they sent me. I look just fine in my own clothes."

And she did look dramatic and dazzling in a long, flowing ivory lace dress with tapered sleeves and a sheer insert at the bodice. "Pretty," I said. "Like you could be a bride yourself."

Behind me Melanie sputtered. I caught her hand as if to control her. "We've got to go find our mother."

Kiki grabbed my arm. The three of us tugged for a second, Melanie and I pulling one way, Kiki pulling the other, like we were back on the playground. "Wait a minute, Ashley. I've got something to tell you."

"What's wrong?" An icy chill froze my insides.

"The wedding's been postponed."

Melanie dropped my hand. "Is our mama all right? She hasn't had another episode, has she?"

"Your mother's fine. But there was a death here this morning, and out of respect for the dead woman, Ms. Miller cancelled the wedding."

"What happened?" I asked.

"One of the patients had a severe asthma attack and she didn't survive."

"Asthma? You're not talking about Mrs. Penry, are you?"

"Yes. That's the name. You know her?"

We found Mama, Mr. Dorfsman, and Ray in the conservatory. Under the curving frond of a potted palm, a harpist in a black gown played lovely tunes. Maids were arranging trays of tea and cookies on small tables. Mama was dressed in a pale pink gown. Mr. Dorfsman had on a tuxedo, as did Ray. Ray looked more handsome than ever. Melanie shrank behind me, fluttering her fingers over my shoulder.

Mr. Dorfsman offered Mama a cup of tea, but Mama didn't respond. I sat down next to her, exposing Melanie and her squashed pumpkin outfit.

Mama's hand was limp and I lifted it to my lap where it disappeared in the deep folds of tulle. "Hi, Mama," I said softly. "You look pretty."

She would not lift her eyes or look me in the face. With my free hand, I raised her chin so she had to look at me. "Mama?"

"Poor Dorothy," she murmured. Tears dribbled down her cheeks. "She's gone. She couldn't breathe. No one could help her. And it's all the florist's fault."

"Mama?"

"I don't want flowers at my funeral, Ashley. Promise me there won't be flowers."

"I promise, Mama. No flowers."

"And get this silly dress off me." She looked up at Maurice Dorfsman. "Who are you? Why are you dressed up like an undertaker?"

I started to get up to take Mama to her room but Mr. Dorfsman stepped forward and offered her his hand. "I'm Maury, Claire, your best friend. Let's you and I take a little stroll down the hall to your room. I think we both could use a little peace and quiet."

Mama smiled at him. "I like that idea, Maury. Peace and quiet."

I sought out Ms. Miller. "Mama's so upset. She had a relapse."

"They're all upset, Ashley. I'm sorry for the way it's turned out. We had such a beautiful day planned. Now . . ."

"What happened? Mama said something about a florist."

Ms. Miller shook her head. "We aren't sure what happened. Someone made a terrible mistake and sent Mrs. Penry flowers. Our receptionist never left her post at the front desk yet somehow the florist's delivery boy got past her. He delivered a huge bouquet of flowers directly to Mrs. Penry's room. We'd never let such a mistake happen. We simply don't understand it. The room number was written on the envelope. And that's another odd thing, we never give out a patient's room number. Whoever sent the flowers must not have known about her asthma and how severely allergic she was to flowers."

Ms. Miller was shaken. "There was a doctor on the premises, and the paramedics arrived within minutes. They tried to revive her. She's been in such poor health. Their best efforts just weren't good enough."

"Whose name was on the card?" I asked.

"We couldn't find a card. In all the excitement, it must have fallen out of the envelope."

32

Christmas Eve service at St. James Episcopal Church was beautiful and inspiring. During readings from the scriptures and carols sung by the choir, I escaped into the comfort of worship. I contemplated God's gift to mankind, the babe in the manger.

The church was crowded with members and their families, and those folk who attend church only at Christmas and Easter. Melanie and I had arrived early to claim our usual seats, since attendance is always big on Christmas Eve. Joel had returned from L.A. that afternoon, but being Jewish insisted Melanie go to church without him. She told me he was napping when she left her house. As if I gave a hoot about Joel's jet lag.

I glanced around for people I knew, recognized the regulars, and saw many new faces. I thought I caught a glimpse of MaeMae and Lucy Lou, but then heads got in the way. At that point the service began.

As I opened my hymnal, a scrap of blue paper fluttered into my lap. Standing to sing, I clutched the paper so it wouldn't fall to the floor. I have a pretty good singing voice, if I do say so myself, and I love singing hymns, especially the old, cherished, well-known songs, like the carols we sing at Christmas. I know all the words to "Silent Night."

Sitting back down, I glanced at the blue paper. A message was written in block letters. My name jumped off the page.

Ashley, I know who killed Sheldon and Rachel. Meet me behind the church, and I'll tell you. Come now. Hurry. I can't wait long. They're watching me. A friend

I looked around, wondering who could have slipped it into my hymnal. All the regulars know where Melanie and I sit. I didn't see a friend. No one was watching me.

I slipped the note into my pocket as I considered the gravity of its message. Who was the author? And who were the ones who were watching? The police? The killer?

The music buzzed like static in my ears and my head spun. I was back in my library, standing over Sheldon's dead body, a frightened Binkie clutching the poker. I was cautiously entering my house, calling Rachel's name, when a cold-blooded killer swung his club at my head.

Inside my wool jacket, I was suddenly overheated, perspiration dripping under my arms and pooling in the small of my back.

"I've got to get some fresh air," I whispered to Melanie. Before she could protest, I ducked out of the pew, tiptoed past rows of worshipers, and hurriedly slipped out the side door.

I stumbled forward, then doubled over, gasping for air. This is no time for a panic attack, I told myself. I turned left, crossing through St. Francis's garden. Pushing through the gate, I followed the sidewalk to the back of the church property.

I approached the graveyard slowly, giving my eyes a chance to adjust to the darkness. Patches of light fell from unshuttered windows. I seemed to be alone. I lifted my head and studied the sky. The night was still. Cold, crisp air revived me. My balance seemed restored. The stars shone down and I wondered fleetingly which was the Star of Bethlehem.

I looked around for my note writer, but the churchyard was empty. My ears perked up. Someone was calling my name. The voice came from deep among the tombstones.

"Ashley. Over here," the whispery voice called.

I made my way down a brick path under the shadowy trees. Dangling Spanish moss brushed my cheek. Tombstones surrounded me. "Over here," the voice called.

"Where are you? I can't see you." I peered into the darkness.

"I'm behind a tree. I don't want them to see me. Come closer."

I moved in the direction of the voice. In the stillness, I felt a swift rush of air near my head. Its passing warmed my hair. What was that? A bug? A bat? I brushed my hair. The ends felt crisp.

"Where are you?" I called again.

No answer.

A sudden pop and again the insect darted at my head, grazed my hair, chipped bark off the live oak tree behind me. Oh my God, no! I threw myself on the ground. Someone was shooting at me. Someone with a gun with a silencer.

The ground near my head ripped open, spewed dirt and leaves into my face. I rolled over, then lunged for the nearest tombstone. With it between me and the shooter, I started to scream.

The swelling of the organ inside the church drowned out my shrieks. I wrapped my arms around my head and crouched behind the tombstone, praying to be spared.

A siren filled the night, drowning out the chords of the organ; flashing lights approached at great speed. How did they know? Who had summoned them?

The shooter sprang away from the tree where he'd been hiding. Scaling the wrought iron fence that enclosed the churchyard, he darted through traffic and crossed Fourth Street. Dressed all in black, he disappeared into the darkness behind Temple of Israel.

I ran to the street. The police car sailed by, not even slowing down. The officer never intended to rescue me. He was on his way to another call. But his near presence saved me.

I limped to my car, tears rolling down my cheeks, dripping from my chin. I gasped for breath, wrenched open the door. Sobbing, I fell behind the wheel, hit the master lock.

I've got to get home, I thought. I've got to get away from that graveyard. I've got to wash the smell of moldering earth off my face. Shampoo away the stench of singed hair. I wanted my shower, my bed. I wanted to be clean and safe. I wanted to turn on the burglar alarm, to bolt my bedroom door. To sleep and sleep until I couldn't remember that my life had turned into a hellish nightmare.

But rest was not for me. When I pulled up in front of my house I saw that my own home had been the destination of the racing police car. I parked in my driveway and waved to the uniformed officer on my porch. My burglar alarm was screaming like a banshee.

"This your house, ma'am?" he hollered, approaching my lowered window.

"Yes," I replied numbly.

"Let me make sure it's safe, then we'll go inside and turn that thing off."

He circled around my house while I waited in my locked car. When he returned to report that there was no sign of a break-in, we walked up to the front door together. I unlocked it and punched in a code on my alarm pad. Blessed silence followed. If the officer noticed my dirty face and disheveled hair and clothing, he didn't comment. He showed me his ID.

"Thank you for coming, Officer Youngblood. I guess the neighbors called you."

"Them and the security people. I'm going to check the doors and windows and do a general search. You wait here." He pointed to the bottom step of the staircase.

"Okay," I mumbled. I knew he wouldn't find anyone. My boogie man was not in my house. He'd been in the graveyard with me after trying to break in here.

I sat down on the bottom step, too whipped to remove my jacket. Pulling a tissue out of my pocket, I wiped fine dust off my face.

The officer was thorough. He made a complete tour of the downstairs. When he opened the door to the kitchen, Spunky scooted out, fur all spiky, and leapt into my lap. Then the officer went upstairs and I heard him moving from room to room, opening and closing doors, probably checking under the beds too.

"I'm going to look around outside again. You got floodlights?"

"Yes," I replied.

"Turn 'em on."

I complied.

Absently I petted Spunky. I ought to tell him, I thought. I need to report this. Someone tried to kill me. Where are you, Nick? I need you.

As if I'd conjured him out of thin air, he appeared, filling my open doorway, looking as scared as I felt. "Nick! Oh, Nick," I cried and flew to the safety of his arms. Now I was home. Now I was safe. No one would dare shoot at me now.

"I came right away, as soon as I heard it was your address. I was on my way here anyway to warn you that Eddie Parker was almost apprehended at his parents' house in Greensboro this morning and they said he was coming here."

Officer Youngblood joined us in the foyer. "There are some scratch marks around the lock on your side door. They could have been made by someone attempting a B&E. I searched your yard. If there was someone, he's long gone."

Try Temple of Israel, I wanted to say, but knew my attacker would be long gone from there too.

"I'm getting to know this property pretty well," Youngblood quipped. "I was here two weeks ago when you found Jimmy Weaver's body. Well, goodnight, Ms. Wilkes. I'll leave you in good hands." He nodded respectfully to Nick.

As soon as he was gone I told Nick about the note in my hymnal and someone shooting at me in the graveyard. He stepped back, livid. "You little fool. Are you trying to get yourself killed? Of all the lame-brain stunts you've pulled, this one beats all."

I sank down onto the lower step again. "Don't yell at me."

But he wasn't through with me. "I rushed over here to warn you about Eddie Parker and now I find out you foolishly set yourself up as his target."

Nick struggled to control his anger. I struggled to control my hurt. The only way I could do that was to concentrate on his words, not the disapproval behind them.

"Do you think Eddie Parker is responsible for all these murders then?"

His shoulders slumped. "I don't know. We're trying to find him so we can question him. The only case we've got against him is drug dealing. But—and hear me loud and clear, Ashley—I don't want you going anywhere near him. And I sure as hell don't want you going into cemeteries to meet someone you don't know."

"I shouldn't have done it, Nick. I see that now. I learned my lesson. I was so scared."

He pulled me up into his arms. "Oh, baby, can't you see how crazy I am about you? The way you take risks scares the hell out of me."

"Me too." I managed a meager laugh. Some of the tension between us eased.

He held me out at arms length. "I can't stay. I just came to warn you. I've got to get back to work. We're checking all Parker's usual haunts. I'll drive you to Melanie's. You can spend the night there."

"I can't do that."

"And why not?"

"Because Joel Fox is there."

"So?"

"So, I hate him. He threatened to have someone slash Melanie's face if I opposed the hotel project."

"Fox said that? I'll look into it. But right now I'm more concerned about *your* pretty face, and the pretty body that goes with it." He managed a smile. "I'll have a patrol car parked out on your street all night. Call Jon. See if you can get him to come over. Call him now, because I'm not leaving until there's someone here with you."

Jon answered on the first ring, like he was sitting by the phone. Waiting for Christine to call, I thought. When I explained the situation, he promised to arrive in fifteen minutes. "Bless you," I said.

The front door was still standing open so we saw Binkie climb the front steps and cross the porch. "I came to help," he said. "I listen to the police frequency on my scanner. I heard there was a possible break-in at your address." He toted a billy club. "I came prepared."

33

Jon, Binkie, and I sat in the library, drinking prepackaged hot cocoa. Our presents were stacked under the tree, but we didn't have the heart to open them.

"What a Christmas Eve," I grumbled. "No wonder the holidays depress me. Now I have another terrible Christmas experience to add to my list. Next year I'm going to the Bahamas in the middle of December and I'm not coming back until after New Year's."

"How about I build a fire?" Jon offered. "That'll cheer you up."

"Please do. I want to thank you guys for giving up your Christmas Eve to babysit me."

"I wasn't doing anything," Binkie said. "And there's no one I'd rather be with."

"Same here," Jon said, kneeling in front of the firewood box. "Christine is with her family."

Spunky sniffed at Jon's heels.

"This is the last of the firewood," he said, dragging out two split logs. "When are they going to deliver your order?"

"Next week."

"Well, this'll burn for a couple hours." He laid the kindling and arranged the logs on top of it. The door to the firewood box remained ajar as he reached in to scoop up wood fragments which he tossed onto the flickering flames.

I rubbed my arms. "Where's that draft coming from?"

Jon closed the firewood box door. The flow of chilly air ceased.

"Why is cold air coming from the firewood box?" I asked. "And where did Spunky go? Jon, you've closed him inside!"

He opened the small door and leaned in. "He's not . . . wait a minute, this tin backing is loose." He was on his hands and knees, reaching toward the back of the box. The rattle of a tin sheet followed.

"The bottom corner's loose," he called in a muffled voice.

"Is Spunky back there?" I asked, alarmed. "If he crawls in between floor joists, we'll have a terrible time getting him out."

Jon backed out of the box. "He's on the other side. I hear him meowing. Get me a hammer with a claw. I'll pry the back off."

The firewood box was about four feet high, two feet wide, and another four feet deep. It merged seamlessly with the fireplace mantelpiece and the built-in bookcases, and was original to the house. Jon crawled back in, claw hammer ready. On his knees, he attacked the tin backing.

I got two powerful flashlights from the kitchen and handed one to Binkie. "Hold that for him."

Binkie said, "Can you see, Jon? Am I aiming the light on the right spot?"

"Perfect," Jon called over his shoulder. "It's coming."

There were more thunderous bangs, then Jon backed out again, pulling the sheet of tin with him.

"That noise has probably terrified Spunky," I worried aloud. "Who knows where he's run to."

Binkie patted my shoulder. "Ashley dear, you're experiencing a delayed reaction to your earlier trauma. Now try to be brave once more and don't worry. You'll soon have Spunky back, safe and sound. Leave it to Jon and me."

Jon took the flashlight from me and entered the box again, hunched over, knees bent, head ducked down. We watched him disappear through the back side. "Okay, I'm inside. There's room to stand up," he called. "Ashley, get our jackets. It's cold in here."

Binkie put on his jacket, and I mine. I carried Jon's leather jacket under my arm, and crawled through, then out the back side of the fire-wood box.

We had entered a small room. Jon and Binkie shone their flash-lights up and down, revealing a space not much larger than a good-sized closet. A door on the far wall stood ajar a few inches.

"There's no sign of Spunky. The noise scared him and he's fled through that door. You know where we are, don't you?" I asked. "We're under the staircase landing. You know how the front and back stairs go up halfway and meet on the landing? Well, we're under the landing now."

Binkie's voice quaked with excitement. "Yes, that is our location, but do you understand the significance of this room? This, I feel cer-tain, was a hiding place for runaway slaves. Reverend Israel Barton was a well-known abolitionist. The literature is replete with references to him, and the belief that he was active in the Underground Railroad."

"You think he hid slaves here?" I asked.

"Indeed I do. Let us explore a little further. Jon, are you game?"

"I'm with you, Professor."

"Don't forget Spunky. We've got to find him."

"I think I hear him meowing on the other side of this door," Jon said.

Binkie aimed his flashlight beam through the open door. "Just as I thought. An escape route. Now be careful, these old stone steps are cracked and worn."

"Let me go first, Binkie." Jon started down. His flashlight beam bounced down the steps like a bright gold coin. I stepped in behind Jon. Binkie stepped in behind me, aiming the second flashlight into the darkness ahead.

Our little parade of three descended the long flight of stone steps that led down, presumably alongside my basement, and tunneled under my garden. At the bottom, we entered a winding passageway. But no sign of my kitten.

"Spunky! Spunky!" I called. "Here kitty, kitty."

"There's a network of tunnels that crisscross under the city," Jon said. "I've been in Jacob's Run, but I didn't know this one existed."

Binkie added, "As the city expanded, the creeks and streams that fed the Cape Fear were bricked over. The sides of the stream were reinforced with brick, and they used rot-resistant cypress to seal the bottoms."

Jon aimed his flashlight up the sides and across the top of the tunnel. "This one has held up well. Let's see where it leads."

We followed the tunnel but I couldn't find my cat. After what seemed like a quarter of a mile, we came to a flight of steps that ascended to another door. Sagging on its hinges, the door had settled onto the stone. It took the efforts of all three of us to push it inward.

"Ohmygosh!" I cried. "I know this place. It's the root cellar I fell into. We're on Palace Street." The hole in the root cellar ceiling was now sealed up, presumably by the police.

The tiny underground room was exactly as I'd left it. I checked all the corners and shelves. No Spunky.

"Binkie, why do you suppose the tunnel leads here?"

"If I may hazard a guess, it was an escape route for runaway slaves. Shall I theorize? Reverend Barton ran a safe house. Slaves slipped in at night, one or two at a time, and were provided shelter and a place to rest. Then ship passage was secured to transport a number of them North."

"But why the tunnel?" I asked.

"Yeah," Jon said, "why not just walk down Nun Street to Chandler's Wharf and board the ship there? Under cover of nightfall, of course."

"A most populated route. While this area, then the outskirts of town, supported small farms and warehouses, and offered less opportunity for observation. Remember that Captain Beery, Barton's neighbor, trained a telescope from the monitor atop his roof on the community. Ostensibly, he was looking for Yankee ironclads, but would he have failed to notice a band of unshackled African-Americans making their way to the river?"

"Your theory sounds good to me, Binkie," Jon said. "Now what are we going to do about our discovery? How can we use it to save the property from being developed into a resort hotel?"

"Let's talk about that later. We've still got to find Spunky," I said.

Back in the tunnel, Jon's light struck a large flat stone fitted into the brickwork. "Hold it a second, Jon. Shine your light back on that stone."

The flashlight beam illuminated a flat slab. "Look," I cried, "an inscription. Someone has noted his passing."

We all leaned in toward the stone for a close look. "Brush off some of the dirt, Jon. Let's see what we have here."

Two names were inscribed in neat cursive, one atop the other. I read aloud, "Israel Barton, Harriet Tubman, March 19, 1862."

"Yikes," I squealed. I grabbed Binkie and danced him up and down. "This is it! This is what we need! Now we can prove the property is of historic significance. Harriet Tubman, herself, conducted slaves through this tunnel in 1862. Oh, this is too good to be true!"

Binkie shared my excitement. "We know that Tubman worked as a spy and a soldier for the Union Army in South Carolina. She was able to slip around undetected for she was a master of disguises. So she was here in Wilmington too! My word, who would have guessed?"

Jon was laughing. "Stop dancing. You're raising too much dust. And if you shake the roof down on top of us, our discovery will be buried with us."

Retracing our path through the tunnel, we chattered excitedly about what our first step ought to be to save the property. "I think we should contact The National Trust," I said. "They'll move fast. I don't know about the state or the city. Too much local politics. The lawyers at The National Trust will file an injunction that'll stop Joel Fox dead in his tracks."

"He won't be able to touch this property," Jon added, "until the archaeologists verify what we've found. There'll be a hearing, and it'll be a grand day for historic preservation."

We returned to the small room under my stair landing. "But where is Spunky?" I cried. "Jon shine your light in all the corners. He might have returned here while we were in the root cellar."

"And so he has. Come on, Spunky, no one's going to hurt you," Jon said.

Spunky had curled up on a pile of cloth sacks and was fast asleep. I gasped. Was it possible? "Binkie, look. Do you see what I see?"

Light from his flashlight pointed downward, reflected off Spunky's upturned eyes. "I see them," he said somberly.

"See what?" Jon asked.

"Sacks," I answered. "I've seen sacks just like these on display inside an old safe at the Railroad Museum. I think Spunky's found the Atlantic Coast Line's stolen payroll."

34

I forced myself to mingle with the other guests at Melanie's party, a regular party girl, something I rarely do. Ordinarily, I find my restorationist buddies and drag them off into a corner where we compare notes about the houses we're restoring. But at this Christmas party, I had a purpose. I was not here to have fun, but to set a daring plan into motion. To that end, I struck up conversations with Melanie's real estate friends and with anyone in the vicinity of Joel Fox and Earl Flynn.

Jon was huddled on a sofa with Christine Brooks. Binkie had not been invited, nor had Nick. That suited our purposes just fine. Late last night, Jon, Binkie, Nick, and I had hatched our little scheme. Nick had not been won over easily, but eventually we convinced him. He was as eager as we were to solve the old payroll robbery and the murders. We persuaded him to admit our plan was sound and no one would get hurt as long as he provided police backup.

"Just take a look at this, Nick," I told him as I opened Sheldon's high school yearbook to a picture of the "Class of Sixty" track team. "Read those names and see if they don't ring bells."

Nick studied the black and white photo of several young men in numbered tee shirts and running shorts, then read aloud from the caption below. "Sheldon Mackie, Earl Flynn, Russell Penry, James 'Jimmy' Weaver, Melvin Cox."

"Cox was the man whose body was washed up on Wrightsville

Beach," Jon said.

"Yeah, I know who he is."

"Don't you see, Nick?" I argued, "They were buddies in high school, the five of them. We think they robbed the railroad that summer after graduation. Remember, three men broke into the payroll office. That'd be Sheldon, Penry, and Cox. There was the inside man, the guard Jimmy Weaver. And my bet is Earl Flynn drove the getaway car."

"Then how do you account for the money being here?" Nick asked.

"Because," Binkie answered with utmost patience, "they were smart enough to know it'd be risky to flash money around. The three of us worked out a scenario while we were waiting for you to come collect those money bags."

"We think," Jon interjected, "they made a pact to wait a few years before divvying up the money. Penry hid the money. Maybe the others knew where it was, maybe not. Maybe they had a general idea that it was stashed somewhere in Penry's mother's library. That'd explain why Sheldon and Rachel were both killed in the library."

I said, "Jimmy Weaver got greedy and demanded his share. He and Penry, or one of the others, or all of them—although I can't believe Sheldon was a part of this—got into a fight. Weaver was killed and buried in the garden. Fearing discovery, they went their separate ways. Then, my guess is, something went wrong.

"Sheldon became successful as a decorator. Maybe he was ashamed of what he'd done, and disassociated himself from the others and the robbery, not wanting to share in the spoils." That would explain his nightmares and the secret MaeMae referred to in her diary.

Jon said, "And Flynn was making big money in Hollywood. Now Flynn's back, and he and Joel are short of cash."

"Joel's in debt to some nasty sorts in L.A. Why, he even had to borrow money from Melanie," I said. "I think Flynn told Joel where he could get his hands on an easy half million, and that they are behind the killings here, caught by Sheldon and then Rachel while they were searching this room."

"And Cox?" Nick asked. "You think he whiled away forty years, bumming around Johnny Mercer pier, not claiming his cut?"

"Maybe he did try to find the money. Why don't you check to see if Mrs. Penry reported any break-in's during those forty years. He couldn't learn its hiding place from Sheldon because Sheldon didn't know. Flynn was living in California, and maybe wouldn't have anything to do with him. Weaver was dead. The only one he could ask was Russell Penry. And that's where we're stumped. Penry's whereabouts is a mystery."

"Not so mysterious," Nick said. "Penry died in a Georgia State penitentiary less than a year ago. He was serving a life term without parole."

"For what?" we three Sherlocks cried.

"For murdering his girlfriend."

And that explained why he had never visited his mother, Dorothy Penry, at Magnolia Manor, I thought, as I selected hors d'oeuvres from Melanie's buffet table and filled my plate. I needed fortification before tackling the gruesome twosome, Earl and Joel, directly.

I started in their direction when Melanie intercepted me. She'd been looking glum all afternoon, somber and downcast, not at all her confident self. And she wasn't hanging all over Joel the way she usually did.

"I've got to talk to you in private," she said. "Come with me."

Lisa Hamilton followed us with her eyes. Again envy skewed her even features.

"What's up?" I asked, after Melanie closed and locked her bedroom door. She led me to the bed and drew me down beside her, then burst into tears.

"Melanie, don't cry. You'll mess up your pretty face." I told her the one thing guaranteed to stop the tears, and handed her a box of tissues.

"You don't know what Joel did," she sobbed.

"Did he hit you!" Because if he had, I was going to go out there and clobber him, in front of the whole damned party.

"No. No. Not that. Something worse."

"Worse than hitting you?" I asked in disbelief. "What?"

She choked on her sobs. "He said . . ." Sob.

I put my arm around her shoulder. "There. There."

"He said . . . I look . . . ooollllddd!"

It was hard to keep a straight face but I did. "Well, he's wrong. You know, I detest that man. How could he say something like that to you?

Why, everyone knows you're the prettiest girl in Wilmington." Melanie is not a girl but that was what she needed to hear.

"He said . . . he said I've got wrriinnkles."

I walked her to a mirror, then gently wiped away tears and streaked makeup from her cheeks. "I don't see any wrinkles. Listen, Mel, you don't need him. You're the best damned realtor this town has ever seen. You make more money in one month than that scrounger makes in a year. You don't need him. And you don't need his resort hotel. In the long run it will destroy the reputation you've worked so hard to build."

Melanie took a deep breath and lifted her chin. She smiled at her reflection. "I am a billion dollar producer. And next week I'm going for botox injections. Wrinkles! Me? Never!"

"That's the spirit," I said, free to smile again. "Now fix your face and let's join the party. We'll show Joel Fox just how classy the Wilkes sisters are."

There was a tap on the door and Jon's voice called, "Ashley? You okay in there?"

"Fine," I answered. "Be right out."

It may have appeared to the other guests that Jon was all wrapped up in Christine, but the truth was Nick had sent him to the party to take care of me. And if anything untoward did happen to me, well, the consequences were just too horrendous to contemplate.

Returning to Melanie's spacious living room, I saw that Kiki and Ray had arrived. I wanted to claim them for my own, but that pleasure would have to wait. I had my assignment, and I don't shirk my duties. I ducked into the kitchen where caterers were piling sliced turkey and ham, cheese straws, ham biscuits, and pickled relish onto serving platters. I picked up a champagne flute and filled it with gingerale, just as I'd been doing all afternoon. Let Melanie's guests think I was tipsy on champagne; that would explain my garrulousness.

I took a deep breath and sashayed up to Joel and Earl. "Look," I began, aiming for slurred speech, "it's Christmas. Whaddya say we call a truce. Let bygones be bygones."

"I'm glad you've come to your senses," Joel said. He was dressed all in black, black silk turtleneck under a black jacket, probably Armani or a good knockoff. "Are you saying you'll stop blocking my hotel?" He lifted his champagne flute to his lips and eyed me over the rim as if indifferent to my response.

"I won't be around to oppose the hotel," I said, swallowing a large gulp of gingerale. I inclined my head toward Kiki and Ray. "I'm going back to New York with my friends. We're leaving right after the party. I can't stand it here another minute." I managed a few dry sobs, then dropped my head on Joel's shoulder.

Joel shook me off. "Don't go having a crying jag on this jacket."

"I don't blame you for wanting to get out of town," Earl said. "It's not safe for you here."

Was that a threat? "How right you are, my friend." I dipped my head and let it fall toward his shoulder now. He took a step back, and I jerked my head up. "And of all times, my burglar alarm's gone kapooey. Keeps going off for no reason. My neighbors are mad. The police are mad. I had to turn the useless thing off."

I giggled, then covered my mouth. "Ooops, I wasn't supposed to say that. Oh, well, you guys aren't going to break in and steal my Victorian cutlery."

"Listen, gotta go." I lifted my flute in a toast and downed the contents. "Merry Christmas."

Tottering across the room to Kiki, I thought about how I'd been spreading that story for the past hour, hoping to ensure that Joel and Earl heard it. From my vantage point at Kiki's side, I watched the two men confer.

"I'm glad to see you're cutting loose, girl," Kiki said. My drunken act had fooled even her.

"I'm sober as a witch," I said, setting down my flute and reaching for a fudge brownie, which I prefer any day over champagne. "Where's Ray?"

Kiki wiggled her eyebrows. "Your sister's gobbling him up like he's Christmas candy."

I watched them. Melanie's hand was possessively attached to Ray's arm. He didn't look like he minded. "They do make an attractive couple."

"I'm thinking of inviting Melanie into the Wiccans," Kiki said. "She's got all the makings of a powerful witch."

35

My house lay in a blanket of darkness. There wasn't a sound to be heard except for an occasional whisper or a meow. I huddled on the floor behind my Victorian Lady's Chair, while Jon crouched behind the Gentleman's Chair. Binkie had slipped in behind the Christmas tree where Spunky crouched on a lower branch. Nick was on the opposite side of the room, pressed against the wall behind the flung-back door. He was the only one of us who was armed.

Nick had strongly opposed our being here, but we'd insisted, reminding him that we were the ones who found the booty. Eventually, he'd given in, but had laid down some ground rules. We were to sit tight, keep our mouths shut, and let him handle everything.

What seemed like an entire platoon of cops were planted around my garden among the trees and shrubs. They'd sneaked in from adjoining properties as soon as darkness fell. Nick communicated with them over a miniature two-way radio pinned to his lapel.

It was Christmas night, the early morning hours of December 26th. We'd left our cars parked on other streets, sneaking one by one through a neighboring garden to my back door. We'd been hiding in my library for what seemed like an eternity, and were getting restless.

Then I heard it. The tinkle of breaking glass. It seemed to come from the dining room where French doors led out onto a side porch. If those clowns had broken one of my irreplaceable stained glass windows, I'd really be mad. "Did you hear that?" I whispered.

"Yes. Ssshhh. This is it. Not a sound. And stay down," Nick commanded.

The sweeping beam of a flashlight moved toward the library. I sucked in my breath and held the blue amulet tight. Floor boards creaked, giving away the location of our intruder. He seemed to be alone. My guess was that the other one was keeping watch out on the side porch.

He must have felt confident that the house was empty, because he didn't make an effort to be quiet. Joel and Earl had fallen for my story.

The flashlight's beam swept past my chair. I gathered myself into a tight ball. Next, he crept to the fireplace. He was tugging at the firewood box door when the lights burst on. Nick yelled, "Hold it right where you are! Hands up."

"What?" cried our intruder.

"What?" I echoed, jumping up. That wasn't Joel Fox or Earl Flynn. That voice belonged to a woman.

"Who?" I cried.

She was dressed all in black, her platinum blonde hair peeking out of a black stocking cap. I recognized my fleeing shooter from the cemetery. "Lisa Hamilton!" I squealed.

Jon popped up, and Binkie stepped out.

"Get down!" Nick cried, as Lisa raised a gun and aimed it at me. But Nick was faster. He launched himself at her like a missile. The gun flew out of her hand, going off with a loud bang. I grabbed my ears and screamed in pain as the roar hammered through my head.

Nick's mouth opened in a scream, but I couldn't hear the sound. His right hand, still holding his gun, flew to his left shoulder. His legs folded under him.

Lisa sprang toward her gun, but I stuck out my boot and tripped her. Staggering to her feet, her eyes darted around the room, frantic for a way out. She was unarmed and there were four of us. She jumped over a footstool and raced for the door. Binkie stepped in front of her, blocking her way, his fists raised in his best pugilistic stance. His left fist jabbed at her face, and she backed up. Binkie could never hit a woman but she didn't know that. Jon rushed forward, flipped her over on her belly, and straddled her back. Even Spunky got into the act, springing out of the tree and onto her stocking cap.

I kicked her gun into the corner, then fell on my knees beside Nick. Blood flowed down his arm and jacket front. I couldn't tell if the bleeding came from his shoulder or his chest. I ripped the radio off his lapel, and shouted into it, "Officer down! Officer down!"

36

"By air and fire
    By water and earth
    By the power of Oya
    By the power of my ancestors
    By the power of women
    And the men who honor them
    By the power of sun
    By the power of moon
    By the power of plants and animals
    By the power of storm and wind
    By the power of all that is sacred
    By the power of spirits that none can see
    By the power of three times three
    I bind you now, away from me!
    Mare, mare, mare!"

Kiki knotted two ribbons together nine times. She set the poppet on a bright sheet of aluminum foil, sprinkled it with herbs, and chanted, "From this moment on, let all evil that you do befall only you."

Balling up the aluminum foil, she placed it in a white paper bag, dropped the bag into a metal trash can, lit a match and dropped it in. Flames shot up, making us gasp. The flames died down, and we laughed, our tension relieved.

Kiki hugged me. "Your home is free of Lisa Hamilton and the evil she perpetuated in it. That means you are free."

"Thanks for that. I'll sleep better now." I didn't tell Kiki that tomorrow Father Andrew was coming to lead an Episcopal ceremony. "Let's go get something to eat."

It was New Year's Day and I joined my friends around my dining room table for feasting and celebration. Everyone I cared about was here. Melanie and Binkie. Jon with Christine Brooks. Kiki and Ray. Nick, whose shoulder wound was healing nicely. Ray was at my side, refilling my wine glass, offering me morsels from the table. The chef at Port City Grill had prepared a variety of buffet foods for us including the traditional black-eyed peas. We sipped red wine and wished each other a happy New Year.

"I always knew there was something phony about that Lisa Hamilton," Melanie declared. "She never would commit to buying a house. I can't tell you how many lunches I sprang for, and all she did was whine about her dreadful childhood."

"It *was* dreadful," Nick said. "She was so full of pent-up rage, she was ranting like a lunatic when we took her in. Fortunately for us, she never did lawyer-up. We got a full confession."

"But who would have guessed she was Russell Penry's daughter?" I said.

"It's a tragic story. You can't help feeling sorry for her. She was as much a victim as her victims," Nick said.

Kiki caught my eye. Her knowing glance was meant to remind me that she'd seen the satyr in the cards, half-man half-goat, and she'd warned me that the goat might also be a scapegoat.

Jon, his arm wrapped possessively around Christine's waist, said, "I don't know the full story, Nick. Tell us what she said."

Nick took a moment to sip from his wine goblet, as if collecting his thoughts. "After hiding the money bags in the secret room, and after the quarrel with Jimmy Weaver and the fight that killed him, Penry fled to Atlanta. If Weaver's body was found in the garden, he didn't want to be within the law's reach. In 1965, Penry fathered a daughter by his live-in girlfriend. When the baby was seven months old, Penry, crazy on LSD, murdered the baby's mother.

"He went to prison. Lisa was adopted by a couple named Hamilton. When she was four, the Hamiltons were killed in a car accident. Lisa's life then became a nightmare. She was shuffled from foster home to foster home, often with people unfit to care for an emotionally scarred child. But she was smart and got a scholarship to the University of Georgia where she studied Criminal Justice.

"Meanwhile, Penry kept tabs on her. Last year, he sent for her and she visited him in prison. She hated him for destroying her life and felt he owed her.

"He must have agreed with her and felt remorse, because he told her where she could find a half million dollars. He also told her that she had a grandmother who didn't know of her existence. That seemed to send Lisa over the edge. To think that rather than growing up with abusive strangers she might have lived with a loving grandmother! She fixated on Dorothy Penry, whom she'd never met, hating her, blaming her for failing to discover Lisa's existence and needs."

"So she was the one who killed Mrs. Penry with flowers," I speculated.

"We think so. We also think she killed her father. Penry died mysteriously after one of her visits. The prison officials record all gifts, and she'd brought home-made cookies. But they didn't know her real name; they knew her as Penry's daughter, Lisa Penry. The address she gave was bogus. They couldn't find her."

"She killed her own father?" Christine asked. You could see she was wondering what kind of group Jon had introduced her to: witches, robbers, murderers.

Kiki nodded sagely. "Patricide is nothing new in the family of man."

Christine's eyes widened and she leaned a little closer to Jon. Binkie grinned.

Nick continued, "Lisa tried again and again to get the money out of your house. While you were restoring it, there were always too many workers around. She saw an easy way to get inside as part of the tour group. She may have hidden in an upstairs bedroom until the tour was over, saw Binkie go into the bathroom, then sneaked down to the unoccupied library. But Sheldon discovered her. We don't know precisely what transpired between them, but she killed him. Then, fearing discovery, she fled before she could get her hands on the money.

"The next time she tried, Rachel discovered her. You must have just driven up."

I dropped my head and closed my eyes, transported to that terrible Saturday afternoon when the Angel of Death battered my head. A shiver ran up my spine. I'd decided to take Nick's advice and talk to a therapist. Ray slipped a strong arm around my shoulders, and I found it comforting. "It's all right, Ashley. She can't hurt you now."

"Thanks, Ray." I smiled up at him.

Melanie was in a foul mood. "A couple of unsavory characters showed up on my doorstep this morning, demanding to see Joel. I sent them packing. I told them I threw the bum out and as far as I was concerned he was dead." A vengeful smirk played on her lips. "They said I was right. 'Fox is a dead man,' were their exact words."

"But where is he?" I asked.

"Joel Fox and Earl Flynn bought one-way tickets to Los Angeles," Nick explained. "And the records show they boarded the plane. We've got a warrant out for Earl Flynn; he's wanted for questioning in the payroll robbery case. I think he's guilty, but we'll never prove it. There's no evidence against him. The FBI's examining DNA samples from Jimmy Weaver's corpse. If they find DNA other than Weaver's, they'll try to make a comparison with Flynn's DNA. If we ever catch up with him. And if a judge will let us. Same goes for Lisa Hamilton. She carries the same DNA as Russell Penry."

"She sure fooled a lot of people," I said. Including you Detective Yost, I thought.

Nick shrugged. "She was a good actress. Her credentials were impeccable. There was no reason to suspect her of anything."

"She didn't fool me," Melanie quipped. "Now what happens to the money? The half million?" Leave it to Melanie to get to the heart of things.

The Wizard of Wall Street speculated, "My guess is the lawyers will battle that out but in the end it'll be returned to the insurers who covered the payroll."

Binkie sighed. "So Suzanna O'Day's bag of gold was just a rumor."

Jon grinned. "Maybe not, Binkie. We haven't searched everywhere." He turned to Nick. "Speaking of rumors, I hear you've been offered a job with Atlanta P.D.."

"Nick!" I cried.

"We've got to talk, Ashley." He led me into the parlor. "I was waiting for the right moment to tell you. It's true. Atlanta P.D. wants me to head up their cold case task force. They were impressed with the way I solved the Atlantic Coast Line payroll robbery." He raised his palms before I could protest. "I told them I had a lot of help from civilians. Their reply was, 'That's how good police work is conducted.'"

I felt a sinking feeling in the pit of my stomach. "You're going to take it, aren't you?"

He smiled at me, displaying those heart-stopping dimples and a bitter-sweet smile. "Yes. I only made up my mind last night. That's why I didn't tell you about it sooner, Ashley. I had to mull it over. I'm sorry you had it sprung on you that way."

His arm was in a sling. He'd risked his life to save mine. He was my hero. Not willing to fire his weapon in the close quarters of my library, he'd offered himself as a target. I'd always love him for the way he'd been willing to take a bullet for me.

Yet the thought of him leaving me was painful. I felt abandoned. My feelings must have shone on my face, because he said, "Look, Ashley, you know how I feel about you. Atlanta is not so far. We can see each other often. I'll come back, and when I do, we won't be bogged down in one of my cases. I'll be able to leave my work behind."

I doubted that. I felt sick, but managed a smile. "You deserve the promotion, Nick. Before you leave, I have a present for you." The painting I'd bought for him was under the tree. "Something to remind you of the North Carolina coast."

"Ashley? You okay?" Ray asked.

"I'm fine, Ray. I'm just wishing Nick well on his new job. He's moving to Atlanta."

Ray stuck out his hand. "Good luck, Nick. Thanks for the way you saved Ashley's life." He took my arm and steered me toward the table. "They're serving dessert. Tiramisu. Kiki said it was your favorite."

From across the table, Melanie shot daggers at me. The botox treatments had smoothed out the planes on her face. How could anyone so beautiful be so insecure? My adorable sister would always be an enigma to me.

Ray spoke softly, for my ears alone. "Kiki and I think it would be great if you'd come back to New York with us. I've got a townhouse on East Sixty-Second Street. You'll be my guest. Your own suite of rooms, of course."

"Ray, that sounds heavenly. But maybe another time. My business is going to pick up now that the holidays are over. I've already got jobs lined up."

Wilmington's next major event was the Azalea Festival in April, and there was much to do to prepare for it.

"Well, what about a weekend then? I've got a box at the opera. You love the opera."

"That would be nice," I replied, smiling, and recalling the magical way the crystal chandeliers in the Metropolitan Opera House ascended to the ceiling with the first chords of the overture.

Ray rewarded me with a heart-melting grin. Gosh, I thought, he's everything any girl could ask for. Why am I resisting?

"Ashley, could I see you for a moment?" Kiki called. Again I was torn from the buffet table and hustled into a corner for a *tete-a-tete*. "I prepared a love potion, like you asked. It's really very simple: patchouli, lemon verbena, vetiver, various oils. I'll give you the recipe. The thing is you have to find a way to get Nick to bathe in it. That's how it works."

"How in the world will I manage that? Men prefer showers."

"Not me," Ray said, coming up to us and latching onto my last sentence. "That old-fashioned claw-and-ball bathtub you've got upstairs is fantastic, roomy enough for a big guy like me. Sis, I hope you don't mind but I borrowed your bath oil. Had a nice natural scent."

Kiki's huge eyes popped open even wider. We exchanged horrified looks. Ray had bathed in the love potion that was intended for Nick. So that's why he'd been hanging around me all afternoon.

"Good lord, Kiki," I exclaimed. "Don't you dare invite Melanie into the Wiccans. She'll turn us into toads."